To Lese

From G

Nov 2013

THE PURSUIT OF TRUTH

THE PURSUIT OF TRUTH

ARTHUR HUGHES

Matador
5 Weir Road
Kibworth Beauchamp
Leicester LE8 0LQ, UK
Tel: (+44) 116 279 2299
Fax: (+44) 116 279 2277
Email: books@troubador.co.uk
Web: www.troubador.co.uk/matador

ISBN 978 1848767 232

British Library Cataloguing in Publication Data.
A catalogue record for this book is available from the British Library.

Typeset in 11pt Garamond by Troubador Publishing Ltd, Leicester, UK
Printed and bound in the UK by TJ International, Padstow, Cornwall

Matador is an imprint of Troubador Publishing Ltd

In memory of Agnes Marianna Hughes
1915-2004

The warm summer night was filled with the throb of disco music. The old woman paused as her dog stopped to pee against the wheel of a sports car. She did not hear the body hit the ground.

SATURDAY

'So you see we return to the point where we began. It is through a formal analysis of the modal verbs that we can best structure, and so most clearly see, their semantic properties. This must always be the basis of linguistic description. And such descriptions in turn provide you, the teachers of English as a foreign language, with the best information on which to base your pedagogical decisions.'

The speaker, who was wearing a pale yellow long-sleeved shirt and baggy beige trousers, paused, glanced at his watch, then pulled back from the lectern. He smiled thinly at his audience, who, realising that the lecture had ended, began to clap loudly.

He was a tall, slim man in his thirties with curly brown hair, a straggly beard and horn-rimmed glasses. As he gathered his papers together, he looked again at his watch.

'I think we have a couple of minutes for questions.' He looked down towards a man of about the same age sitting in the front row between two attractive young women.

'If the course director agrees,' he added. 'Is that all right, Peter?' The course director nodded his assent.

'So, do we have any questions?' asked the lecturer.

In the few moments of silence that followed he looked

round the faces in front of him. Most of them belonged to women, the majority of whom were young. His gaze settled finally on one of the two sitting beside the man who had nodded. She was particularly pretty, he thought, her ash blond hair and striking blue eyes suggesting that she might be Swedish, or maybe German. She stared back up at him with what might have seemed a look of admiration, but which could equally have been one of wonder at the dark stains below his armpits.

A hand went up at the back.

'Yes?' said the lecturer, woken from his reverie.

'Professor, thank you for a most interesting and illuminating lecture. I am sure we are all very grateful.' The corpulent, middle-aged man who offered these thanks was of Middle Eastern appearance and spoke with an unmistakably Arabic accent. He stood up.

'I would like to put to you a question. You have told us about all of the model verbs, but can you tell me please which of them you believe is the most important? This is a very great question in our profession.'

'I take it that you are speaking of *modal* verbs and not *model* verbs?' There was a slow nod from the questioner accompanied by transparent incomprehension. There were sniggers from others in the audience.

'Even so, I'm afraid that I don't know what kind of answer to give you. Do you really mean which modal verb, or do you mean which *use* of a modal verb? And what do you mean by important? I may be able to tell you which was most frequent in our corpus, but I can hardly tell you which is most important. I'm sorry, but your question doesn't really make sense to me. I'm afraid I can't give you an answer.'

Everyone in the room turned to look at the questioner, who remained standing. 'I think you know what important means, professor. We cannot teach everything at the same time. So we must teach the most important first. And in order to do that, first we must know which *is* the most important. That is why I seek the opinion of a learned scholar as yourself.'

The lecturer gave a derisive snort. 'Ah, the mighty must! Well it is *you* who must do these things. As a linguist and not a language teacher, I needn't … and indeed I mustn't!' Amidst much laughter, some of which it might be thought was at his expense, the questioner sat down.

There were two more questions, which the lecturer answered to everyone's satisfaction, including his own. The man in the front row then uttered a few words of thanks, joined in the brief applause that followed, and then reminded everyone that they would now be meeting in groups with their tutors to analyse the use of modal verbs in recorded conversations. Eventually he was left alone with the lecturer, who was wiping what he had written from the blackboard. 'That was excellent, Chris. Thanks. I'm sure they got a lot out of it.'

'Even our friend?'

'There's always one like that.'

'Makes you wonder.'

'Certainly makes *me* wonder. Till I remember that it pays for our holidays.'

'Or goes into the pension fund. Well, Peter, I'll be getting along. See you tonight. In the meantime, back to the book.' He clapped his hands together and a cloud of chalk dust was caught in the slanting sunlight. He stepped towards the door, then turned back. 'By the way, who was the cutie sitting next to you, on your right?'

'You noticed! That's Silvia.'

'Swedish?'

'Italian actually.'

'Another reason for doing summer schools, eh, Peter? Droit du seigneur and all that.' The lecturer grinned and scratched his beard. Before the course director could respond,

3

the door opened and the woman that they had just been talking about came in.

'Excuse me, I'm sorry to interrupt, but Dr Crouch is not there. What should we do? We don't have the recordings.'

'Really? All right, Silvia.' The director put his hand lightly on the woman's shoulder and motioned her towards the door. 'I'll come and see what's happening.'

No longer grinning, the lecturer followed them out.

* * *

have they found him yet?
did I leave anything? … no I'm sure I didn't … but I have to get rid of them
that's good … that's easy

* * *

Detective Chief Inspector Healey signalled a right turn, slowed down almost to a stop, and then swung into the drive of his house. As he did so, he noticed with a feeling of guilt the dead cypress that he had still done nothing about except learn that the disease which had killed it was probably already at work at the roots of the next one in the line that separated the garden from the road. He stopped the car in front of the door, which was immediately opened by his thirteen-year-old daughter.

'Dad. Telephone for you.'

'Okay, love. I'll get it.'

He walked round the car and into the house, where he picked up the receiver from the wicker table beside the door.

'Richard Healey.' He listened in silence, his eyes fixed on a framed photograph of Liverpool Pierhead on the wall. The clock on the Liver Building showed three o'clock. He glanced at his watch.

'Yeah … yeah … okay … I'll go straight there. Who've I got with me? … Teague? Yeah. Okay.' He put the phone down and walked through to the kitchen.

His wife turned from the sink. 'You've got to go out again?'

'Sorry. No choice.'

'What is it?'

'They've found a body at one of the University halls.' As ever, it pained him to tell his wife anything about his work, though he would have found it difficult to say why. He'd only said this much because he was taking the car and she would have to walk to collect their son from the judo lesson where he had just left him.

When he told her this, she stared at him. 'Couldn't they have sent a car to pick you up?'

'It would have been difficult.'

'Difficult? Don't you think it's difficult for me to walk to Whiteknights to get Jamie, with everything I've got to do? God! It's always the same with you. Whatever happens, your work has to come first.'

'You know it's not always.'

'Always.'

'It's not always. How can you say it's always when you know it isn't?'

'Always.'

Healey had already turned away. He squeezed the shoulder of his daughter, who stood thumb in mouth in the kitchen doorway.

'Bye, Dad.'

'Bye, love.'

As he drove out onto the road, Chief Inspector Healey did not see the dead cypress. Nor did he think about the shopping that he'd bought before he dropped Jamie at his judo class and which was still in the boot of the car.

5

'Miss Colgan will see you shortly, Inspector.'

Healey had already seen the body. It lay spread-eagled on its back on the band of paving stones that ran along the foot of the six-storey wing of the red brick building that was a university hall of residence. It was of a short, stout, middle-aged man, dressed in an open necked lime-green shirt, beige cotton trousers, and solid brown shoes, lying in the shadow of the wall. Dead at least nine hours, according to the pathologist, who was still there when Healey arrived. That meant not later than one o'clock that morning.

'How?'

'I can't say yet, of course, but …,' the pathologist looked up towards the top of the building and then down to the body, 'that would have to be most likely.' He leaned forward and put his plastic-gloved hand to the side of the head, where blood had caked in the thinning hair. 'And the skull's obviously taken a tremendous blow. Anyhow, I'll let you know when I can examine it properly.'

In the open top floor window directly above them a head and shoulders appeared. 'Morning, sir.'

Healey looked up to see the fair hair and round, pink, moustachioed face of his sergeant. 'Morning, Teague.'

'This was his room, sir.'

'Okay. I'll be with you. I'm going to see the Warden first.'

As Healey sat waiting in the Hall Warden's outer office, a small, scruffy, sandy-haired terrier emerged from behind the secretary's desk. It looked at him and wagged its tail.

'Yours?' he asked the secretary.

'Sorry?'

'Is it yours? The dog.'

'Oh! I didn't see her. No, she's not mine. She belongs to Miss Woods, the lady with Miss Colgan. Come here, Daisy.' The dog hesitated.

'It's all right,' said Healey. 'Come here, girl.' The dog, clearly not young, waddled forward and put its paws on Healey's seat. He scratched the back of its neck. 'You're a friendly thing, aren't you? Aren't you just?' He looked up at the secretary. 'Does Miss Woods work here?'

'Oh no. She lives just around the corner. She's always popping in about one thing or another. Usually to complain. To tell you the truth, I think she comes for the company as much as anything. She hasn't got anyone at home. And most of the people around here are young. They've got their own lives.'

Healey tried to guess the secretary's age. Middle fifties, probably, but well preserved.

'Is she here to complain this time?'

The secretary nodded. 'Noise. The summer school had a disco last night. It went on later than it should have done. And it was so hot they had the windows wide open. I'm surprised there haven't been more complaints.'

'What time did it finish?'

'Well it should have finished at twelve-thirty, but I think it was gone one before Mr Bird managed to close it down.'

'Who's Mr Bird?'

'Our senior porter. He was on duty last night.'

Her pronunciation of 'last' was the first indication that she was from the north. He wondered where she came from.

'You haven't always lived in the south?'

'No. I'm from Manchester. Well, Poynton actually. Cheshire. But I've been here nearly twenty years.' As she said this, the door of the Warden's office slowly opened. A small old lady appeared, presumably Miss Woods. Behind her loomed a much larger female figure.

'Ah, good morning, Chief Inspector. Do come in.' Healey waited while Miss Woods edged past him, her dog already in the corridor outside.

'Do come in,' repeated the Warden, a broad smile revealing a set of large yellow teeth. 'Tea, please, Enid, if you wouldn't mind.'

She followed Healey into her office, gestured to him to take a seat, and sat down behind a desk covered with what looked like architectural drawings. 'An extension,' she explained, 'and something of a headache.' At this Healey couldn't help thinking of the head of the body he had seen lying outside.

'It must be quite a job looking after a large hall like this.'

'It's not as easy as some people think, including members of the University, I'm sorry to say.' She paused as if to give greater emphasis to the words she was about to utter. She pulled herself upright in her chair. Healey was reminded that she was a magistrate. She carefully folded her hands, as if in prayer, her elbows resting on the desk.

'Let me first tell you what I know and then I can arrange for you to see anyone else who may be able to help.' Healey nodded. 'The body is that of Neville Crouch, as I'm sure you are already aware.' Healey did not contradict her. 'He was a lecturer at the University of Berkshire.' This was the former technical college on the King's Road, still known as the 'Tech' by most people in the town, as opposed to the 'real', long established university.

'He wasn't from here then?' By 'here' Healey meant the original university.

'No. The summer school is organised by people from their Communications Studies Department. They use this hall of residence because they don't have one of their own.'

'How long does the summer school last?'

'Three weeks. It ends on Saturday morning. A week today.'

'How many people teach on the course?'

'Three full-time and the course director. Then there are various occasional lecturers.'

'Who's the course director?' Healey took out a notebook.

'Dr Peter Farrell.'

'Is he here now?'

'I doubt it. They have classes on Saturday morning, over on the main campus. Our campus, that is. Here, Chief Inspector, you should have this.' She handed Healey a booklet, on the cover of which he read 'British Council Course 936: Communicative English Language Teaching'.

He flipped over the pages until he came to the course programme. There, sure enough, was the disco scheduled for the previous evening. This morning there was a lecture on 'Modals and Modality' by Professor Christopher Carter in the Sutton lecture theatre, followed by workshops with tutors. After lunch at twelve-thirty there was to be a coach trip to London.

Inside the front cover he found the names of the tutors:

Dr Peter Farrell	*University of Berkshire (Course Director)*
Dr Neville Crouch	*University of Berkshire*
Mary Walters	*University of London*
Tim Wright	*University of Berkshire*

At the back was a list of the course participants and the countries they came from. He counted. Forty-six, coming from at least ten different countries. Healey put the booklet down.

'Who found the body?'

'Mr Bird.'

'When was that?'

'Just after half past nine.' The Warden peered at her watch. 'Nearly an hour ago.'

'Who else knows about it?'

'I should imagine just about all the Hall staff, Chief Inspector. Though I don't think anyone else has been to the body. Your people were here within ten minutes of my telephoning, and Bird was still with me.'

'What about you?'

'Yes, I went to look. I wanted to be sure that it really was Dr Crouch. Bird might have made a mistake.'

'But he hadn't.' The Warden looked at him without responding. 'And what did you think?' he asked.

'Think?'

'When you saw the body. What was your first thought?'

'I thought, poor man.' Healey waited for her to continue but she said nothing.

'That was all?'

'You asked about my first thought. That was it.'

'And your second?'

'I thought ... how unfortunate that this should have happened in the Hall. It may not sound very pleasant, Chief Inspector, but that was my second thought.' Healey had in the past often seen Miss Colgan on the bench. He had always been struck by the apparent lack of doubt with which she made judgements. He could never be sure in that way himself. He was reminded of this now, as she answered his questions directly and without any apparent temptation to go beyond what was required of her. Despite himself, he found himself looking fixedly at the strings of large amber beads that hung from her broad pink wrinkled neck and lay across her outsize paisley blouse.

Before he could ask her another question, there was a tap at the door. 'Come,' called out the Warden. Enid stepped in with two cups of tea, a bowl of sugar and a plate of biscuits, from which Miss Colgan immediately took a chocolate digestive. Only then did Healey feel able to continue.

'What can you tell me about Crouch?'

Miss Colgan swallowed what remained of the biscuit, ran her tongue round her upper teeth and smiled. 'Very little, I'm afraid. I only know him from the summer school, which he's taught on each year since they first came here. This is the third year, but I can't say I've got to know him. He always kept very much to himself. Married to a woman from the Philippines he met when he was working there. They have a daughter, about four years old, I think.'

'What sort of person was he?'

'As I said, I didn't really get to know him. He seemed to be a very particular person, finicky even, tended to worry about what I regarded as rather trivial matters.'

'Such as?'

'The fact that the beer in the bar wasn't quite as cold as he thought it should be. That the coffee wasn't strong enough. Things of that order.'

'He complained?'

'He did. But I'm not saying, Chief Inspector, that he had no grounds for complaint, simply that he was always the one who found fault. And having made his complaint, he persisted with it until he was satisfied that things had been put right.'

Healey pictured the body beneath the open window. 'Would you say he was a happy man?'

'Who can say for sure that someone is a happy person? But in my estimation, no, he wasn't. He rarely smiled, if ever, and he went about as if he carried the world's worries on his shoulders.'

'Did you notice any change during the course of the summer school?'

'No, not really. He seemed very much the same as ever.'

'How did he get on with the other tutors, do you know?'

'Well enough, I think. I didn't see any evidence of ill feeling.'

'And with the students?'

'I don't know. I see very little of them myself. I could ask my staff, if that would help?'

Healey hesitated before replying. 'Yes, that would be helpful, Miss Colgan. One last thing, what time does the Hall close?'

The Warden smiled again. 'It doesn't close.'

'So anyone could come in off the street, at any time?'

'They'd have to come through Reception, where there's always a porter on duty. They'd need to have a key to get in through any of the other entrances.'

Healey nodded and stood up. 'Now, if I may, I'd like to see Crouch's room.'

* * *

Shit, we need to get our stories straight

* * *

When Healey knocked at the door of what Miss Colgan had referred to as Crouch's 'study-bedroom', Teague opened it. Healey stepped inside.

Teague looked pleased with himself. 'I've found something, sir.'

Healey put his hand on the younger and shorter man's shoulder. 'All right. Just a minute. Let me find my bearings.'

Healey looked round the room. It contained a single bed with a heavy dark green bedspread, neatly turned back to reveal white pillows and the folded-over edge of a white sheet. On the floor at the foot of the bed was a long maroon sports bag. There was an armchair covered in the bedspread material, a desk and chair, with a black leather attaché case open on the desk. On a glass shelf above a washbasin, an upturned toothbrush and a tube of toothpaste stood in a white plastic mug. Dabs of blu-tack on the grey walls betrayed the former presence of attachments of some kind. With pictures and a few personal touches, the room could have been quite cosy. Now it seemed cheerless. Almost all of the external wall was taken up by one very large upward-tilting window, which was open to its widest extent, leaving ample room for a man's body to pass through. Curtains, also in the same green bedspread material, were drawn back.

Healey approached the window. Between the tall chestnuts that stood in the Hall grounds he saw in the middle distance the gas-holders beside the river in Newtown. Beyond them and the Thames (which he couldn't see) was the green of rolling Oxfordshire countryside. The room must be looking north-west. By evening the sun would be coming through the window. Could be very pleasant. Nice for a student. For a moment he thought about his daughter, who at thirteen was already talking about going to university. He looked down to the ground below the window and saw that the body had been taken away.

Hearing a cough, he turned and saw Teague looking even more than usually smug. 'Well then, what is it?' asked Healey.

Teague took out a handkerchief and, like a conjuror about to produce a rabbit, slid open the top drawer of the desk, to reveal a folded sheet of white paper. 'It's a letter, sir, addressed to Crouch. Typed. Or done on a computer.' He passed it to Healey, who, having already slipped on a pair of thin white gloves, carefully unfolded it, and began to read.

```
Neville
     Yes, its from me. Surprised? Yes, its a
long time since my last letter, isnt it?
     You  should  have  thought  that  I  would
leave  you  alone  now?  No,  never.  I  shall
```

never forget what you did. Soon EVERYONE will know and you know what that will mean!! You gave me much pain and now you will SUFFER in your turn. There is nothing that you can do. Just wait and think about it. BELIEVE ME! I am near you.

Healey looked up from the letter to see Teague's watery pale blue eyes fixed upon him. 'What do you think, sir?'

'What do *you* think?'

'Well, it's a threat.'

'And?'

'If what he was going to reveal was something really bad, that might have been enough …'

'To make him jump out of the window?'

'It might be.'

Healey read through the letter again, put it down open on the desk, then walked back to the window. Teague followed him. They both leaned forward and looked down to the spot where Crouch had landed.

'Not the way I would choose,' said Healey.

'Nor me, sir, but he wouldn't be the first.'

'That's true.' Healey nodded his head in the direction of the letter. 'Anything strike you about the letter?'

Teague walked back to the table and peered at the letter without touching it. 'No date.'

'Mmm.'

'No name. No address.'

'What about the style?'

'Sorry?'

'The way it's written. The English.'

'Well it's a bit funny.'

'Meaning?'

'It doesn't sound natural.'

Healey did not pursue the matter further. He sat on the bed, picked up the attaché case, and set it on his knees.

'Has anyone told his wife yet?'

'No, sir.'

'Okay. I'll do that. What I want you to do is to speak to everyone on the course, tutors as well, and the Hall staff. Find out where they were between eight last night and nine this morning. Anything they can tell you about Crouch's movements.' Teague's mouth opened as if he were about to speak, then slowly closed. From the inside pocket of his suit jacket he pulled something which Healey recognised as the course booklet. Teague flicked through the pages.

'Do you know how many …?'

'Four tutors and forty-six participants. No problem. Get all the help you need. On my authority. And try the neighbours. See if they noticed anything. Okay?'

Teague hesitated. 'Yes, sir.'

As he went out of the door, he paused. 'Would you like to have this, sir?' He offered the booklet, which was still in his hand.

'I've already got one. But where did you put that letter?'

'It's on the desk,' said Teague, not pointing out that it was Healey who had placed it there. Healey went over to the desk, took out a note-pad, into which he started to copy the contents of the letter, being careful to reproduce the errors accurately. When he realised that Teague was still in the room, he turned.

'You can go now, Teague,' he said. Teague went out, closing the door behind him.

Healey was pleased to be alone. Teague wasn't bad at his work but he wasn't the most congenial company, despite his cheery chappy manner. Narrow-minded, cynical, chauvinistic, and a reader of the Sun, he was also ambitious, someone to whom brown-nosing was second nature. When Healey finished copying the letter, he saw that there was a set of keys on the desk, one with a tag marked 'Office', next to a neatly folded copy of the previous day's Guardian. Turning his attention to the attaché case, he opened it and surveyed its contents. Three Pentex pens: one red, one blue and one black, each held in a loop of imitation leather. A book of first-class postage stamps. A book of second-class stamps. A copy of the course booklet, in which all references to Crouch were highlighted in yellow.

There was also a book: *RP Revisited: emerging variation in Received Pronunciation*, whose authors were Christopher Carter and Neville Crouch. He opened it from the back and glanced at the index ... 'glottaling, glottalization, glottal stop ... monophthongization'. Not a gripping read, he thought. He flipped through the pages and from the book fell a small sheet of paper covered in very neat but tiny writing. It was headed 'Meanings of the Modals', beneath which was a list of numbered notes. The only other object in the case was a Casio miniature tape recorder, which Healey slipped into his pocket. He set the case aside and, sitting down on the bed, pulled the sports bag towards him. From it he took out a pair of batting gloves, a pair of pads, a pair of neatly folded whites with grass stains at the knee, a pair of rather battered but perfectly white cricket boots, a plastic protector and a jock strap.

As he began to put them back there was a tap at the door. It was Enid, the Hall secretary. 'I'm terribly sorry to bother you, Chief Inspector, but your wife just phoned. She says you've got all the shopping in the car.'

* * *

A curtain twitched in the house next door. Healey was at the door of a semi-detached house in Falstaff Avenue. Beside him on the step stood a bottle of milk. He rang the bell, for a second time. It was eleven o'clock and already very hot, though the nature of his visit had made him put on a jacket and tie. A strong scent reached him from the lavender at his feet where bees were busying themselves. He had never liked the smell of lavender. It reminded him of long Sunday mornings as a child when he sat with homework he couldn't do, while his mother attacked the furniture around him with lavender-scented polish. Still no answer. Shit. He should have phoned. He pressed the bell once more and turned to walk to his car, a new silver-green Cavalier.

Leaning against the car he surveyed the house in which Crouch had lived. The brickwork was reddish brown, the woodwork painted bright yellow and white. All the curtains were drawn. Just as he was about to open his car door, the curtain of an upstairs window was pulled back and a face appeared, then disappeared. Healey returned quickly to the door, where through the frosted glass he saw movement and heard the lock turn. The door opened as far as the chain attached to it would allow.

Half a face looked out at him. 'Yes?'

'Mrs Crouch? Good morning. I'm Chief Inspector Healey, Thames Valley CID.' He put his warrant card in front of the face. 'I need to speak to you. May I come in for a moment?'

'My husband isn't here.'

'No, I know, Mrs Crouch, but could I come in for a moment?' The door closed briefly and then opened wide. If Healey thought of a word at that moment, it was 'beautiful'. The woman was beautiful. Shiny black hair, big brown eyes, shapely lips, slim, quite tall, signs of a good figure inside the dark blue dressing-gown which she held closed at the collar.

She looked worried. 'Is there a problem? I wish my husband were here.'

There was just a trace of a foreign accent, Healey thought,

though he didn't recognise it. Presumably a Philippine – or was it Filipino? – accent. He followed her into a rather gloomy, sparsely furnished room that ran from the front to the back of the house and smelled of stale cigarette smoke. Picking up a cloth doll from a dark brown imitation leather armchair, she sat down and Healey sat opposite her. Behind her was a French window, through which he saw a lawn running back to fruit trees at the bottom of the garden.

'Mrs Crouch, I have some bad news for you.' She held the rag doll to her chest. He waited for her to say something but she didn't.

'It's about your husband.' Healey bit on his lower lip. 'I'm afraid he's dead.'

Her hands went immediately to her face, dropping the doll into her lap. She made a whimpering sound. Her head still in her hands, her elbows resting on her knees, she began to pant. Healey got up. He went to the sideboard, where there was a decanter and some chunky cut-glass tumblers. He lifted the stopper of the decanter, sniffed it, then poured a large shot of brandy into one of the glasses. He went over to where she was still sitting and put his hand on her shoulder. 'Here, have this.'

She looked up at him as if in alarm, then down at the glass he was holding, and shook her head. Still looking down, she asked, 'What was it? What happened?'

'It was at the University. At the Hall. He fell. As far as we can tell, he appears to have fallen from the window of his room there.' He put down the glass of brandy.

'Can I make you some tea?' he asked after a few moments. She didn't answer but slowly stood up, and walked unsteadily into the kitchen. Healey heard water pouring from the tap into the kettle.

She came back into the room. 'Was it an accident?'

'It may have been. We don't know yet.'

'When did it happen?'

'We think early this morning.'

She walked to the front windows and pulled back the curtains, allowing the sun to stream in and fill the room with light. She turned, and without looking at Healey went back into the kitchen. When she emerged, it was with a tray on which there was a green teapot, jug and cups. She poured out two cups of tea. Healey reached towards the cup she had put on the low table beside him, then paused.

'When did you last see your husband?'

'When he left to go to the summer school yesterday morning, about half past eight.'

'He didn't come back?'

'No.'

'Did he telephone you at all?'

She hesitated. 'He phoned in the evening to say he would be staying at the Hall.'

'What time was that?'

'About eight o'clock.'

'Did he say why?'

'No.'

'It isn't very far to come.'

'No.'

'So why not come home?'

'I don't know. He wanted not to disturb me, perhaps.'

'Did he make the call from the Hall, do you know?'

'It should have been from the Hall, I think. Yes, I'm sure. He said I'll stay *here* tonight. He said 'here'.' She bit her lip as she looked at Healey through eyes which he noticed were still dry. 'It wasn't an accident, was it?'

'I honestly don't know, Mrs Crouch.'

'But all these questions.'

'Just routine. I have to ask them. Just in case.'

'He said that the party would finish very late.'

'And after that telephone call from your husband, did you stay here at the house?'

'Yes.'

'All evening?'

'Yes.'

'You didn't go out?'

'No.'

'So you were by yourself?'

'Except for my daughter.'

'Your daughter? And how old is *she?*'

'Five.'

'Did anyone come to the house? Is there anyone who could confirm that you were here?'

Mrs Crouch shook her head. 'No.'

Healey picked up the cup of tea, paused, then put it down again. 'Was there anything bothering your husband, do you know? Did he seem worried lately?'

'He was always worried. He worried all the time.'

'What about?'

'About work ... about money ... about ... about everything.'

'Why did he worry about ...?'

She interrupted him. 'It was his nature.'

Healey nodded. 'But was he particularly worried lately?'

She looked down for a few moments, as if trying to remember. But what she said made Healey think that she had been making up her mind whether to tell him or not.

'Yes, he was. For the last two weeks he has been very preoccupied.'

'Since the summer school began?'

Again she hesitated. 'Yes. I suppose it was.'

'Do you know what it was that was worrying him?'

'No.'

'You have no idea?'

'No. He told me nothing.'

Healey put his hand towards the cup of tea and pushed it slowly away from him. He stood up stiffly, wincing slightly.

'Well if you think of anything that may have been worrying him, please call this number.' He handed her a card. 'Leave a message if I'm not there.' He rubbed the knuckles of his right hand up and down the small of his back, before moving towards the door.

Behind him, Mrs Crouch glanced at the card he had given her. 'Chief Inspector, do you want to see my husband's things?'

'No I don't think so, thank you. Not now. But just one thing. Your husband called. Did anyone else?'

Before she could reply, the phone rang. She picked it up. 'It's for you.'

She stood close to him as Healey listened intently. 'What's that? Not sure? Okay. Yes, ask them to set it up. In the Hall if possible. You just carry on. I'll be back in an hour. Oh, and by the way, you can tell them their trip to London is off.' He put the phone down.

'Perhaps I will look at your husband's things after all, Mrs Crouch.'

* * *

Healey parked his car in the unmade road at the side of the Queen's Head, or the 'Knob', as it was known to the students who were its principal customers. He didn't like the place. Or the people who ran it. But it was on his route from the Crouches' to the Hall of Residence, and he was hungry. Ordering a cheese toastie and an orange juice and tonic in the gloomy and almost empty public bar, he sat down on a bench in the corner under the dartboard. The battered, grimy wooden floor had not been swept, the tables were covered with greasy smears, and the smell of stale beer hung in the air.

Putting on his white gloves again, he took from his jacket pocket the tiny black tape recorder which he had found in Crouch's attaché case at the Hall. He turned it over in his hands, pressed a plastic switch marked with an arrowhead, and put the recorder to his ear. Nothing. He found a knurled wheel beside the letters 'VOL', turned it as far as it would go, and put the recorder back to his ear. Still nothing. He took out a pair of gold-rimmed spectacles and put them on, stood up, held the machine beneath the dartboard light, and squinted to see if the tape inside was moving. But there was no cassette there. Healey remained standing, motionless. You idiot, he said to himself.

It was only when a woman's voice called 'cheese toastie' that he slowly stuffed the tape recorder back into his pocket, walked to the bar, and took the proffered plate. 'Sauce?' the woman asked, but he was half way back to his seat before he heard the question, and when he turned to say no thanks, he saw the woman's back disappearing into the lounge bar. As he chewed his toastie, which he now noticed was burned at the edges, Healey's mind went back to what had happened less than an hour before.

Mrs Crouch had led him upstairs, past a mobile made of dozens of sea-shells hanging from the ceiling, and into what she announced as her husband's study, a box room with a window onto the back garden. She immediately excused herself and went into the bathroom opposite. Against one wall of the study was a small white melamine-covered desk with a computer on it, a shallow drawer on either side. The opposite wall was lined with shelves filled mostly with books but which also held what looked to Healey like dozens of audio-cassette cases. Attached to the shelves were sticky labels on which were typed various categories of book: *Psychology, Language, Research Methods, Other.* Within these categories the books were in alphabetical order according to author. Each of the cassette cases, numbered 1 to 62, was marked with a three-letter code. He put on his glasses, opened one of them and saw that the cassette itself was marked with the same code and number as the case, and also a date. He thought of the cassette player in his pocket that he had taken from Crouch's room in the Hall but these cassettes would have been too large for it.

Healey pulled out the black swivel seat that was resting against the desk and sat down. He switched on the computer, which rumbled into action. As he waited for it to boot up, he pulled open the two desk drawers in turn. The first contained envelopes, pens, pencils, an eraser, blue and green highlighters, and a box of apparently unused floppy computer disks. In the second were a chequebook, a paying-in book, and a set of bank statements, the latest of which showed a credit balance of £103.33. Looking through the entries, Healey noticed with some satisfaction that Crouch's monthly salary payment was little more than half his own. Buying the computer must have been a big investment for Crouch, he thought. But perhaps it wasn't his but the University's.

He looked up at the monitor. Despite the computer's clicking and whirring, the screen was blank. It took him a moment to realise that the monitor had been switched off, not something that anyone bothered to do at headquarters, at least as far as he was aware. He switched it on and was soon browsing through Crouch's WordPerfect files. Most of these seemed to be concerned with his work: lecture notes, summaries of articles. There was a directory containing the outline of a book he seemed to be planning which had not been modified for more than three years. There was also a directory for correspondence, which contained letters, including more than one addressed to a publisher, explaining why he wasn't yet able to send any of the promised chapters. In a further directory was a single file which, because it demanded a password, Healey was unable to open. It was while he was wondering how he might get into this that it had happened.

As he looked through Crouch's things, Healey had been vaguely aware of what sounded like a shower running, the opening of the bathroom door, the closing of another door, and then the scent of a perfume that he didn't recognise. Now that scent was in the room again and with it Mrs Crouch herself, dressed in a pale blue silk cheongsam, split to the thigh. She came up behind him and put her hands on the back of the seat. Healey turned to look up at her. As he did so, her right hand slid from the seat to his shoulder.

'Yes?' Healey asked abruptly, as if addressing one of his detectives who had spoken out of turn.

She immediately pulled her hand away, and a look of alarm, almost of fear crossed her face. 'I'm sorry,' she said.

Healey turned back to the computer screen and tried to concentrate on the words in front of him. After a few seconds, without another word, Mrs Crouch left the room. He heard the tinkling of the hanging shells as she brushed against them and, a few moments later, the sound of the front door opening and then closing. He quickly took a floppy disk from the desk drawer, onto which he copied the file with the password protection and slipped it into his jacket pocket. He closed down the computer and hurried downstairs, opened the front door, walked half way down the path, and looked up and down the street, hoping that he would see Mrs Crouch.

The only person he saw was a middle-aged woman in the front garden of the house next door where the curtains had twitched earlier. The woman leaned on her fork and stared at him. He turned back to close the door behind him, only to see Mrs Crouch framed in the doorway. In one hand was a lighted cigarette and in the other was the bottle of milk that she must have picked off the step when he had heard the door opening and closing. She held up the bottle as if in explanation. Healey started to tell her why he had rushed out, stopped, muttered a thank you, and, under the watchful eye of the lady gardener next door, made his escape to the car, where he sat motionless, trying without success to understand Mrs Crouch's behaviour upstairs. How could she have acted that way within a few minutes of being told that her husband was dead? Eventually, he shrugged and put the key in the ignition. As he started the engine, he realised that he hadn't asked about Crouch's diary and cricket bat. He also realised that he hadn't seen the Crouches' daughter.

As he remembered this in the Queen's Head and continued to wonder, Healey felt in his pocket for the floppy disk. It was still there. And there was a lot to do. He took off his reading glasses, put them away, and walked out of the dark pub into the bright sunshine. He left his car where it was parked, and strode off in the direction of the Hall of Residence.

Even though it was only a quarter of a mile to the Hall, when Healey got there, he was sweating and he wished that he'd driven. Before he opened the door to reception, he sniffed his armpits and then slipped on his jacket, which he had been carrying over his shoulder. There was no one in reception but the sound of voices led him to what turned out to be the incident room that Teague must have set up, where uniformed policemen and policewomen were talking to course participants across trestle tables. There was no sign of Teague. 'You might try the bar, sir,' suggested one of the constables.

And that was where Teague was, leaning against the bar, a half empty pint glass beside him, a half smoked cigarette in his hand. 'Just a shandy,' he volunteered.

'How's it going?' asked Healey.

'All right. A few interesting things. Should be finished within an hour, sir.'

'Have they finished in Crouch's room yet?'

'They're just finishing now.'

'Good. Give them this.' He passed Teague the miniature tape recorder. 'It was in Crouch's briefcase. Have we interviewed all of the tutors yet?'

'All except one, the course director. Farrell.'

'Is he around?'

'That's him there.' Teague nodded his head in the direction of a tall, dark bearded man with hair down to his collar, probably in his thirties, who was leaning against the glass emergency exit at the far end of the room and talking animatedly with a pretty, young, fair-haired woman, who was wearing a simple cream blouse and what looked like expensive jeans. Healey went over to them.

'I'm sorry to interrupt, but I'm Detective Chief Inspector Healey. You're Doctor Farrell, I believe. I wonder if I could have a word.'

'Of course,' replied the man. He turned towards the woman, who Healey now saw had bright blue eyes. 'I'll get back to you on that later, Silvia. Maybe after supper?' He turned back to Healey. 'How can I help you?'

'If we can find a quiet corner, I'd like to ask you about last night.'

At that moment, the Hall secretary came up behind Healey. 'Chief Inspector,' she said, 'there's a call for you.' As she led him away, she added, 'You can take it in Miss Colgan's office.'

Healey came back from taking the call to find Teague talking to the Silvia woman. 'Teague,' he said, 'there's a tutor called Wright. What was he …' He stopped as he noticed that the woman was listening intently to what he was saying. 'Excuse me,' he said, 'I need to speak to my sergeant.' She looked at him blankly. 'Would you mind leaving us?' he added.

'You are so polite,' she responded and, with a toss of the head that Healey would have found funny in other circumstances, she stalked off.

Healey looked back at his sergeant, who had a silly smile on his fat pink face. 'So, Wright, where was he last night?'

Teague stopped smiling and consulted papers attached to his clipboard. 'Er yes, I thought it was him. That was one of the interesting things. He says he was at the party until ten and then he went round to the Crouches'. Spent the night there.'

'That's exactly what Mrs Crouch has just told me on the phone. After telling me this morning that she was on her own. Except for her daughter.'

'Did she explain why she said she was on her own?'

'Because she was embarrassed at having a man in her house all night.'

'So why did she change her story?'

'Says because she realised she should tell the truth.'

'Yeah, yeah – after Wright phoned her and let her know what he'd told us.'

'That could well be it, Teague. We need to talk to her again. This time, you do it. By the way, is Wright around?'

'I'll check, sir. Do you want to speak to him?'

'I do. But I'll talk to Farrell first.' He walked over to Farrell, who seemed not to have moved since the Hall secretary had come for Healey.

'I'm sorry about that, Doctor Farrell. Can we talk now? The Warden's office is free.'

Once inside the office, Healey gestured for Farrell to take one of the two seats facing the Warden's desk, closed the door, and sat down in the other seat himself, with his back to the window. He saw that, despite his almost black hair and beard, Farrell had pale grey eyes, which were now looking directly into his own.

'Well,' Healey began, 'I'd like you to tell me …' He slapped his hands against his chest. Damn. He didn't have a notebook with him. 'I don't suppose you've got something I can write on …'

Farrell grinned. 'I don't, but I'm sure Miss Colgan will.' He got up and went round to the other side of the desk, pulled open a drawer, and produced a sheaf of headed letter paper. 'This do?'

'Thanks.'

'And a pen?'

'No, I've got one, thanks.'

Farrell returned to his seat and Healey began again. 'Can you begin by telling me where you were at eight o'clock last night?'

'I was here, at the party.'

'What time did you leave?'

'A quarter to ten.'

'Where did you go?'

'To the Three Tuns. It's a pub on the …'

'Yes, I know it. How long did you stay there?'

'Till closing time.'

'And then?'

'I went home.'

'And?'

'I stayed there.'

'All night?'

'All night, yes.'

'If I had to check what you've told me, who would I ask?'

'About the Hall, anyone on the course, I guess. The pub, I was with a friend.'

'Whose name is …?'

'Chris Carter.'

Healey wrote down the name then pulled the course booklet from his pocket. 'The same Chris Carter who gave a lecture this morning?'

'Yes.'

'All right. And at home?'

'Chris Carter went back with me. He stayed until nearly two. After that, my wife, I suppose, though she was asleep when I went to bed.'

'You didn't wake her up?'

'No.'

'Well, thanks for that. Now, about Doctor Crouch. What can you tell me about his movements last night?'

'He was at the party too.'

'He was still there when you left?'

'I think so.'

'How did he seem?'

'I'm not sure I can tell you. It was a party. It was noisy. People were dancing and drinking. To be honest, I didn't really take much notice of him.'

'Was *he* drinking?'

'I suppose so.'

'But not so much as you'd notice?'

'No.'

'Was he dancing?'

'At one point he was. I saw one of the Bulgarian women dragging him onto the floor.'

'But only that once?'

'That's the only time I remember.'

'Did you notice anyone in particular talking to him?'

'Not really. He was sitting with the Bulgarians. And some other East Europeans, I think.'

Healey folded the one sheet of paper on which he had written, and put the others on top of the architectural drawings that still lay on the Warden's desk.

'Thank you, Doctor Farrell. That's all I need to ask you for the moment.'

Farrell stood up as if to leave, then paused. 'May I ask *you* a question?'

'Yes, though I don't promise an answer.'

'Do you know if Neville ... whether he did it himself, or ...?'

'No, we don't.' No longer writing notes, Healey noticed that not only were Farrell's open neck shirt, corduroy trousers, and socks dark blue, but also his shoes. The brown leather belt he wore seemed an anomaly.

'Was Crouch a friend of yours?'

'Not exactly. I always got on well with him but I wouldn't call him a friend. I never went to the pub with him, for example. Except in a crowd.'

'Do you know who his friends were?'

'No. No one in the Department, I'm pretty sure. He kept very much to himself.'

'But he wrote a book with Professor Carter, didn't he?'

'That was a long time ago.'

'Were they friends then?'

'Perhaps.'

'But they aren't now? Or, they haven't been lately?'

'I don't think so. But you could ask Chris, of course. If you need to know, that is.'

Healey stood up and opened the door. 'Thanks again,' he said as he ushered Farrell out of the door. 'Oh, and could you give your home address and phone number to one of the officers in the games room?' Farrell was halfway down the empty corridor when Healey went to the door and called after him.

'One last thing. Do you know Mrs Crouch's first name?'

'Teresa.'

'Teresa. And the lady you were talking to just before. Silvia I think you called her. Is she teaching on the course?'

'No, she's just a course member. Why?'

'No reason. I just wondered. Well, Dr Farrell, no doubt we'll be seeing each other again.' As it turned out, they saw each other rather sooner than Healey expected.

* * *

It was after nine and beginning to go dark when Healey got home. Through the open front window he saw his wife and the two children watching television, one of those awful game shows by the look of it. Jamie, he thought, should be in bed. Once inside, he opened the door of the front room to say hello. The children giggled and pointed at their mother, sitting upright in an armchair, glasses on her nose, fast asleep. 'All right, you two, straight to bed when this finishes.' He went upstairs, changed into jeans and T-shirt, and stopping only to make himself a gin-and-tonic, went out into the garden.

As he drank, he looked with satisfaction at what he had achieved since they had moved there five years before. The garden looked good. The pleasing curves of the lawn, the beds of floribunda roses, the rockery, the judas tree set amongst pink flowering bushes, the small apple orchard at the bottom, and the corner where he had put up a Wendy house for the kids. In the gloom it was easy to ignore the weeds, his wife's one responsibility in the garden. From the shed he took a pair of long-handled shears and began to carefully trim the edge of the lawn where it met one of the flower-beds. As he did so, he began to think about the new case.

He was fairly confident that Crouch had not committed suicide. There was evidence of his having received a blow to the head before he hit the ground. With the proverbial blunt instrument. It was this information, relayed to him at Mrs Crouch's by Teague, that had caused Healey to set up the incident room. Crouch, he felt sure, had been murdered, pushed, possibly unconscious, from the fifth floor window of the Hall. But there was no sign of a struggle in the room. Who could have done it? Someone who knew him. Mind you, it wasn't long since that Open University lecturer had been killed on a campus by a complete stranger. That was a summer school too. But this was different.

Be methodical, he told himself. Who had the motive? Who had the opportunity? 'Cherchez la femme,' Teague had said that afternoon when he got back from interviewing Mrs Crouch. 'What a little cracker she is. Well worth cherching her, and no mistake. Our Teresa.' He said her name as if eating a sweet, and Healey saw spittle ooze from his mouth onto his lips.

'I wonder what *she's* cherching,' Healey had said to himself, remembering her behaviour towards him. Now, in the garden, he thought again of his encounter with her. Could she have killed her husband? No, of course not. At least, not by herself. Wright? He still hadn't managed to speak to him. Must do that in the morning. The image of Teresa Crouch came back to him and he tried to remember the scent of her perfume.

Anyone watching the chief inspector at this moment would have seen a tall and rather heavily built middle-aged man standing motionless, shears in hand at the end of the garden, a pose he held for more than a minute. With a sudden shake of the head, he crossed over to the other side of the garden, where, shuffling sidewards, he began to work his way up the side of the lawn towards the house, cutting away the blades of grass that hung over the rose bed. Halfway along, he stopped abruptly, took the shears to the shed and, glancing up to the windows of the children's bedrooms, which were now lit, strode purposefully into the house.

Having said goodnight to the children, he went into his own bedroom, where he found his wife sitting up in bed with two pillows behind her, still with her glasses on and a book resting open in front of her, but again asleep. 'Jill. Jill,' he said, 'I'm just going along to the pub. Won't be long.' One of his wife's eyes opened; there was a faint smile on her face. 'All right, love,' she said. 'Don't forget your key.'

* * *

The Three Tuns, a 1930s brick building standing close to the busy Earley crossroads, was Healey's nearest pub. It wasn't the greatest, but it was only ten minutes' walk, and the Guinness was as good as anywhere in Reading. Out of term time, with the students away, it wouldn't be too crowded. It was where Farrell had said he'd been for a drink on the night of Crouch's death, something he could perhaps check at the bar, as well as have a welcome pint or two before closing time. Then back for the test match highlights. The best idea he'd had today.

As soon as he got close, Healey realised his mistake. From across the road he heard the confused sounds of talk and sudden shouts of laughter from the open windows and saw people sitting at the wooden picnic tables that had recently been put in what was previously a car park. The place must be packed. Still, there was nowhere else to go now that he'd come this far on foot. He crossed the road and went into the lounge bar and immediately recognised the reason for his mistake. It was full of Open University students, who also attended summer schools at the University. In their thirties and forties, the men far outnumbering women, and all of them apparently drinking pints, the men showing much more interest in the women than was usually the case in pubs, they had taken over the bar.

Healey was reminded of how close he had come to registering with the Open University a couple of years before. If only he had, what might he be doing now? Chatting up a young woman? Sitting with his books? More likely just what he *was* doing, what he always seemed to be doing, going for a pint by himself. He pushed his way to the bar, where he had to wait while others got served. Eventually a hot and tired barmaid, dressed in a half unbuttoned white lace blouse, was ready to take his order.

'Pint of Guinness, please. Straight glass.'

He felt a hand on his shoulder and a voice from behind said, 'Make that three, will you?' Healey looked round, to see Peter Farrell, who greeted him cheerily.

'Hello there. Checking my story are you?'

'No, not really. Just felt like getting out for a drink.'

'I was joking.'

'Oh.'

'Chris Carter's here. Why don't you join us? I'll get these. That's him there, with the beard. I mean, that's if you're allowed to fraternise with your suspects.'

'You aren't …' began Healey, until he realised that Farrell was joking again, or at least he thought he was. 'All right, thanks, but take this.' He offered Farrell the five-pound note that he had already taken from his pocket.

'Absolutely not. You're our guest.'

Healey eased his way between bodies to the corner where Carter was sitting. 'I've just seen Peter Farrell at the bar. He asked me to join you. Richard Healey.' He held out his hand to Carter who, half standing, shook it vigorously and gave his own name.

'Can you squeeze in here?' he asked.

Healey ensconced himself on the green velour bench tight between Carter and a large-breasted young woman in a pink T-shirt which, with the aid of a red heart and black lettering, advertised her love of mathematics. The woman, apparently engrossed in a paperback, remained immobile and Healey felt the warmth of her thigh against his. He looked at Carter, who peered back at him through the thick lenses of horn-rimmed bifocals.

'It's *Professor* Carter, isn't it?'

'Not quite. I don't become a professor until October, the beginning of the academic year.'

'Oh, it's just that I saw it in the course booklet.'

'The course booklet? Oh, the summer school booklet. That was just Peter's little joke.'

'Well, congratulations anyhow,' said Healey, wondering what was funny about giving someone their title a couple of months early.

'Thank you.' Carter looked round as Farrell edged towards them through the standing crowd, raising the tray of drinks to chin level in order to pass a laughing and gesticulating man with an almost bald head. 'You should congratulate Peter too,' he said, loud enough for Farrell to hear. 'He's just been made a reader.'

Farrell sat down and they all three took up their glasses. 'Cheers,' they said.

'And congratulations to you both,' added Healey.

They took long draughts of Guinness. Farrell drew the back of his hand across his mouth, collecting creamy foam from his beard.

'Have you two introduced yourselves?'

'Yes,' responded Carter. He looked at Healey, who said nothing.

'The Chief Inspector …' Farrell began, at which the woman next to them looked up from her book.

'Richard,' Healey muttered.

'Sorry.' Farrell paused. 'Richard is investigating Neville's death.' At the word 'death' the woman looked at Healey more closely.

'Oh, really?' said Carter. 'How interesting. You aren't here to check up on us, I suppose?' He chuckled and scratched his beard.

'I've already asked him,' volunteered Farrell, 'and the answer apparently is no.'

Healey watched as, in the following silence, Carter picked up his glass, drew it towards his mouth, leaned his head forward as if to drink, then put the glass down again.

'Poor old Neville,' said Carter, slowly shaking his head. 'Do we know how it happened?'

'No,' replied Healey, uncomfortably aware of the interest being taken by the young woman. 'I was wondering if I might talk to you about it tomorrow.'

'Of course. When?'

'Morning?'

'Fine. I'll be in the Department from about nine.'

'It's Sunday.'

'Oh yes, I do realise that. Best time of the week. No students.' He glanced at Farrell. 'And just as important, no colleagues.'

'Fine. I'll call by about ten, if that's all right.'

'I'll be there.' Carter lifted his glass again, this time taking several gulps before addressing Healey. 'Richard, you're from the north, I take it.'

'Yes.'

'Let me guess. St Helens.'

'Not quite. Widnes.'

'Widnes.'

'Yes. Wide nose.'

'Sorry?'

'Widnes … wide nose of the Mersey. At least that's what we were told at school. In geography.'

'Well I'll be blowed. I would never have thought that.'

'May not be true, of course. Our geography master also told us that changing weather was the explanation for what he called the English genius.' Healey paused, waiting for laughter or at least some comment, but none came. To break the silence, he asked, 'And where are you from, Chris? Not so far from Widnes yourself, I imagine?'

'Manchester. And Peter's from Liverpool.' He lengthened the last syllable of Liverpool and rhymed it with *cruel*. 'What are we all doing living down here?' He laughed. 'Taking advantage of the poor southerners.' As he spoke, the landlord called last orders. Healey stood up.

'Another pint?'

'No thanks,' replied Carter. 'We've got to be off. We're going back to Peter's to watch the cricket.'

'I was planning to watch it too,' said Healey.

They made their way to the door, Farrell calling an unanswered goodnight in the general direction of the bar. They stood outside in the still warm air.

'Can we give you a lift?' asked Carter.

'No thanks. I live just down the road.'

'Where?'

'Beech Lane.'

'But that's where we're going. Peter lives at 22. Come on. The car's here.' Carter put his hand on Healey's back and led him to a large saloon car that looked orange under the neon streetlight. They got in what Healey now recognised as an old Rover and the heavy doors closed with a pleasing clunk. Carter started the engine.

'Why don't you watch the cricket with us?' said Farrell, as the car nosed its way onto Wokingham Road.

'Oh no, I couldn't …'

'Of course you could. And you could check the rest of our story at the same time.'

From the back seat Healey could see only the back of Farrell's head but it wasn't difficult to imagine the grin on his face. Why not, he thought. Couldn't do any harm. It would be more fun than watching the cricket by himself. And it would be a chance to find out a bit more about Crouch and the people who knew him.

'All right. Thanks,' he said.

The car pulled into the drive of Farrell's house. As the three men got out, a light came on in the hall and the door opened. Healey saw a small female form silhouetted there.

'You forgot your key,' said the woman.

'Did I, love?' said Farrell. 'Sorry. Did you wait up?'

'No, I was watching that Ruth Rendell thing on ITV. The cricket's just started, by the way.' Farrell stepped inside. Carter motioned Healey forward. He found himself facing a small sharp-faced woman with red hair and green eyes. He would have guessed she was in her late twenties. Farrell spoke.

'Oh, Pam, this is Chief Inspector Healey. Richard, my wife.'

'Hello,' she said in what struck Healey as a posh Liverpool accent. 'This isn't an official visit, I hope.'

'No, I …'

'He's come to watch the cricket with us. He's our neighbour, would you believe?'

'Yes, I would actually.' She turned to Healey. 'I've seen you walking past with your dog, haven't I? A terrier.'

'Yes, probably. I take her on the campus.'

Farrell pushed the door of the front room and held it open.

'Cricket, gentlemen.'

Healey smiled at the woman. 'Nice to meet you.'

'Nice to meet *you.*'

The room the men sat down in was almost square with a small rectangular bay. The whole of the dark green wall opposite the door was covered with books on white shelves. In one corner, below the books, was the television. In the other corner stood a black cupboard, on which there was a tape recorder and stacks of audio cassettes. The remaining walls, all white, sported various framed prints and a small oil painting of a beach scene. In front of the men was a glass topped black metal table on which were two tumblers, a bottle of whisky, cheese and biscuits. Farrell's wife came in and put another tumbler and a plate on the table. Farrell picked up the bottle.

'You'll have a drop, won't you?' he said to Healey.

Healey looked at the bottle. 'Teacher's,' he said. 'That's quite appropriate.'

'Funnily enough,' said Farrell, 'that's how we started drinking it. The students on the summer school a couple of years ago thought it would be amusing to give their teachers each a bottle of Teacher's. And we've been drinking it ever since.' He poured three very large whiskies.

The men drank whisky, ate cheese (Healey more than the others – he hadn't eaten since lunchtime) and, largely in silence, watched New Zealand build up a big lead over England, whose batting then collapsed. After the smiling (smirking, Healey thought to himself) Australian presenter of the programme bade them good night, there appeared on the screen the logo of the Open University.

'That's it,' said Carter. 'They're going to lose, first time ever against New Zealand in England.' No one responded. Healey looked at his two companions. They were both of similar build, tall and slim, and they both had beards. Otherwise they looked quite different. Carter had greasy curly brown hair, pasty pockmarked skin, a somewhat bulbous nose, and fat lips, and his beard looked as if it hadn't been touched for weeks, except by food, of which there were obvious traces. There were pronounced bags under his hazel-coloured eyes that looked enormous through the lenses of his spectacles. Not a picture of health, thought Healey. Farrell by contrast had long, straight, almost black hair, smooth tanned skin, light grey eyes, an aquiline nose, and a wide, almost pretty mouth. His beard was neatly trimmed. He looked several years younger than Carter.

The Open University logo was still on the screen. 'What do you two think of the Open University?' Healey asked.

'Best thing Harold Wilson ever did,' replied Farrell.

'Really?'

'I'm a bit biased. Pam is doing a degree with them. It's changed her life.'

'Your wife?'

'Yes, sorry, I didn't introduce you properly, did I? Too keen to watch the cricket. Yes. She felt she'd missed out, not going to university. Decided to do a degree with the OU. Now she feels, well, fulfilled, I suppose, if that doesn't sound too pretentious.'

'I was thinking of doing a degree with them myself.'

'Why not? If you want to, that is. Would it help your career?'

'Bit late for that, I'm afraid. But that wouldn't be the reason. It's just that I'd like to be able to study something in depth, really get to the bottom of it. Something completely different from my work.'

'But isn't that just what you do in your work?' broke in Carter. 'Search for the truth. Get to the bottom of things. When you think about it, your job is not that dissimilar to ours really. We're all seekers after truth.'

Healey was about to protest but Farrell spoke first.

'The pursuit of truth,' he said. 'Where does that come from? I mean, who said it? Or who wrote it?'

'Don't know. But tell me when you find out,' said Carter as he stood up. 'Anyhow, Richard, the point is, we're in the same business really. And if I don't get to bed very soon,' he affected a long and noisy yawn, 'I won't be in a state to pursue much truth tomorrow morning.' He beamed at Healey and moved towards the door. 'Good night, Richard. See you tomorrow.'

'Good night.' Healey stood up himself. He heard the other two exchange words in the hall, the car door clunk shut, the tyres crunch on gravel, and the front door close. Farrell came back in.

'Sit down, Richard. Have another scotch.' He went over to the television, where an earnest young man in a double-breasted blue blazer was attempting to show how mathematics could explain the outcome of a naval battle, and turned down the sound.

Healey sat down. He sensed that, however unusual the situation he found himself in, he might learn something useful. 'Did Dr Crouch play cricket?'

'Yes. He was very keen. In fact he played yesterday afternoon. For the academic staff. Against Berkshire second eleven, I think.'

'So he was pretty good?'

'Yes. Opening bat. Very dour. Very Yorkshire.'

'Not *another* northerner?'

'Afraid so.'

'Was anyone else from the Department playing yesterday?'

'In that match? No.' Farrell sat down beside Healey, then suddenly put his hand to his brow, almost as if saluting. 'Wait a minute. *Tim* played. He's not staff but he was playing too.'

'Tim?'

'Yes. Tim Wright. He did an MA with us this year. English Language Teaching. Got a distinction. I asked him to be a tutor on the summer school. That's why he stayed on.'

'Instead of going home?'

'Home? I don't know about that. He's been trying to get a job over here. He thought we might find something permanent for him but there's no chance. He'll probably have to go overseas again.'

'Overseas?'

'He was in Manila for five years before he came here. I imagine he can go back to a job there if he wants.'

'The Philippines? Isn't that where Dr Crouch was before he came to Reading?'

'Yes.'

'Did they know each other before?'

'I think so. In fact I'm sure they did. I remember Neville saying that Tim asked him to be one of his referees. When he applied for the MA.'

'Would you say they were friends?'

'Not really. At least I don't think so.'

'But they played cricket together?'

'No. Oh you mean yesterday. That was an exception. They were one short and Neville asked Tim to make up the numbers. He asked Chris first, but of course he was too busy.'

'But they got on all right?'

'Neville and Tim?' Healey nodded.

'I think so.'

Healey stood up. 'Sorry, I need a pee. Can I use your …?'

'Of course. Up the stairs, turn right, and it's the door in front of you.'

Healey paused at the door. 'Is there anyone Dr Crouch *didn't* get on with?'

Farrell shook his head.

Healey persisted. 'Someone who might have something against him?'

Again Farrell shook his head. 'No. Not that I'm aware of.'

Healey made his way upstairs. As he walked across the landing, he heard a familiar voice coming from a room on his right, the door of which was ajar. It was the radio. World Service, he thought. But the man's name, what was it? When he got downstairs, Farrell had switched off the television and was gathering newspapers from the shelf under the coffee table.

'I'll be on my way,' said Healey. Farrell offered no objection.

'I'm sorry,' said Healey, 'I shouldn't have taken advantage of your hospitality to ask you about Crouch.'

'That's all right.'

'It's just that …'

'You're in pursuit of the truth.' Farrell smiled.

Healey smiled back. 'Thanks very much. I enjoyed it.'

'You're welcome.'

'Goodnight.'

'Goodnight.'

When Healey reached the road and looked back at the house, the downstairs lights were already off and one came on in the room from which he'd heard the radio. It suddenly came to him. John Timpson. That had been the voice on the radio. The Open University, he thought, perhaps that's the way to go. Feeling happier than he had for some time, he walked the fifty or so yards home and went straight to bed, where he dreamed that he was opening the batting for Lancashire.

SUNDAY

Though he had gone to bed happy, Healey did not sleep well. Something was troubling him. He woke at five minutes to four, at twenty past five, and again at a quarter to seven. On the first two occasions he went to the bathroom to relieve his bladder and, dehydrated, to slurp up water from his cupped hands, which he held under the cold-water tap.

On the third occasion he went down to the kitchen and put on the kettle. He dropped an English Breakfast teabag into a mug, put it beside the kettle, and went out into the garden. As he did so, a green woodpecker rose from the lawn where it had been eating a breakfast of ants. If only it would eat all of them; Healey's attempts to exterminate them from the lawn and rockery by pouring boiling water into their nests had resulted in failure and a sense of guilt for what he had done. Still, today was another cloudless day, a beautiful day. Healey found himself looking at the mostly yellow roses in the bed next to the terrace (or what they called the terrace; in fact it was just a broad strip of concrete that ran along the south side of the house, which he planned to tile some day, when he had more time and his back wasn't so bad). These roses, which the previous evening had glowed modestly in the twilight, were now revealed to have leaves covered with black spot, which both disfigured them and foretold their imminent death. In fact some of the leaves were already dry and withered, ready to fall to the ground – amongst the weeds – at the first breath of wind.

Healey felt an unfocused anxiety. It always seemed to happen these days when he'd been drinking the night before. He never knew whether it was because of the alcohol or because of whatever had caused him to drink. Or because of what drinking had led him to do or say. Well, last night he hadn't felt a desperate need for drink. And he hadn't drunk much. But he did feel uneasy about what had happened. Meeting Farrell and Carter at the Three Tuns had provided a good opportunity to find out more about the people involved in the case. He had taken advantage of this, and maybe they – at least Farrell – felt he had taken advantage of them, of their hospitality. He had felt comfortable with them, even flattered to be in their company, until, by asking too many questions, he had shown what Farrell must have felt was his real interest in them. He didn't expect to be invited to the Farrells' again in the near future.

Was that what was bothering him? That was part of it. And …? Few of his colleagues, probably none of them, would have gone back to Farrell's house, even if it *were* only a few yards from their own. 'Thank you, but no, I must be getting back.' It wasn't thought wise, in fact it was positively forbidden, to fraternise with anyone involved in a case, however obliquely. At least not without getting authority for it. When he'd done it before, it had sometimes led to a breakthrough in a case that was going nowhere, and nobody worried about it. But that wouldn't help him if anything ever went wrong. He certainly wouldn't say anything to Teague about last night. To another sergeant perhaps – to Teague no. That ambitious little toad wasn't above telling tales if he thought it would be to his advantage.

Was that all that was troubling him? No, but … He went back into the house. The kettle had stopped boiling and he switched it on again.

Fifteen minutes later, after a crap, a shave and a shower, and now wearing a white shirt with narrow blue stripes, Healey was sitting at the wooden picnic table on the terrace, drinking his tea and eating toast smothered with butter and French apricot jam. Though it was still early, the sun was hot on the side of his face and neck. A wasp landed beside his toast and he waved it away. He began to make a list of the things that he had to do that day. At ten he had the appointment with Carter. Before that, though, he would go to the Hall. There were things to check there, and he would see if he could get to speak to Wright. He also needed to go over with Teague everything they'd got so far, something they hadn't managed to do the previous day.

Back in the kitchen, he made a cup of sweet milky instant coffee for his wife, which he took upstairs and put on the table beside the bed, where she lay on her back, still asleep. He pulled back the curtains. 'Jill,' he said. There was no response. 'Jill,' he repeated. She stirred slightly. 'Coffee,' he said.

Without opening her eyes, his wife smiled. 'Thanks, love,' she said. As he watched, she turned on her side and snuggled under the sheet. Thinking that the coffee would be cold long before she woke up again, Healey went out onto the landing. The door of his young son's bedroom was open and Healey looked inside. Jamie too was fast asleep, lying on his back, completely naked, with the covers in a pile at the bottom of his bed. Healey then tapped lightly on his daughter's door.

'Hello?' he heard. He quietly turned the handle and opened the door. The room was filled with a warm glow from the sun shining through the red curtains. His daughter was sitting in bed, her knees drawn up, reading a book. Above her head Paul Young looked down from a poster. Their terrier, curled at her feet, eyed him warily. His daughter smiled.

'All right?' he asked.

'Yeah.'

'What are you reading?'

'Agatha Christie.'

'Is it good?'

'It's great.'

'Do you want me to open the curtains?'

'All right.'

He pulled back the curtains and the room was filled with sunlight. He didn't want to leave. 'I've got to go,' he said. 'Tell Mum I'll be back for lunch if I can.' She nodded.

He went to the door.

'Bye, love.'

'Bye, Dad.'

On the way out he tugged the Sunday paper from the letterbox and put it on the kitchen table. He got in the car and drove off down Beech Lane, noting as he did so that the curtains of Farrell's front bedroom had not been opened. It didn't occur to him that he still had the previous day's shopping in the boot.

* * *

The Hall stood on the corner of two roads. As he drew near to it and began to slow down, Healey saw a coach parked in the smaller of the roads. A line of what seemed to be mostly young women were climbing aboard. Healey parked on the opposite side of the road and stayed in his car. He took out the course booklet, which he still had with him, and saw that this must be the day trip to Bath. At the back of the queue he noticed the woman who had complimented him sarcastically on his politeness. Silvia, was that her name? She was clearly agitated, changing her weight from one foot to the other, looking up and down the road, looking at her watch twice in the two minutes that Healey was watching her. She was wearing a cream blouse – again – and a sage coloured skirt, a jacket of the same colour over her arm, with a beige canvas bag hanging from her shoulder. An attractive woman, he thought, stylish, elegant, probably in her mid-thirties. He wondered what it would be like to be with a woman like that.

He was jolted from his musing by the sound of a horn behind him. He looked in his mirror and saw a blue open-topped sports car, signalling a turn that would take it into the Hall grounds, but which would not be possible until either the coach or Healey's car moved and left enough space for it to pass. Healey started his engine and moved forward a few yards. From behind he heard an acknowledging toot from the sports car and, tilting his mirror so that he could see the Hall entrance, Healey watched as the car turned, then stopped. The woman stepped towards it, leaned on the door with one foot off the ground, and spoke animatedly to the driver, before the car moved on into the Hall grounds, parked, and the driver, a slightly built young man with long fair hair, emerged and took the woman's arm. They both got on the coach, which drove off almost immediately.

As Healey entered the reception area, the old man on the desk asked if he could help him. Healey told him who he was. 'And you are …?' he asked.

'Mr Bird,' was the reply.

Very apt name, thought Healey, for such a thin and bony man. Long scrawny neck and beaky nose too. He noticed that Bird pronounced the 'r' in his name, as most older people in Reading would, though very few young ones. Healey showed him his warrant card.

'So it was you who found the body?' he asked.

'It was.'

'Did you recognise who it was right away?'

'I did. His face was very familiar to me.'

'Why was that?'

'Cos he was always coming to me complaining about something or other, right from the start. This wasn't right. That wasn't right. I tell you, I got really fed up with him. I said to him one day, I said, Tell me, Doctor Crouch, are you the director of this here summer school? No, he says, why? Why? I says, well you know who the director is so why don't you tell '*im* what's wrong and then he can take it up with the proper authority. Then you won't have to keep bothering me. Well, he didn't have an answer to that.' Bird paused. 'Poor bugger, though. No way for anyone to go.' He shuddered.

'Did you notice if Dr Crouch spent time with anybody in particular?' asked Healey.

'No. No, but he did have an eye for the ladies, I noticed. They seemed to have time for him too. Funny really, him being such an ugly bugger. I thought it must be to do with them being foreign or something.' Bird shook his head in apparent wonder. 'Some really nice-looking ones too.'

'But no one in particular?'

'Not that I saw.'

Healey started to move off, then stopped. 'There's a blue sports car parked outside. Do you know whose it is?'

'Parked where?'

'Just outside the door.' Healey pointed to the door through which he had come into the building.

'Bloody hell. He knows he's not supposed to park there.'

'Who?'

'Mr Wright.'

'The tutor?'

'Yes. The Warden told him he wasn't to park there. It's for senior Hall staff only.'

'Was it here last night?'

'I didn't see it at all last night.'

'What about the night before, the night of the party?'

Bird scratched his head before replying. 'It *was* there, yes. Until I made him move it. Got him out of the party I did.'

'When was that?'

'Just after nine.'

'You're sure?'

'Yes. The nine o'clock news had just started on the telly. I saw it when I come through the bar. There was nobody around here so I went out for a fag and there it was, his car in Miss Colgan's place.'

'So where did he move it to?'

'Onto the road. Just round the corner.'

'Did it stay there?'

'All night. At least it was there when I went off duty at one. And it was there when I came back on at eight.'

'Well thanks, Mr Bird. Where was Miss Colgan's car, by the way?'

'She was at home. She doesn't like to be around when there's a party on.'

'Oh, I see. Thanks again, you've been very helpful.'

Bird looked pleased with himself. 'Can I ask you a quick question, sir?'

'What's that?'

'What exactly is the law on street parking? Only I don't think it's right that people who don't live in an area should take up space that doesn't belong to them.'

'I'm afraid I can't help you on that one, Mr Bird.'

Bird seemed surprised.

'But,' added Healey, 'I'm sure my sergeant will know. Why don't you ask *him?*'

When Healey entered the incident room, it was empty except for one constable.

'Morning, Gifford.'

'Morning, sir.'

'Any sign of Sergeant Teague?'

'I haven't seen him, sir.'

'Can I have what we've got so far?'

Gifford handed him two fat folders, which Healey took to a table near the window. He was leafing through the contents of the first folder when Teague appeared. 'Morning,' he called cheerily. As he approached Healey, he added, 'That porter's a bit weird, isn't he? Wanted to know all sorts of things about street parking. Said you told him to ask me.' Healey did not respond and Teague continued 'Yeah, weird, what you might call a funny old bird,' at which he chortled loudly.

Healey, still annoyed at having missed Wright, gave him what he thought of as an old-fashioned look. 'Can we get some work done. I'm seeing Carter in less than an hour.'

By the time Healey left the Hall to call on Carter, he and Teague, though they were still waiting for a report from Forensics, had agreed on what they ought to follow up. They had to talk to Wright, give him a hard time if necessary. They needed to know whether he had really been with Mrs Crouch on the night of Crouch's death. They knew that Mrs Crouch, since she had changed her story, had lied to them but not why. When Teague interviewed her, she had simply repeated what she had said to Healey on the phone: that she had been too embarrassed to admit to having a man in her house all night when her husband was away. If she had in fact told the truth in the first place, then Wright had lied. Why would he have done that? Teague was confident that Wright hadn't been at Mrs Crouch's when he went there the previous afternoon. Downstairs there was only the living room and the kitchen, and he had used an unnecessary visit to the loo to go through all the rooms upstairs.

Wright wasn't the only person whose movements on the night of what they now mostly referred to as the murder demanded further investigation. Teague was particularly interested in one of the few male course participants, first because he was from the Philippines, where Crouch had lived, and second because he told Teague, who happened to interview him, that he had been with friends in London and then had gone to Heathrow to see them off on a flight to Paris, where they would begin four weeks touring through a number of European countries. The man did not have a contact address for them, and said that they wouldn't be coming back to Britain before they went home to the Philippines. 'Very convenient,' said Teague, at which Healey told him to speak to the man again at the earliest opportunity.

The second person with what Teague referred to as 'a dodgy story' was Mary Walters, one of the tutors. She had said that she had left the party at about 8.30 and gone back to her flat in Ealing. But one of the other participants said that she had seen Walters in the communal bathroom on her floor not long before midnight. This discrepancy only came to light when stories were being collated and compared late the previous evening and no attempt had so far been made to look into this further.

The other obvious essential matter was motivation. Who would want to kill Crouch and why? Healey would concentrate on this, interviewing Crouch's colleagues and family (and friends, should there be any). Teague would speak to Wright, Walters and the Filipino, as soon as that proved possible, bearing in mind that at least one of them, Wright, and possibly all three, had gone to Bath for the day.

Healey had some other possibilities in mind, but it wasn't his practice to let his sergeant know everything he was thinking.

As he left, Healey nodded in the direction of Gifford. 'Where's everyone gone, by the way?'

'Sorry, sir, I meant to tell you. They rang last night just before I left. Wanted to know if we still needed them, and I said just one would be enough for now, seeing as all the interviewing was finished. I hope that was all right.'

'All right, but call me next time.'

* * *

Healey parked his car next to Carter's big Rover, which in daylight turned out to be maroon in colour, in the otherwise empty car park on the King's Road campus of Berkshire University. Getting out, he surveyed the long dreary brick building that ran parallel to the road, just twenty or thirty yards from it. He had never been there before and he realised that he had no idea how he was going to find Carter's office. He went to the main entrance and pulled on the handle of the heavy glass door and found that, as he had suspected would be the case on a Sunday morning, it was locked. He looked at his watch. Four minutes to ten. He had just stepped back from the door and was scanning the windows above in the hope of seeing some sign of life, when he heard the rattle of keys in the lock. Carter came out, a smile on his face, took Healey's hand and shook it as vigorously as he had the night before.

'Good morning, Richard,' he said. 'Another beautiful morning.'

'Yes,' agreed Healey, a little taken aback by Carter's cheerful manner. 'It's supposed to last another week, they say.'

'Is it indeed? No doubt it'll turn nasty then. That's when I go on holiday.'

They entered the building, climbed a flight of stairs and were walking along a narrow corridor with doors on each side.

'Where are you going? On your holiday, I mean,' asked Healey.

'South of France. We've got a little place there, above Cannes.'

'Very nice,' said Healey, wondering what relevance British weather had for a holiday in the south of France. 'Going with the family?'

Carter smiled. 'Yes. Wife and the two kids, one from my previous marriage. What about you, Richard? Are you going away?' Carter pushed open the door and ushered Healey into a room which was much smaller than he had expected.

'Not sure. We tend to do things at short notice. Occupational hazard. This case for instance ...' Healey's voice tailed off.

Carter waved his arm in the direction of a chair where Healey might sit and sat down behind his desk. Immediately he stood up again.

'Before I forget, take a look at this.' He pushed a large open volume across the desk towards Healey. 'Remember last night we were talking about the pursuit of truth?' he said. 'It's part of the title of a book. Well you can see for yourself.'

Healey put on his glasses. 'You'll need this too,' said Carter, handing him a magnifying glass. 'It's the compact edition. Of the OED,' he added.

Healey squinted at the text. 1956 J. Wilson *Language and Pursuit of Truth* ii. 57 Men make .. protests against particular types of privilege .. for instance, against class-privilege, he managed to read.

'And there's another,' said Carter. 'Let me show you.' He opened the dictionary at a page marked by a yellow Post-it. This time the quotation was from a book on Buddhism.

'Different pursuit. Different truth,' said Carter.

'Yes.' Healey continued looking at the second entry. 'I'm impressed. I wouldn't have expected you to have time to find these.'

'Well you know what they say; if you want something

doing quickly, give it to a busy man. Or woman, I suppose we have to say today.' He picked up his spectacles and began to clean them with a tissue he took from a box. 'And, to put it kindly, Peter isn't the busiest man on this earth.'

'What about Crouch? Was he a busy man?'

'Ah, well, there you have a different case altogether. If you believed what Neville said, he was the busiest man in the Department. But it was all show. If you look at what he actually produced, there's nothing there.'

'Didn't he write a book with you?'

'Oh, you know about that. That was me. He contributed very little.'

'But his name's on the cover.'

'Oh yes, but that doesn't mean much.'

'Doesn't it mean that you don't get full credit for what you did?'

'Yes.'

'I wonder why you did it then.'

'Out of friendship, as much as anything else. He was new in the Department. He seemed a nice enough guy. He was certainly bright, but he wasn't getting anywhere. I just thought he needed a bit of help to get going. That's why I suggested we do the book together.'

'But it didn't work out the way you expected?'

'No, not at all. At the beginning he was full of enthusiasm, reading a lot, making notes, writing outlines for his chapters, but not producing any text. After a few months of this, when I'd more or less finished my half of the book, I got fed up and said that unless he did produce something quickly, we'd better scrap the idea. I'd do it by myself.'

'And?'

'He did eventually write a chapter but it was almost unreadable.'

'So what did you do?'

'I rewrote it and the rest of what he did. And made up my mind not to do anything of a collaborative nature with him again.'

'Did you fall out?'

'Not at all. He was happy to be getting half of the credit. And half of the royalties. While I was happy to put the matter behind me. No, there was no ill feeling. I felt a bit sad that it hadn't worked out more as I'd anticipated, but that's all.'

'Did you remain friends?'

'Truth is, we were never very close. I know when you asked me I said I did it out of friendship. It would have been more accurate to say out of friendliness. The only real friend I have in the Department is Peter.'

'What about Crouch? What friends did he have?'

'In the Department? I don't think he had any. He seemed completely wrapped up in his home life, as far as I could see.'

'Did he have any enemies?'

'Not that I'm aware of. His inefficiency may have annoyed people but not to the extent that they became enemies. Or would throw him out of a window, if that's what you're thinking.'

Healey didn't respond. Despite the windows being open, he was becoming aware of a faint but acrid scent of sweat. He looked around the room, at the three walls lined with books, at the small table on which stood a computer, at the whiteboard covered with what he thought must be some foreign script, and finally at Carter himself, with his elbows on the desk, his head resting in his hands, looking directly through his spectacles into Healey's eyes. Carter's own hazel eyes were magnified, as were the bags beneath them. His beard still had the same traces of food on it as the previous night. His hair did not seem to have been washed either.

Not a particularly attractive man, thought Healey. But

attractive to whom? Healey had to admit that he was often surprised by what women found attractive. It certainly wasn't just appearance. Carter was energetic, successful, presumably quite well off – he had a house near Cannes, he'd said – and apparently self-confident. Healey wondered what his wife was like. What each of his wives was like. But he asked a different question.

'How did Crouch get on with his wife?'

'As well as people usually do when they're married to each other. I mean, he seemed devoted to her, couldn't do enough for her. They had the child, of course. She didn't have to work.'

'He earned enough to be comfortable?'

'Nobody earns a fortune in universities, but yes, enough to be comfortable, I'd say.'

'And they got on well?'

'Yes, at least …'

'At least what?'

'It may not have anything to do with their marriage at all, but I sensed that something was bothering Neville over the last couple of months. I told you that he always gave the impression of being busy. Going from office to office with a stack of papers, sending out dozens of memos about nothing in particular, generally wasting people's time. Well, perhaps two, no probably three months ago he stopped doing that. All of a sudden you'd hardly see him, and when you did, he didn't want to say more than hello. And not always that. I can remember a couple of occasions when he walked straight past me, as if I weren't there.'

'Do you have any idea what might have caused this?'

'None at all.'

The scent of sweat was getting stronger. Healey produced a notebook. He hesitated before speaking, knowing that he shouldn't call Carter professor, and didn't want to call him

Chris, so what should he call him? Nothing, as he'd been doing all morning.

'As a formality, can I ask you about your movements on the night that Doctor Crouch fell? I just need to know where you were from eight o'clock on Friday evening until nine o'clock on Saturday morning.'

Carter told him that at eight he had been working here in his office. Just before ten he had left for the Three Tuns, where he met Peter Farrell. At closing time they'd gone in his car to Farrell's, as they had the following evening with Healey. He'd stayed until two o'clock, then driven home, where he went straight to bed, and that was it. He left the house next morning at eight-thirty and at nine was starting his lecture to the summer school.

While Carter gave his account, Healey had been looking at a pair of large framed photographs on the wall behind him. Now he asked, 'So, that's you, is it, the young cricketer?'

'Lancashire schoolboys.'

Reminded of his dream, for a moment Healey thought to tell Carter about it but decided not to. 'Really?' he said. 'You must have been good.' Carter did not demur.

'And the other picture. Is that judo?'

'Karate, actually. But I was pretty useless. I put it up there just to keep the students in order.' Carter chuckled and his eyes glinted as he grinned at Healey.

After thanking Carter for his help, Healey stood up to leave. Carter came round the desk to shake his hand again, pausing on the way to switch on his computer. Closing the door behind him, Healey pulled back his jacket and sniffed under his arm. All he smelled was the anti-perspirant, whatever it was called, that his wife bought him. As he walked along the corridor, the nameplate on one of the doors caught his attention. On white plastic, printed in black, was 'Dr N. Crouch'. Next to it, attached to the door by a drawing-pin was a folded piece of paper on which were typed the hours that Crouch was available to see students. Healey pulled the paper from the door and slipped it into his pocket. He tried the door but it was locked.

* * *

When Healey got back to the Hall, Gifford, the constable that he had spoken to in the morning, was still there, reading a newspaper. 'Sergeant Teague asked me to tell you that he had to nip out but would be back soon,' he said, pushing away the newspaper across the table he was sitting at. Healey was reminded of Carter pushing the dictionary towards him.

'Is there something you want me to read in that?' asked Healey.

'No, sir,' said the man, 'I was just …'

'Just give me the key to Crouch's room, will you?'

Armed with the key, he climbed five flights of stairs to the floor on which Crouch's room was to be found. On his left were the rooms, with their views over the sports field; on his right was a series of windows looking down into a courtyard. As he stood outside Crouch's room, the nearest to the stairs, he heard sounds coming from the half-open door of the next room, heavy breathing and the occasional grunt. Curious, he put his head round the door and saw a diminutive woman tucking in the bedspread that she must have just thrown into place.

'Oh, my God,' she gasped, when she saw Healey, 'you frightened the life out of me. I didn't hear you come in.'

Her hair was black and tightly curled, her eyes bright blue, and her lips painted scarlet. The lines on her face suggested she was in her fifties. Dyed hair, thought Healey.

'I'm sorry,' he said, 'I didn't mean to shock you. Are you all right?'

'Yes, I'm fine.' She put her hand to her chest, gulped and put her tongue out over her lower lip. Like a gargoyle, thought Healey. 'At least, I think I am,' she added and sat down on the edge of the bed.

Healey told her who he was and why he was there. 'Do you do all the rooms on this floor?' he asked.

'Yes.'

'So you did Doctor Crouch's room?'

'I did.'

'Did he stay there every night?'

'No. In fact, he never stayed in the Hall – unless you count Friday night, of course.'

'Do you know why he had a room at all?'

'I've no idea. Unless he thought he might strike lucky with one of the women on the course.'

'What makes you say that? Was he trying, do you think?'

'I don't know. I don't think so. He didn't seem the type.'

'What type is that?'

'You know, after the women.'

Healey nodded. 'Whose room is this by the way?'

'Doctor Farrell's.'

'Does he stay over at the Hall?'

'I'm not sure.'

'Why aren't you sure?'

'Should I be telling you this? It isn't very nice talking behind someone's back.'

'I'm sorry, what's your name?'

'Rita. Or do you mean my surname?'

'Rita,' Healey adopted the most serious tone he could muster, 'I'm investigating what may turn out to be a murder.

It's your duty to tell me anything that will help me find out exactly what happened.'

The woman seemed pleased to be able to continue without any sense of guilt. 'Well, the first week he didn't use to use it at all. Except to keep his mac here.'

'His mac?'

'Yes, it used to be lying there on the bed. Never moved. I suppose he thought it might rain one day. It's gone now, though, and it still hasn't rained.'

'And since the first week has he used the room at all?'

'Well he's used the bed all right but I'm not sure it's at night.'

'Go on.'

'The talk is that he comes up here in the afternoons.'

'And?'

'When I come the next morning, the bed clothes are all over the place.'

'Is that *it?* Nothing else? No evidence of someone else being here with him?'

'No. Well, sometimes I've smelled perfume on the pillow but that could be Doctor Farrell's aftershave, couldn't it, things being unisex and all these days?'

Healey went to the head of the bed and lifted a pillow to his nose. It did smell of some scent or other but he was at a loss as to whether it was a man's or a woman's. He put the pillow down.

'So are all the rooms on this floor for the tutors?'

'Yes. I mean no. The one at the far end is Sam's.'

'Sam?'

'The course assistant.'

'I didn't realise there was one. What's his second name?' As he asked, Healey pulled out his course booklet.

Rita laughed. 'It isn't a he, it's a she. Samantha. Samantha Black. She's a student.'

Healey found her name in the booklet.

'All right. And who's in the next room to this?'

'That's Miss Walters. Or *Ms* Walters, as she likes to be called.' Rita pronounced Ms with a long drawn out zzz sound.

'And then?'

'Mr Wright.'

'And then?'

'An empty room. Then Sam.'

On the blank inside cover of the course booklet Healey made a quick sketch.

Crouch	Farrell	Walters	Wright	——	Samantha

STAIRS

Putting the booklet back into his pocket, he asked, 'You say you clean all the rooms on this floor?'

'Yes.' The cleaner nodded.

'Do you remember if any of them wasn't slept in the night that Dr Crouch fell?'

'Ms Walters' wasn't. I'm sure of that. Doctor Crouch's wasn't, of course.' She looked at the ceiling and held her mouth open. 'That's all, I think,' she said eventually. 'I had to make the other beds, though, like I say, I never know if a bed's used at night or before. Or actually slept in.' Her eyes twinkled. 'I don't come nosing up here at night, Inspector.'

'No, I'm sure you don't. Does *anybody* come round at night?'

'I don't know. You'll have to ask Mr Bird to find that out.'

'I'll do that,' said Healey.

Healey left Rita to carry on with her cleaning and let himself into Crouch's room. At first glance it looked just as he had left it the previous morning. Then he noticed traces of graphite left by the scene of crime people where they had been looking for fingerprints. He saw too that the attaché case and the letter had gone, which reminded him that he had to ring about the letter, unless there was already a report on it downstairs. He'd check that before he left.

He moved to the window and looked out. He heard the buzz of a moped and looked down to see the little red helmet of its rider flash repeatedly between the chestnuts that lined the road. On the other side of the road were the hedge-lined University playing-fields, a car park and tennis courts to the right of the entrance, a pavilion and cricket pitch directly ahead. After weeks without rain, the grass was the colour of straw. Over the roof of the pavilion he could see a man on the cricket square with a hand-mower preparing a wicket. The boundary had already been marked with white metal disks on spikes. Healey glanced at his watch. He guessed the match would start in a couple of hours and last at least until six or seven in the evening. He would pass by the pavilion in the afternoon to see what he could find out about Friday's game. Crouch's last game, he thought. 'Krapp's last tape,' he said aloud, and wondered why.

* * *

At the priest's signal, the congregation rose and made its way slowly towards the altar to receive communion. Just one figure at the rear of the church, head bowed, remained seated.

* * *

'Come on, Dad.' Jamie was calling to him from the garden, where he was standing with his cricket bat. 'Come and bowl to me.'

Healey had just got back from the Hall and brought in the shopping that had been in the boot of the car and put it on the kitchen counter. Luckily, there had been nothing that could have gone off. His wife, who was making lentil soup, had acted as if she hadn't noticed and he had picked up the Sunday Times from the table where he'd left it a few hours earlier. 'I want to look at the paper,' he called through the open window.

'Aw, come on, Dad.'

Healey remembered how much it had meant to him when *his* father had played with him. He put down the paper. 'Okay. But just five minutes.'

'Yes!' His eight-year-old son punched the air.

In the cupboard under the stairs Healey found a cardboard box that had held bottles of wine. He took this and an old tennis ball out onto the lawn. Using the box as the wickets, and having placed Jamie's hands in more or less the right position on the bat handle, Healey proceeded to lob the ball gently in his direction. Jamie swished at it, missed it completely, and the ball bounced twice before hitting the box. Jamie picked up the ball and rolled it back to him. Collecting the ball, Healey walked up to his son.

'Look,' he said, 'try and hit the ball just after it's bounced. See where it's going to bounce and step towards it.'

He put the ball on the ground two feet in front of them. Leaning over him, he put his hands round Jamie's on the bat.

'Imagine it's going to bounce there. So take a step forward, and *bang,* you hit it.'

He stepped forward himself, dragging Jamie with him. 'Do you see?'

Jamie nodded, without looking up at him.

'Let's give it a try then.' As Healey stood up, he saw his wife watching them from the kitchen.

'Jill, why don't you come and play too?'

'I can't. I've got to watch the soup.'

Healey went back to where he had bowled the first ball from. He lobbed another down. Jamie took a big step forward, swung his bat, and the ball went flying over the fence and into the garden next door.

'That's it,' said Healey. 'You've got it.'

Jamie glowed with pleasure.

'That was really good,' said his father. 'Now, do you want to go round and get the ball back?'

* * *

Later that afternoon Healey stood outside the Crouches' house in Falstaff Avenue. He had rung the bell twice but there was no answer. He had deliberately not phoned ahead; he didn't want her to have time to prepare herself. A ground floor window in the house next door opened.

'She's in the back garden.' It was the woman who had been gardening when he was there the previous time.

'Thanks,' said Healey. He stepped to the gate between the house and the garage, pressed the latch and pushed. The gate didn't move.

'Can you tell her I'm here?' he said. 'The gate's bolted.'

'Go through the garage,' said the woman. 'It isn't locked. The lock doesn't work.' She continued to watch him.

Healey turned the metal handle and tipped the yellow garage door upwards and over until it was half open. He stooped and peered inside. Directly in front of him was the sunlit front end of a grey Mini. In the wall to the right of the car he made out a door. Standing up inside the garage, Healey edged round the car, took hold of the handle of the door he had seen, turned it, and pushed.

The door swung open and he saw before him Mrs Crouch sitting in a deck chair with a young child on her knee. The chair was set at an angle to him and Mrs Crouch did not see him but the child, presumably her daughter, was looking directly at him and began to tug at her mother's arm, pointing in his direction. Mrs Crouch turned her head and saw him too. Healey stepped forward.

'I'm sorry, I rang the bell but there was no answer.' He was conscious that in the morning he had already apologised for arriving unexpectedly in a woman's presence. At least Mrs Crouch didn't perform the same pantomime act as the cleaner had.

'Oh, Inspector,' she said and made as if to get up.

'Don't get up.'

Mrs Crouch eased the girl from her knee onto the concrete ground, where she stood, looking up into Healey's face.

'Your daughter?' he asked.

'Yes. Gia.'

As Healey looked down at her, Gia took her mother's hand and pressed her hip against the side of the deckchair. 'Mrs Crouch,' he began, 'I need to talk to you seriously. I don't suppose Gia could ...' He gestured in the direction of the house.

'Not really, there's no one else to look after her.'

'All right, but could we go inside?'

'Do we need to? Can't we talk here?'

'Very well.'

'You'll find a deckchair at the back of the garage. Do you mind getting it?'

After what had happened on his previous visit to the house, Healey had made up his mind to be very formal and keep a distance, physical as well as psychological, between him and Crouch's widow. Now, within a minute of arriving, he found himself sitting opposite her in a deckchair and, despite himself, looking at the opening at the top of her blouse, where he saw a heavy gold chain and crucifix. This won't do, he thought. He put his hand to his mouth, coughed,

sniffed, and then proceeded to produce a notepad, which he opened, and appeared to study what was in fact a blank page. He looked up and fixed his eyes on hers. He spoke quietly in order not to alarm the child.

'Mrs Crouch, when I came here yesterday you told me that you had spent the previous evening and night alone with your daughter.'

'Excuse me,' interrupted Mrs Crouch. 'Gia, why don't you take dolly to the bottom of the garden and show her the flowers?' The girl seemed reluctant but picked up the cabbage patch doll that lay at her feet and carried it by one of its legs as she walked slowly down the lawn.

'Yes, you were saying?'

'First you told me that you were alone with your daughter. Later you telephoned to say that you hadn't been alone, that Mr Wright was here all night.' Even as he said this, Healey was conscious of the rhyme of *night* and *Wright,* and even worse, that *Wright* could be interpreted as *Right.* Spend the night with Mr Right! Mrs Crouch, however, did not smile and continued to look at him intently. He pressed on.

'The reason you gave for changing your story was that you lied at first because you were embarrassed at spending the night with a man who was not your husband. That's what you told me and that's what you told my sergeant when he questioned you. You also told *him* ... ' At this point Healey hesitated, glancing in the direction of the child who was now too far away to hear if they spoke quietly.

He continued, 'You told him that Mr Wright was just a friend, that you did not have sexual relations with him, that you slept in your bedroom and he slept downstairs on the sofa. Am I ... er ... correct?' He had just managed to stop himself saying 'right'.

'Yes.'

'And you stand by your new story?'

'Yes.'

'Well I have to tell you, Mrs Crouch, that I find it difficult to believe.'

'It isn't a story. It's true.'

'All right. How often has this happened before? That he's spent the night here when your husband was away.'

'It was the first time.'

'What time did Mr Wright arrive?'

'About ten o'clock.'

'What time did you go to bed?'

'I don't know. Perhaps midnight.'

'So you spent two hours together. What did you do during that time?'

'We talked.'

'What about?'

'Many things.'

'Such as?'

She hesitated. 'About the Philippines,' she said eventually.

'And?'

She looked at him blankly.

'And?' he repeated. 'What else did you talk about?'

She did not answer.

'So Mr Wright is a tutor on a summer school, where there's a party in progress. He leaves the party, comes here, talks to you for two hours about the Philippines, then you go to bed. And what does he do? Does he go back to the party? Does he go back to the Hall where he's got a bed? No, he spends the night on your sofa, during which time your husband falls to his death at the Hall. Are you surprised I find it difficult to believe?'

As he looked at her, tears began to well up in Mrs Crouch's eyes. She stood up and felt inside the pockets of the cut-off jeans that she was wearing.

'Just a minute, please,' she said and went towards the

house. Healey noticed that, despite her slim figure, Mrs Crouch's hips were wider than he had remembered. Her daughter went running after her, a pink carnation that she had picked for her doll falling from her hand.

As she came out of the house, Mrs Crouch was still dabbing her eyes with a tissue.

'I'm sorry,' she said. She sat down. 'I've left Gia watching television. I don't want her to hear what I'm going to tell you.' She put the tissue to her nose and sniffed.

'So are you going to tell me what really happened?' asked Healey.

'What I said is true,' she replied. 'He did stay all night on the sofa. But we did not speak about only the Philippines.' She sniffed again. 'You see, I asked him to come because ...'

'Because?'

'Because I was afraid of my husband ...'

'Go on.'

'He was being very violent with me.'

'He was hitting you.'

'No, not hitting, but shouting, shouting so loud, in my face. He said terrible things.'

'Why?'

'I don't know why. He was becoming crazy.'

'What terrible things did he say?'

'He called me a bitch. A whore. He said I was sleeping with other men.'

'Is that true?' Healey's curiosity was not exclusively professional.

'No. Of course not.'

'And how long had that been going on for?'

'For months. It started after Easter.'

'But you waited until last Friday before you felt the need to talk to Mr Wright.'

69

'No. I have told him before. But this time was different.'

'In what way?'

'The night before, Neville told me that he hated me, really hated me, and he would like to kill me. I was frightened. That's why I asked Tim to stay with me.' Mrs Crouch burst into tears, put her hands to her eyes, and rocked backwards and forwards, sobbing. At which, Healey's first thought was to make a pot of tea. He forgot to ask about her husband's friends.

* * *

his wife, his child
what have I done to them?

* * *

Healey parked his car in the sports ground car park, and ambled over to the pavilion. He watched as a bowler tore in at great speed and released the ball, which bounced half way down the pitch. The batsman planted his right foot outside off stump and hooked the ball fiercely in Healey's direction. The ball was still three feet above the ground when it reached him and he caught it in front of his midriff. He signalled a six, quite unnecessarily, he realised, and there was a ripple of applause. He tossed the ball to the fielder who had come from square leg to collect it, and continued on his way to the pavilion. As he got there, he was greeted by a small, bearded grey-haired man with a jutting chin, dressed in whites and holding a nearly empty pint glass.

'Good catch,' he said.

'Thanks,' responded Healey. 'It's been a long time.' His hands were still stinging but he wouldn't mention that.

'The bar's open,' said the man, 'if you fancy a drink. Just through there.'

'I won't, thanks. But what about you?'

'Very kind. Pint of Directors, please.'

While Healey was being served, he heard a loud 'Howzat?' from the field. There were groans from the front of the pavilion, and, a few moments later, brief clapping, which Healey suspected, was sympathetic in nature. When he emerged from the pavilion, the bearded man was engaged in putting on the pads that the outcoming batsman had just taken off. Healey placed the glass of beer on a nearby table.

'Many thanks,' said the man, and continued to struggle with the straps.

Healey let him finish padding up before he asked him if he knew Neville Crouch.

'Neville! Of course I do. He played for us the other day. He a friend of yours?' The man picked up the pint Healey had bought him and began to swig from it.

'Not really. Actually, I'm with Thames Valley CID.'

The man put down the glass.

Healey continued, 'I don't know if you've heard …?' The man did not react. Healey realised that he was doing this all wrong. He couldn't tell a man who was about to go out to bat that someone he possibly knew well had been killed.

'It's just that I have to check up on the movements of a number of people. You told me that he played for you the other day. Would that be Friday afternoon?'

'Yes.'

'What time did you start?'

'Half past one.'

'And finish?'

'Towards seven.'

'Did Doctor Crouch seem well that day?'

'I suppose so.'

'Nothing unusual about his behaviour?'

'No, nothing I can think of. What's happened, anyhow? Is Neville all right?'

Before Healey could reply, there was another triumphant shout from the centre of the field. One of the stumps at the far end was leaning back, and a disconsolate batsman was already trudging back to the pavilion. The little bearded man slipped on his gloves, put his bat under his arm, and set off in sprightly fashion for the wicket. After perhaps ten yards, he stopped, turned, and called back to Healey, 'He did get a bang on the head, if that's the sort of thing you mean,' then continued on his way.

'Retired hurt,' Healey heard a voice behind him say. He looked round and saw that it was the scorer who had spoken.

'You were talking to Jim about Neville, weren't you? He ducked into a bouncer that didn't bounce. Hit him on the head.' The man flicked over the pages of the scorebook.

'Look, here it is. Retired hurt, thirteen. Unlucky thirteen. We all had a laugh about that. Except Neville, of course.'

'Was he badly hurt?'

'I don't think so. It was his pride that was hurt more than anything else. It didn't bleed. Just a bump.'

'Where was the bump exactly?'

The man leaned towards Healey and placed a finger at a point above his own left temple. 'Just about here.'

'Did he have it checked out, go to the hospital, do you know?'

'I don't think so. He took a couple of paracetamol. Said he was going home to have a lie down.'

'Did he say *home*?'

'Oh, I'm not sure. Maybe not.'

Healey waited while the man concentrated on making an entry in the scorebook. 'By the way, do you know if Dr Crouch had his own bat?'

'You mean on Friday?'

'Yes,' replied Healey quickly, realising that he shouldn't have used the past tense.

'I imagine so. I'm sure he did.'

'I don't suppose he could have left it here, could he? I mean, after being hit.'

'No. If he had, someone would have noticed when we all left.'

Healey was about to thank the man, when he heard shouting from the middle of the pitch. He recognised the voice of the bearded man, who was waving his bat in the direction of the sightscreen, in front of which stood a woman with a dog on a lead. 'Get out of there,' the bearded man called. It was only when one of the fielders ran over and presumably explained what was wanted of her, that the woman moved. She headed slowly in the direction of the car park and exit.

'Thanks,' said Healey to the scorer, setting off for the car park. He and the woman met almost beside his car.

'Excuse me,' he said. 'It's Miss Wood, isn't it?'

'Woods,' replied the woman. 'With an ess. Do I know you?' She stood feet apart, both arms behind her back. Though she was only small and apparently frail, she gave the impression of someone who was used to more than holding her own. She looked Healey in the eye.

'No,' said Healey, 'but I was at the Hall when you were talking to Miss Colgan yesterday. I saw you come out of her office with your dog. Maisie.'

'Daisy.'

'I'm sorry. Daisy. I believe you live just by the Hall.'

'Yes.'

'And when you saw the Warden yesterday you were complaining about the noise on Friday night.'

'Was I?' replied Miss Woods. 'I really don't know.'

'I'm sorry?'

'I don't remember what I was talking about. In fact I don't remember speaking to … Who did you say I was speaking to?'

'Miss Colgan.'

'Oh, yes.'

'But you don't remember what you talked to her about?'

'What are you? Police?'

'Yes, I am actually. Thames Valley CID.'

'Shouldn't you have told me that at the beginning?'

'I'm sorry.'

'And don't you have a badge or something?'

Healey produced his warrant card and showed it to her.

She examined it carefully. 'Well, Chief Inspector. Now I know who you are. What was it you were asking me?'

'I was asking about your visit to the Hall. I believe you were complaining about the noise on Friday night.'

'Oh, the noise. Yes, there's often noise from there.'

'And on Friday night?'

'Friday night.' She paused. 'Friday night. What day is it today?'

'Sunday.'

'So Friday would be …'

'The day before yesterday.'

'The day before yesterday.' Again she paused. 'No, I'm afraid I don't remember, Chief Inspector. It's my Alzheimer's, you see.'

'You've got Alzheimer's?'

'Yes.'

'So you can't remember if you perhaps took …' Healey nearly said 'Maisie' again, the name of his own dog. 'Daisy?'

'Yes. Daisy.'

'Daisy out for a walk.'

'Well I always take her for a walk before bed.'

'And do you bring her this way?'

'Yes.'

'Past the Hall?'

'Yes.'

'So you probably brought her this way on Friday night. Do you have any idea what time that might have been?'

'No, not really.'

'Do you remember noticing anything unusual at all? In the area of the Hall.'

'I can't even remember coming out.'

'Not at all?'

'No, not at all.'

'Well, if you do remember anything, please let me know.' Healey handed her a card. 'The number is there,' he said.

Miss Woods put the card into a pocket, gave Healey a pinched smile, tugged at the lead, and set off with Daisy in tow. When she was about twenty yards away, she turned abruptly. 'Is this to do with the murder?' she called. Healey pretended not to hear, opened the door of his car and climbed in. In the rear mirror he watched Miss Woods and Daisy make their way out of the playing fields onto the road, and turn left.

Once they had disappeared from view, Healey turned his attention to the cricket. The little bearded man was striking the ball all over the field. Through the open car window, Healey heard spasmodic clapping as the ball went for a four or a six. At one point the ball was struck in his direction, crossed the boundary and came to rest not far from his car. Healey sat and watched as a tired and red-faced fielder came lumbering up, picked up the ball, and trotted back onto the pitch, before bowling the ball underarm in the general direction of the wicket. Hot and tired himself, Healey yawned. He would go to the Hall, check what had been happening, and then go home. With luck he would be able to have a nap before supper.

But he was out of luck.

* * *

'What? Lentil bake?'

'Yes, lentil bake. What's wrong with that?'

'We had lentil soup for lunch and now we're having lentil bake for supper.'

'And so?'

'Christ Almighty. I give up.' Healey turned away from the kitchen door, resisting the urge to slam it shut.

His wife called after him. 'You give up? What if I gave up? Let's see how you'd manage.'

'Well I wouldn't do lentils for lunch and supper,' he muttered to himself. He went into the front room, where the two children were on the sofa watching television. They looked round at him but said nothing. Nor did he. Why did it happen so often like this, he thought. He had come home quite cheerful, thinking he'd take the paper to bed and doze off while reading it. He had popped his head into the kitchen to ask what was for supper, and immediately they were having a row again. He knew that the real cause wasn't lentils – he'd enjoy the lentil bake – but he didn't want to think about the source of their problems now, though his mind was burning with the injustice of it all. He looked down on the children, who had turned back to face the television. He put a hand on each of the heads and ruffled their hair, before going into the hall, out through the front door, then through the gate at the side of the house and into the back garden. He wasn't ready to go through the kitchen yet.

He stood at the bottom of the garden and looked back at the house. It was detached, but only just (the house on the right was no more than six feet away from his) and had been built, badly, in the early sixties. Through the kitchen window on the left he could just make out the figure of his wife, leaning over the stove, not moving, listening no doubt to whatever happened to be on Radio 4. A few moments later he saw her cross to the Welsh dresser, gather plates and cutlery, then disappear into the hall, to reappear at the table beside the French windows in the dining-cum-sitting room. As he watched her lay the table, thought of the children in front of the television, looked round the sunlit garden and back at the house, he was aware that these images belonged to the picture he had had in his mind since childhood, a picture which he had worked hard to create in real life. But he was also aware that in his imagination it had been a silent picture and one over which he had exercised complete control. It had been a child's picture. He suddenly wondered what pictures of grown-up life his wife had had as a child. Feeling more tenderness towards her than he had for some time, he went back to the house to tell her he was sorry.

* * *

After supper Healey sat in his study, a small room with bright orange walls, part of an extension to the ground floor of the house, built before they had bought it. The cursor on his computer, into which he had just tried unsuccessfully to insert the floppy disk he had taken from Crouch's house, blinked at him incessantly. Why the hell did they make different sized disks, for God's sake? He turned the machine off and took from a drawer of his desk a large sheet of paper, on which he wrote down a series of names, placing them apparently at random on the page. Against each name he proceeded to write in green ink the supposed whereabouts of that individual around the time of Crouch's death, next to which, in several cases, he drew a large question mark. He then took a red pen and to a small number of names added a possible motive for murdering Crouch. Finally, still using the red pen, he drew a large circle round three or four of the names.

As he stood up from his desk, Healey groaned. Even in this warm weather his back was giving him trouble. Not something to talk about. He'd already been approached about possible early retirement. Give them a chance, and he'd soon be gardening full-time. And that would be no good for his back, he thought ruefully. He went into the next room, poured himself a scotch, and sat down at the table where they had eaten supper. Normally they ate in the kitchen, but on Sundays they had supper here in the dining-cum-living room that gave onto the garden through French windows, using their best silverware and red paper napkins, and listening to the top forty on Radio 1.

It was Jamie who had raised the question of the lentils. 'Dad, why were you annoyed we were having lentils?'

Healey looked round the table before pinching the end of his nose between his thumb and first finger.

'What?' asked Jamie.

Healey held his nose again.

'What? What d'you mean?'

'Farts,' said Healey. 'Lentils make you fart. The more you eat, the more farts you do.'

Jamie giggled.

'Shurrup, Dad,' said Meg. 'We don't want to hear about farts when we're eating.'

'And,' Healey continued, 'we already have enough farts in this house. Three at this table for a start.'

'Four,' said his wife.

'Oh, so you admit you're one, do you?'

'No, I mean you.'

'But if there are four at the table, one of them must be you.'

'No,' shouted Jamie. 'What about Maisie?'

'Maisie's not at the table,' said Healey. 'Where is she, by the way?'

'In the garden.' Meg pointed through the window and Healey, who was sitting with his back to the window, turned to look out. He winced.

'Your back?' his wife asked.

He shook his head. 'Hey, you kids, you'll never guess what happened to me. I met a dog just like Maisie. And guess what her name is.'

'Maisie,' the two children said together.

'No, not quite. It was Daisy.'

After he had told them just how like Maisie the dog was, and who its owner was, and how he had found it hard to remember its name, the conversation had wandered over a variety of topics before Meg asked them to be quiet for the top five hits at least. When these were over, so was the meal, and Healey had gone into the study.

Now he was back at the table, sipping his scotch. The phone rang and he listened as his wife went from the kitchen to the hall to answer it. 'It's for you,' she called.

It was Teague, telling him that neither the Filipino nor Mary Walters had been in the Hall, that the coach which had taken the participants to Bath was due back at the Hall about nine o'clock, and did Healey want him to meet it and interview Wright, and see if the other two were on it, or would tomorrow morning do? To Teague's obvious relief, Healey said that tomorrow morning would do.

Finishing his whisky, Healey went back into the study. Glancing repeatedly at the sheet he had already been working on, he quickly made three lists. One was headed 'CHECK'; the second was headed 'FIND OUT'; and the third, which represented his plan for the following day, was headed 'MONDAY'. Having written the lists, he looked through them, nodding at various points with approval. Satisfied with his work, he clipped the sheets of paper together and laid them down neatly on his desk.

He went into the next room, poured himself another whisky, and slumped into an armchair. From the low table in front of him he lifted a heavy hardback book on modern art by an Australian, whose television series on the same subject – and with the same title – he had already watched. He put his hand upwards and behind him to turn on the standard lamp. As his fingers searched for the pull-cord, he felt a twinge in his back. 'Bloody back,' he said to himself. 'What a pain.' Not for the first time he found himself smiling at his use of the expression. It reminded him of a period, several years before, when he had been involved in the training of new recruits, talking about legal sanctions of various kinds, and had seemed unable to stop using the word 'fine' as an expression of approval.

That work hadn't lasted for long. They had decided that he wasn't the most suitable officer for recruits to meet. Too idiosyncratic, he had been told. He had been told worse. A maths teacher at his grammar school had summed him up in his report book with a single word – *Lazy*. On the same page, his French teacher had referred to his *'dilettante attitude'*, an expression which he had found quite attractive and felt almost flattered by. He glanced down at the book on his lap and grunted. A dilettante still, he thought, conscious that he had bought at least a dozen such volumes through the book club

but had hardly got further than looking at the pictures in any of them. No change there.

There had been a change, however. He had been in the police for nearly twenty-five years. And done pretty well. Not many people who had known him as a teenager would have predicted that. Leaving school after a few months in the sixth form when he missed more classes than he attended, he had worked for nearly five years as a trainee personnel manager in a chemical factory in the centre of Widnes, next door to the knacker's yard. He had gone to night school, first to get qualifications in personnel work (something at which he had been singularly unsuccessful), and later to take 'A' levels with the intention of getting into university. He finally did pass one 'A' level, but with such a poor grade that he knew no university would accept him. It was soon after this, when he woke one winter morning and heard the rain hammering against his bedroom window, that he decided he wouldn't go to the factory that day. Or any other day. Within a week he had left home, rented a room in Liverpool, and gone on the dole.

It was at the Employment Exchange that he saw the advertisement for the police. He wasn't in the least attracted by it at first, but as weeks went by and he didn't get any work except casual labour, he began to think of it more and more as a possibility. Eventually he applied and, somewhat to his surprise, was accepted for training. Looking back on it now, he was pretty sure that it was the 'A' level that attracted them. Apart from that, he couldn't have looked such a good prospect. Anyhow, he survived the training, getting by on the physical side, being outstanding on the academic. When he graduated, he was told that he had a great future ahead of him in the force. You could be a chief constable one day, they had said. Well, he had known for a long time now that he wasn't going to be a chief constable, or anything like it. It had taken him several years to see it clearly, but for him the police wasn't a career; it had never been more than a job. A job that he mostly enjoyed, especially from the time he became a detective, and one that he was good at. But it was just a job.

As he reflected in this way, Healey turned the pages of the book, stopping here and there to look at a picture or to read a few words. He had begun to read about how Matisse in old age was unable to hold a paintbrush, when the print began to go out of focus, and Healey knew that he was about to have the snooze that he had hoped to have before supper. The room was soon filled with the sound of snoring and the predictable effects of eating too many lentils.

When he woke up, Healey wandered into the front room and switched on the television. He might just catch the cricket highlights, he thought. But no, it was Sunday and they weren't playing.

* * *

Someone, somewhere, sat up in bed, and switched on the light.

> *thank God*
> *I didn't do it*

> *but I did ... I did*
> *that was just a dream*

MONDAY

Healey woke early to another sunny day. While he drank a mug of tea, he completed the 'Quick Crossword', as it was misleadingly named, that his wife hadn't managed to finish the previous day. He took the dog for a walk, shaved and showered, drank another mug of tea, collected the papers he had left on his desk the night before, and left the house just before seven. As he was getting into his car, he thought for a moment of going back to take a cup of coffee to his wife who was still in bed, but decided not to. He was moving and he needed to keep moving. And, anyhow, she'd be glad not to be disturbed this early. He swung out of his drive into Beech Lane and immediately recognised the figure of Farrell walking in the same direction he was driving. He pulled up alongside and wound down the front passenger window. Farrell's beard, Healey noticed, had been subjected to a severe trim, though his hair still hung over his collar.

'Can I give you a lift?' he asked.

'I'm going to the Hall.'

'So am I. Jump in.' Healey lifted his papers from the seat and stuffed them in the glove compartment.

Farrell climbed in and fastened the safety belt around him. 'Thanks. You're starting early.'

'I was going to say the same to you.'

'Well, I'm giving a talk at nine and I'm afraid I haven't done much in the way of preparation. I've got to look through stuff that I left in my room in the Hall.' He glanced sideways at Healey. 'What's your excuse?'

'I'm a policeman.'

'Oh.' Without this time looking at Healey, Farrell went on, 'Er, I wonder if … I know I shouldn't be asking you this, but have you made … is there … I'm not even sure how to ask the question …'

'You mean, have we made any progress? Yes, we have actually. But you wouldn't expect me to tell you what form that's taken.'

'No, of course not.'

Healey had stopped at the traffic lights at Christchurch Green. 'I suppose *you* must have been thinking about it too?'

Farrell hesitated before replying. 'Yes, I suppose I have.'

'And?'

Again Farrell hesitated. 'I can't see who would have wanted to do it.' He turned towards Healey, who was looking directly at him. 'Assuming that Neville didn't do it himself.'

Healey did not respond but continued to look at Farrell. A car immediately behind them hooted and Healey looked up to see that the lights had turned to green. He moved forward and made the turn into Elmhurst Road. A few seconds later they were outside the Hall. Farrell got out and, holding the door open, leaned down. 'I've been thinking,' he said. 'You know we were talking about the OU the other night. Well, we offer part-time courses at our place and I was wondering if you would like me to let you have details of them. There might be something that you'd be interested in.'

'That's kind of you. Yes, I would, if you don't mind.'

'No problem.' Farrell looked as if he might say more but only smiled, held up his hand briefly, as if in thanks for the lift, and closed the door.

Healey watched him cross the road and go into the Hall. He opened the glove compartment and took out his papers. As he did so, there was a tap on the window beside him and the pink smiling face of Teague appeared. Healey made a semicircular movement with his hand to indicate to Teague that he should go round to the passenger side of the car. Teague did this, opened the door and dropped into the seat, an audible puff of air coming from his mouth.

'Morning, sir.'

'Good morning, Teague. And how are you?'

'Wide awake and ready to go. Unlike the driver ahead of me at the lights back there.' Teague chuckled.

Without appearing to have heard the remark, Healey promised himself revenge before the day was out. 'Right,' he said, 'let's agree what we're going to do today. I'd like you to talk to the Filipino again. Go through every detail of his movements, every little detail. Doesn't matter how long it takes. Okay? Check tickets, credit card slips, everything. Well, you know.'

'Yes, sir.'

'And go through all the statements again to see if he's mentioned by anyone else. Look for mentions of Wright and Walters too. Get the latest from the lab. We haven't had a report, have we?'

'I'll check.'

'And get this to them.' Healey took from his breast pocket the folded piece of paper that he had taken from Crouch's office door the day before. Ask them to compare this with the letter we found in Crouch's room. Find out when the inquest's going to be.' Healey became pensive, put his hand to his mouth and chewed at the nail of his thumb.

Teague waited a few moments before asking, 'Is that all?'

'What? Oh, yes. I'll take Wright and the Walters woman, since you didn't manage to do it yesterday. I'll see you at the Queen's Head at one.'

* * *

Wright drew deeply on his hand rolled cigarette, paused before blowing smoke out of the corner of his mouth. Through narrowed eyes he looked directly at Healey and asked in a surprisingly deep voice, 'So what is it you want to know?'

Wright had still been asleep when Healey knocked at his door, but now fifteen minutes later he sat in the armchair, looking neat in a mauve shirt and dark pink trousers, with nothing on his noticeably small feet. He had grey eyes, a wide, rather delicate mouth, and shoulder length dirty blonde hair. Healey, sitting opposite him on the upright chair, wondered what kind of woman would find him attractive. Hadn't he been thinking more or less the same thing about Carter the previous day? There was no reason why Wright shouldn't appeal to Teresa Crouch, especially if he gave her support with the problems she said she was having with her husband. Could there be something between them? There must be. Even if he hadn't spent the night with her – and Healey doubted that he had – she was willing to lie for him. So there must be something. But then he had seen the Italian woman waiting for him to go on the trip to Bath. What was going on there? The thought crossed his mind that Wright could also be attractive to men. The powerful scent of the sweet smelling aftershave or deodorant that filled the room may have brought this possibility to mind, as well as his choice of clothes.

To Healey, Wright's languid manner and an accent which struck him as posh made him distinctly unappealing. He began by asking Wright to tell him everything that had happened on the Friday evening. Wright said that he had been at the party from the start at eight o'clock, had left around ten and walked to Falstaff Avenue, rather than take his car, because he'd had a few drinks and thought he might be over the limit. He talked with Mrs Crouch until she had gone to bed and then slept on the sofa, coming back to the Hall early the next morning.

Healey then asked Wright to describe in detail the route he had taken to Falstaff Avenue. At various points in Wright's account, Healey asked him if he had seen anyone on that part of the journey. Wright hadn't. When asked if he expected Healey to believe that a two-mile stretch of the town had been completely deserted of people at that time of a Friday night, he said no, perhaps not, but he had been thinking about the problems between Crouch and his wife, and so he hadn't noticed anyone. You're a liar, thought Healey but didn't say it.

Instead, he asked about these 'problems'. Did they really exist? Wright replied that he was sure they did but he didn't know why Crouch accused her as he had. Nor did he know how long it had been going on. He had been completely absorbed in his studying for the MA. It was not as easy as some might imagine to complete an MA in nine months. But yes, he had visited the Crouches occasionally over the previous months, though he hadn't noticed tension of any kind between them. When Healey observed that he didn't seem to be very good at noticing things, Wright smiled briefly, revealing more teeth than there seemed room for in even such a wide mouth. 'It's not my job,' he said. 'I'm not a policeman.'

Not rising to the bait, Healey switched his questioning to Wright's days in Manila. Wright told him that he had worked in the same British Council language school as Crouch for three years before Crouch got the job in Reading. They had always got on well and it was Crouch who had encouraged him to do the MA at the University of Berkshire. Healey asked how Crouch had met his wife. It was through Teresa's younger sister, who was one of Crouch's students at the school and to whom Crouch had taken quite a fancy, according to Wright. Crouch had a thing about young oriental women, not that he had done much about it, as far as Wright knew. But when his student invited him to her apartment and he met Teresa there, that was *it*, so to speak. They latched onto each other immediately and six months later they were married.

'Was Teresa a student too?' asked Healey.

Again he was treated to a brief smile. 'No, certainly not. I mean she had *been* a student – she trained as an English teacher – but she was working in a bar at the time he met her.'

'In a bar?'

'As a hostess.'

'Which means?'

'That she made a lot more money than she would have earned as a teacher.'

'That's not what I meant.'

'No, but it tells you what you want to know, doesn't it?'

Healey wasn't sure that it did but he let it pass. 'So Crouch changed her world?'

'You could say that.'

'Was she grateful to him?'

'I'm not sure that she thought in terms of gratitude. But she appreciated what marriage to him had done for her.'

'When was it they got married?'

'Seven or eight years ago. It must have been around seventy-six, I suppose.'

'Since they got married, was she tempted, do you think, to find someone, well, more attractive. I mean, she's a very good looking woman, and he was, how can I put it, rather unprepossessing.'

'I really don't know about that. Though I doubt it. You know, you've got to look at him the way she did to know that. Through different cultural eyes.'

Healey did not like being told this by a man not much more than half his age. 'So why did he accuse her of being a whore?'

'I don't know.' Wright looked at his watch. 'Is this going to take much longer? I've got to be at a lecture at nine.'

'Did she ever try anything on with you?' Healey was deliberately crude.

'I beg your pardon?'

'Did she?'

'No, she didn't.'

'Never?'

'Never.'

'Not at all?'

'No, not at all. Look, what's the point of these questions?'

'Well, think about it. You arrive in the country. Visit their house off and on. You're young and good looking. He gets suspicious and accuses her of carrying on with … someone. He suddenly falls out of a window at a time when the lady says you were with her but really you were still in the Hall …'

'But I wasn't.'

'Wasn't what?'

'In the Hall.'

'Where were you then? Why don't you tell me?'

'I was with Mrs Crouch.'

'Oh yes. Of course.' Healey looked intently at Wright for a few seconds before saying, 'You played cricket with Dr Crouch on Friday afternoon, didn't you?'

'Yes.'

'When Dr Crouch was hit by the ball and left, do you know where he went?'

'No. I was batting myself at the time.'

'So you wouldn't have noticed whether he took his bat with him?'

'No.' Wright stood up, yawned noisily, and walked to the window. He picked up a guitar that was leaning against the wall, turned towards Healey and lightly brushed the strings.

'Where did you go after the match?' asked Healey.

'To the Hall.'

'How long did you stay there?'

'Until I left the party to go to Teresa's.'

'What did you do between arriving at the Hall and leaving the party?'

Wright went still for a moment, his brow furrowed. Then he smiled. 'I had a shower, went to bed, had a snooze, got up to have supper, and then it was the party.'

'There is another thing,' said Healey, who remained seated. 'There's a Filipino on the course.'

'Reyes.'

'Do you know him?'

'Yes, we taught in the same school. Why?'

'So his English must be very good, to teach for the British Council.'

'It's excellent. As good as yours or mine.'

'Really? Do you know where he is right now?'

'I've absolutely no idea. Why should I?'

'Who's his tutor on the course?'

'I am.'

'But you don't know where he is?'

'I'm not his keeper.'

'Was he there on Friday morning?'

'I think so. Yes, I'm sure he was.'

'Did you see him at the party on Friday evening?'

'I'm not sure.'

'Think.'

'No, I don't remember seeing him, but he could have come later, after I left.'

'Of course. Do you know where I might get information on Mr Reyes? His background, that sort of thing?'

'You could try the British Council in Oxford. All the applications come through them. They should have something on him.'

Healey ignored this suggestion. 'Did Dr Crouch and

Mr Reyes work at the school at the same time?'

'They must have.'

'Did they know each other well?'

'I can't say. Not that I'm aware of.'

'Did Mr Reyes know *Mrs* Crouch? Before she was married?'

'I really don't know. I think it's unlikely.'

'Why?'

'Ricardo Reyes is an old-fashioned catholic, a God-fearing man. Not at all the sort of person to frequent bars of the kind that Teresa worked in.'

'I see. Well, thank you for your time, Mr Wright. At some point we'll ask you to describe your movements again and make a formal statement. But that's all for now.' Healey stood up and turned towards the door. Without looking round he said, 'Nice car you've got.'

'It's not bad.'

'Must be expensive to run.'

Wright did not reply.

'Especially on a teacher's salary.'

'My parents help.'

Now Healey did turn towards Wright. But he resisted the temptation to say anything.

* * *

Healey sat with his chin in his hands at the end of a row near the front of the room as the lecturer, a tall bald man with a pronounced squint, droned on about the play, Othello, which the participants were going to see at Stratford the following evening. It took a special talent, thought Healey, to make a play like Othello sound so boring. He looked round to see if the participants showed signs of sharing his puzzlement but, as far as he could see, they seemed fascinated by what they were hearing.

Healey's thoughts turned to the case. After talking to Wright, he had telephoned the British Council to ask about Reyes. All the information they had on him, said the young lady he spoke to, was on the forms that they had sent to the Course Director in Reading and they hadn't kept copies. She was sure that Dr Farrell would still have them. When Healey explained the seriousness of the case, she volunteered to get in touch with the British Council in Manila, since they were his employer, to see if they could say more about him than was on the form. Healey was tempted to say that he would call them himself and ask his own questions but for the moment decided to let them do it for him.

His next task would be to interview Mary Walters. He was pretty sure he knew who she was, sitting just in front of him, with a wicker basket containing books and papers balanced incongruously on her knees, and wearing an equally inappropriate pink woolly hat. When the lecture ended she was the first person to ask a question. Something about Desdemona being treated as property, the fate of all women until very recent times. Silly woman, thought Healey but the lecturer, to his surprise, thanked her for a good question, took up the point and expanded on it at some length.

Healey looked around the room for Farrell, from whom he hoped to get the form for Reyes, but didn't see him. But then he had said he was giving a lecture himself at nine? Where could that be? Eventually there were no more questions, the lecturer thanked the audience for their attention and interesting questions, and they clapped him. There was a rustling of papers, banging of seats, and a general movement towards the door. Healey leaned forward.

'Excuse me,' he said. The woman turned round. She looked younger than Healey had expected, no more than thirty at the most. Her face was plain and covered in freckles.

'Is it Ms Walters?'

'Yes.' She managed to answer in a tone that suggested he had been impertinent to ask.

'I wonder if I could have a word with you. I'm Chief Inspector Healey. I'm ...'

'I have a class now.'

'Yes, I know, but this won't take long. Couldn't you give them something to do while we talk?'

'Can't this wait?'

'I don't think so. If you wouldn't mind.'

'Oh very well. Where do you want to talk?'

Healey looked round the room, which was now empty. 'Here is as good as anywhere.'

'I'll be back in a minute.'

When Ms Walters came back, she no longer carried the basket and had removed her hat, to reveal straw coloured hair held in a blue crocheted snood. She was wearing a flowery short-sleeved blouse which hung outside her jeans. After taking a seat in the same row as Healey but a few feet away, she was the first to speak. 'You probably want to ask me again where I was on Friday evening.'

'I do actually.'

'I was in the Hall.'

'But you said ...'

'Yes, I know I did. I was foolish.'

'But why ...'

'I thought I was protecting someone. It seems I needn't have bothered.'

'One of the participants?'

'Yes.'

'Did you know that another participant told us you were in the Hall on Friday evening?'

'Yes. She told me herself.'

'And the person you thought you were protecting?'

'Was with me.'

'In your room?'

'No. Hers.'

'And who was that?'

'Do I have to say?'

'Please.'

'Helga Braun.'

Healey wrote *Helga Brown* in his notebook and snapped it shut. 'And why did you think Miss Brown might need protecting?' he asked.

'She's from the GDR. I thought it might be something that could be used against her once she got back home.'

Healey chose not to ask what they had been doing in the room. 'So you preferred to lie to the British police?'

A small pink patch appeared above Miss Walters' breastbone and spread up her throat. She said nothing.

'Thank you, Ms Walters,' said Healey. 'I think you can go back to your class now.' As she went out, he opened his notebook and added the word 'check' to the name Helga Brown.

* * *

After talking to Mary Walters and searching, unsuccessfully, for Peter Farrell in the same building, Healey drove to the University of Berkshire site on King's Road. He quickly found Chris Carter's office, the door of which was open. Carter, his back to the door and hunched over his computer keyboard, was tapping away at what to Healey seemed phenomenal speed. Healey knocked but Carter did not respond. Healey coughed loudly and stepped into the room but it was only when he spoke that Carter turned round. 'Well, Richard, how nice to see you again.' He smiled expansively. 'What can I do for you?' Healey asked if Peter Farrell happened to be around. It seemed he had been there but had left just a few minutes before. Healey then said that he would like to look in Crouch's office, if that could be arranged.

Five minutes later Healey was sitting at Crouch's desk, which faced a window through which the sun shone brightly. He loosened his tie, opened the top button of his shirt, and ran a finger round the inside of the collar; it was only 10.30 yet the room was already uncomfortably warm. On the desk were two framed pictures: one of Crouch's wife and one of his daughter, both of which Healey picked up and inspected closely, before putting them back in the positions where they had been standing. He then began to look through the drawers of the desk. They contained only stationery, an internal telephone directory, and an unopened pack of cassettes for the kind of mini-recorder that Healey had taken from Crouch's room. After looking briefly at the titles of the books on the shelves that lined one wall of the room and seeing nothing of interest, he went to the filing cabinet standing against the opposite wall.

Above the cabinet was a notice board, empty except for a child's crayon drawing of a man, to which someone had added the word 'Daddy'. Without warning, tears came to Healey's eyes. He had found himself crying more and more often lately, something which hadn't happened to him since childhood. It was often provoked by an item on the news, the death of a child, pictures from the Falklands war the previous year, or even a sentimental scene in a film that he knew was nonsense. Tears came before he even thought that something was sad. Not a good sign. He took a handkerchief from his pocket and dabbed his eyes.

Sniffing, he opened the top drawer of the cabinet, which had hanging files relating to departmental and faculty meetings.

The next drawer down contained what appeared to be files devoted to lecture notes. Healey slid these towards him, one by one, looking briefly inside each of them. As he reached the ones towards the back of the cabinet, however, they did not slide easily along the rail that they were hanging on; their movement was obstructed by something beneath them. He forced two of the files apart from each other and slipped his hand down between them. At the bottom of the drawer he felt a sheaf of papers which he drew out and looked at.

They were statements from a bank in the Isle of Man. Unlike those he had found at Crouch's house, these were in his name only, and they were for a deposit, not a current account. Healey went through the statements carefully, beginning with the earliest, from six years before, which were at the top. The statements showed more or less regular three-monthly payments into the account of amounts which began as a hundred pounds but which during the last year had increased to two hundred and fifty. All were in cash. The balance of the account, from which nothing had ever been withdrawn, was now over four thousand pounds.

Folding the statements and putting them into a large manila envelope taken from Crouch's desk, Healey took one last look round the room, noticing for the first time a computer on a table in the far corner, before leaving and locking the door behind him. He took the key, as he had been asked to, to Carter's office. There was no one there. He put the key on the desk. As he left, he paused at the door, sniffed the air, pulled a face, and then went on down the corridor.

Sitting in his car, he leaned towards the passenger seat to pick up the sunglasses he'd dropped there when he arrived, and cursed. They had slipped between the seats, and wedged beside them he saw the disk with the file that he'd copied from Crouch's home computer, which hadn't fitted in his own computer and which he'd intended to give to Teague to try in one at headquarters. He'd give it to him when they met for lunch.

* * *

It was ten to one and Teague hadn't arrived at the Queen's Head yet. Healey bought an orange juice and tonic, sat down at an empty table by the window, and flipped open his notebook. The morning had gone well, he thought. He'd done everything he'd set out to do and he'd made the discovery of the payments into Crouch's deposit account. But he had already forgotten about the disk that he had left in his car.

He didn't believe that Wright had spent Friday night at Falstaff Avenue, but neither did he think that he was responsible for Crouch's murder (suicide was no longer considered a possibility, at least not by him). But he had something to hide. What could that be? Where had he been that night? Thinking of Wright reminded him of the smell, almost hidden by the scent of deodorant or whatever it was, which he noticed as he left his room. Was it marijuana? Could have been. If Wright had been smoking the stuff, he might have tried to hide the smell by spraying deodorant about. But it wasn't something, surely, that he'd go to the length of creating an alibi for.

And there was the other smell of the morning. The acrid body scent in Carter's office. Again. He may be a very clever man, thought Healey, but he's got one problem he doesn't seem to have solved. Or perhaps he doesn't notice. Or care. His wife would though, surely.

Then there were the bank statements. He had put the envelope that contained them onto the table in front of him, and was in the process of taking them out when he saw Sergeant Teague walking jauntily towards him, a grin on his face and a brimming pint glass in his hand. 'What's he got to be so pleased about?' wondered Healey. To judge from what Teague told him, not a lot.

He had been unable to find Reyes. He had spoken to the porter, Bird, who was pretty sure that Reyes hadn't been around at all over the weekend (which could not have been the case, since Teague had interviewed the man on Saturday afternoon). A cleaning lady had said that his bed hadn't been slept in since, she thought, Thursday. So why was he around on the Saturday?

'I've changed my mind about Bird, though, sir. Officious little git I thought, but he turns out to be quite a wise old you know what.'

'I don't know what. What?'

'Bird!' Teague uttered the word as if in triumph.

'Christ, Teague, you made that joke yesterday. If you could call it that.'

Teague appeared chastened. 'Sorry, sir. But, seriously, he's no fool. Knows a lot that's been going on. That Ms Walters, for example. Her and a German woman are a pair, he says.'

'Yes, I know that. Walters told me herself this morning.'

'Oh.'

'Did he say anything about Wright?'

'Stuck up little bastard is what he said. Nothing else.'

'And Crouch?'

'His name didn't come up.'

'What about Reyes?'

'Wouldn't trust him an inch.'

'Did he say why?'

'Greasy oriental.'

'That's helpful. Did you find anything new in the statements?'

'No, not really, sir.'

'When you see him next, ask him if anyone on the staff does the rounds at night. Did anyone go up on the tutors' corridor on Friday night. Now why don't we get something to eat?'

While they waited for their food – a prawn sandwich for Healey and a double cheeseburger and chips for Teague – Healey told his sergeant what he had learned that morning. They were the only people in the lounge, and when he spoke about the bank statements, he took them out of the envelope and pushed them across the table. 'Why don't you look at them yourself and see what you think.' Teague took them and studied each of them carefully.

'Well?' asked Healey. Before Teague could respond, the barmaid arrived with their food, planting it on the table, together with salt, ketchup and brown sauce. Teague took the plastic ketchup container and began to shake it vigorously, before suddenly stopping.

'Sorry, you asked me …'

'Never mind. Let's eat first.'

They had hardly begun to eat, however, when over Teague's shoulder Healey saw the door open and Peter Farrell appear. 'Put them away,' muttered Healey. Teague looked puzzled. 'The statements,' hissed Healey. As Farrell approached, Teague rolled them up and stuffed them into his inside jacket pocket.

Farrell stopped a few feet short of them. 'You're working,' he said.

'No,' replied Healey. 'Sit down. Let me get you a drink.' He motioned towards the seat beside him. 'What'll it be?'

'Half of shandy would be nice, thanks.'

While Healey went to the bar, Teague ignored Farrell and concentrated on his food. When Healey got back, he handed

Farrell the shandy and raised his own almost empty glass. 'Cheers,' he said.

'Cheers.' Farrell sipped at his drink. 'I had to get away from the Hall. Everyone's after me. Now we haven't got Neville, I've had to distribute his participants among the other tutors but they're all complaining. The tutors, I mean. Seem to think I should take on his group myself. Ha! As if I didn't have enough to do. I asked Chris this morning if he'd help out, but he says he's too busy working on his book. Don't blame him really, though the BC would pay him.'

'BC?' asked Healey.

'British Council.'

Healey nodded. 'That reminds me. The forms they send you on the participants, I wonder if I could look at the one for the Filipino, Reyes.'

'You're welcome to, but I don't have it myself. Tim will. I gave them to the tutors.'

'Oh!'

'A problem?'

'No, it's just that I spoke to him this morning and he could have told me he had the form.'

'I suppose he just didn't think.'

'Perhaps not,' said Healey, though he thought exactly the opposite. 'Do you think you could get it from him for me?'

'Of course.' Farrell stood up. 'Thanks for the drink. I'm going to walk back home now. Time for a siesta, I think.'

'Do you want a lift?'

'No thanks. The walk will do me good.'

'Then do you mind if I walk back with you? I could do with the exercise myself.'

'Not at all. But what about your sandwich? Do you want me to wait?'

'No, I don't really want it.' Healey stood up.

At this point Teague, who had thus far studiously ignored their conversation, looked up at Healey expectantly.

'I'll catch you later, Teague,' was all that Healey said.

* * *

On the way back to their respective houses, Farrell asked Healey if he fancied meeting up for a pint later. Healey was initially non-committal, but as they got to Farrell's gate and were about to separate, he said that yes, he wouldn't mind going for a pint and Farrell said that in that case how about going at ten. 'Ten's fine,' said Healey. 'I'll call by for you.'

Once in his house, Healey called out his wife's name. There was no answer. He slipped off his shoes, went into the front room, and switched on the cricket. He could watch a few minutes and then walk back to the Hall to check the incident room, speak to Teague, and pick up his car. The next thing he knew, however, his wife was shaking his shoulder. 'Dick,' she said. 'Didn't you hear the phone? It was the Super. You were supposed to meet him at three.'

'What! No I wasn't.'

'Well he thinks you were.'

'Oh, no.' Healey staggered to the phone in the hall, feeling suddenly quite sick. It took him a moment to realise that the receiver had already been put back on its cradle. 'What did you say to him?' he called out.

'I said I didn't know where you were.'

Healey followed his wife into the kitchen, intending to tell her that as usual she had said the wrong thing, but when he saw that she was already making him the cup of tea he so desperately needed, he said nothing.

The sensible thing to do now would be to go back to the

Hall, call the Super from there, and hang around, browsing through the files. But what would be the point, except to make him look better in other people's eyes? Whose eyes? The Super's? Teague's? Gifford's even? No, to hell with them. He would phone the Super from home and then sit down and think the whole thing through and plan for tomorrow. That was what he was paid to do, and whether he did it in the office, at the Hall, or here at home didn't matter one jot. He'd leave the car where it was, down the unmade road beside the Queen's Head.

* * *

better … better … better today
Crouch, that shit
I had to
I was right to

* * *

After supper, Healey went down to the bottom of the garden, through the gap in the Leylandii, and into his shed. After the heat of the day it was stifling in there and smelled strongly of the pine that it was built from. He took the handles of his old rotary mower and backing towards the door pulled the machine out with him. He pushed it through the gap and onto the lawn, and then proceeded to walk with it up towards the house and then back again, making the stripes that gave him such pleasure. Methodically, as the box on the front of the mower filled with clippings, he took it off and carried it down to the bottom of the garden and emptied its contents onto the compost heap, pulling out the last few blades of grass, enjoying their warmth on his hands. The lawn mowing ritual was soothing, and he remembered watching his father doing just the same thing thirty years before. He paused as he thought of this, and of his wife saying that he was becoming more like his father every day, which was not intended as a compliment, but was not something that troubled him.

Standing there, he became aware of the scent of burning wood. Looking over the fence to his left, he saw a plume of smoke rising lazily and uncertainly from a garden perhaps fifty yards away. Could well be Peter Farrell's, he thought. Funny to think of them having lived so close for years and never spoken to each other, and now, all of a sudden, it was as if they had known each other for ages. As he continued up and down the lawn, and was thinking of cutting along the edges of the curves of the flower-beds, the light began to fade and lights went on in the children's bedrooms. He pushed up towards the house and saw through Jamie's bedroom window his son jumping up and down, using his bed as a trampoline. So much zest for life, he thought; I hope he doesn't lose it.

By the time he had finished the lawn, it was almost ten and time to go out. He had a quick wash, put on a clean shirt, and looked into the telly room, where his wife was watching a film. 'Just off, love,' he said. 'Going to the pub with Peter Farrell. Won't be late.'

'Okay. You won't bring him back here, will you?'

'Shouldn't think so. Why?'

'It's just that I'll have to clean the bathroom and tidy up and …'

'No, don't bother. I won't ask him in. See you later.'

Parked near Farrell's house stood the big old Rover in which Carter had driven them from the pub on Saturday night. Healey looked at it admiringly before approaching the door and ringing the bell. Pam Farrell answered.

'He's in the back garden.' she said, 'Just go through.' Healey went through the side gate, past the kitchen door, and into the garden, which was given over entirely to a scruffy, patchy lawn, near the bottom of which stood Farrell, beside a rusty old incinerator in the form of a metal basket on legs, from which smoke was billowing, obscuring most of the shed that stood behind it. So he'd been right. Farrell strode towards him.

'Sorry, I hadn't realised the time. Been talking to Chris. Did you see him? He just left.'

'No, but I saw his car.'

'Oh, he must have gone through the house. I won't be a minute. Why don't you come inside.'

'Thanks, but I'll wait here, if you don't mind.'

'Of course not.'

Farrell went into the house and Healey walked down to the incinerator. The smoke no longer smelled of wood but of the grass clippings that must have just been put on the fire. In the fading light, Healey thought he saw a glimpse of something red beside the incinerator and stooped down to look. At that moment, however, Pam Farrell appeared behind him. 'Peter said to give you this,' she said, handing over three or four slim booklets. 'He said you might like to have a quick look at them before you leave.' It was too dark to read in the garden and Healey followed her back to the house, glancing at the booklets once he got to the light coming from the kitchen. They were for the part-time courses that Farrell had spoken to him about.

The Three Tuns was largely empty, most people having chosen to sit at the benches on the tarmac at the side. Healey and Farrell were sitting in a corner near one of the doors that had been jammed open in an attempt to create a draught through the otherwise hot and airless lounge. After two pints of

Guinness, and with a third in front of them, they were feeling comfortable, untroubled by the heat. 'So did you ever see the Beatles at the Cavern?' asked Farrell.

'Just once. I'm not sure I'd even heard of them. A girlfriend took me. Said I had to see them. It was that very cold winter. There was thick snow. The buses stopped running and we had to walk home. 'Love me do' they sang. I can remember the walls running with condensation, people jumping up and down, Coke bottles in their hands – don't know what was in them, though. Did you ever go?'

'To the Cavern, yes. But I didn't see *them*. A bit too young. Still, great days.'

Healey laughed. 'You make us sound like old men.'

'Well, we aren't that young. How old are you, Richard?'

'Forty-three. And you?'

'A mere thirty-five.'

'Lucky man. Life doesn't begin for you for another five years.'

'Four years and a few days, actually.'

'How old is Chris Carter?'

'A year older than me.'

The two men lifted their glasses in silence, as if pondering these revelations. It was Healey who spoke first. 'How long have you been married, Peter?'

'Fourteen years.'

'Do you find, I mean, I do … '

Farrell grinned. 'Find what?'

Even emboldened by drink, Healey wished he hadn't begun to ask the question but he had to go on with it. 'That as you get older and you've been married longer, other women seem more and more attractive?'

'Than?'

'Than they did before, I suppose.'

Farrell shook his head. 'No, I can't say that's true for me.

But that's something to do with the fact that since the age of ten I've spent most of my life thinking about them.' He grinned again. 'And in our job there's plenty to make you think. A new batch every year. I don't know how I get through a lecture sometimes, seeing them there sitting in front of me.'

Healey knew he couldn't ask Farrell the question he wanted to. Instead he said 'Does it ever happen, between students and staff, I mean?'

'Well it happened to Chris. That's not a secret by the way. It was my first year here and I didn't really know him. He kept very much to himself, as he does now mostly. Anyhow, there was a young Moroccan lady on the MA. They took to each other. Nobody knew it was going on, at least not among the staff. It seems the students all knew but they were very discreet. Anyhow, a year after the course ended she came back to do a PhD. And not long after that she became Mrs Carter. Mrs Carter the second. She works in the Department now.'

'And Mrs Carter the first?'

'She had a breakdown. She's been hospitalised ever since. Fair Mile.'

'The psychiatric …'

'Yeah.'

'They must have divorced.'

'Yes.'

'Willingly on her part?'

'Who knows?'

'Terrible thing. Presumably it was because of what happened?'

'That she had a breakdown?'

'Yes.'

'Chris doesn't talk about it. The only thing he ever said to me was that she was always like that. The affair didn't change anything.'

Healey took their now empty glasses and stood up. 'Another?'

'Thanks.'

The pub had filled up and Healey had to queue at the bar. It was a while before he got back with their Guinness. 'OU again,' said Farrell. 'Must have just finished a meeting or something.'

Healey sat down, took a long drink, then asked, 'So, Chris Carter, he's quite a powerhouse, isn't he?'

'Certainly is. Makes me tired just to think of the work he gets through.'

'What drives a man to work so hard?'

'Ambition, but don't ask me where that comes from. I know I don't have it. But you've also got to have good health, the right metabolism, and a lack of inhibition – know what you want and go for it.'

'So you've thought about it.'

'You couldn't help but think about it, seeing it in front of you every day.'

'And don't you need to enjoy what you're doing? And believe in it?'

'I suppose so, though I'm not sure. I suspect believing in yourself and enjoying your success is probably enough. One thing I'm sure of, though, is that it's like a drug, for Chris at least. I've seen him once or twice when he wasn't able to work for one reason or another, and he was in a miserable state. Withdrawal symptoms. I suppose you get people like that in the police as well.'

Healey thought immediately of one former colleague who was now the youngest assistant chief constable in Britain. 'Yes. I imagine you get them in all walks of life. What about Neville Crouch? Was he ambitious?'

'Neville? He *may* have had ambitions but he was never going to achieve them. I said about inhibitions. Well he was riddled with them. He was a perfectionist but he didn't have the ability to get even near what he thought was perfection. He never finished anything. I hate to say this now he's dead, but he should never have been given the job. Even his lectures, which he spent days preparing, the students didn't like. If you don't do good research, you have to be a good teacher to survive. And Neville was good at neither.'

'And the book he wrote with Chris Carter?'

'You know that Chris rewrote most of what Neville had done?'

'Yes.'

'In fact, I think that was hard on Neville. I know he found it humiliating but he was so keen to get published that he just accepted it. Actually, he showed me what he had written and I didn't think it was too bad at all. Pretty solid really. But not up to Chris's standards. He can be quite ruthless in things like that.'

Healey digested this information before asking, 'What about women?'

'What do you mean?'

'Was he keen on them?'

'Neville?'

Healey nodded.

'I suspect Teresa was the first woman he ever had. Without paying, that is. Have you seen her?'

Healey nodded and Farrell continued. 'I don't think he could believe his luck. A woman like that. No, he wasn't going to risk losing *her*, even if he had the chance, which I doubt. He did everything for her. Was always buying her presents, a lot of jewellery apparently. At least that's what I heard. And then there was his daughter. He was besotted with her.'

'What about Teresa? Do you think she ever thought of … of other possibilities?'

Farrell seemed to stiffen slightly. 'I don't know, but somehow I doubt it. He'd rescued her from a fate worse than death, by all accounts, or at least from life as a Manila bar girl. Besides, she never seemed to go out, so I don't know who she could have met. Never came to departmental parties. Neville always came on his own. They never had people to their house either.'

'You say he bought her lots of presents. Jewellery. Presumably not cheap. Where would he get the money for that? Did he do outside work?'

'Not that I know of. He got a bit on top of his lecturer's salary for the administration he did. You knew he was the Departmental Administrator?'

Healey shook his head. Farrell continued, 'Yes, Rex, that's our esteemed Head of Department, decided a couple of years ago that he had too much administration to do, so he invented this title 'Departmental Administrator' and got faculty agreement to pay someone five hundred a year to take it on. The deal was this extra five hundred, and less teaching. I wouldn't have touched it with a bargepole but Neville jumped at it.'

'For the money?'

'Perhaps. But also to busy himself with all kinds of inconsequential things, so he had an excuse for not doing others. And poke his nose into areas that didn't concern him. At least, that's what I think.'

'He was nosy?'

'I'd never leave him in my room by himself. I always had the feeling that he'd go rooting through my things. And then there was the big hoo-ha over the secret recordings he was making of colleagues.'

'When was that?'

'It all blew up a couple of years ago but God knows how long he had been doing it. Used to sit and chat and all the time he'd have his little tape recorder going. Of course he said it was for research and that he'd never reveal anything sensitive about anyone if he published his findings. He published bugger all so that wasn't a problem, it was just a breach of trust between colleagues. You probably think I'm being sanctimonious. But everybody felt that way.'

While Healey denied that he thought him sanctimonious, Farrell finished his beer. 'Another?' he asked.

'No, thanks. But are you …? Well, all right. But just a half.'

It took Healey and Farrell nearly an hour to walk the three quarters of a mile back to Beech Lane. They talked all the way, and whenever they became particularly involved with what they were saying, they would stop and stand, occasionally shifting their feet about, for minutes at a time. Farrell told Healey more about the Department and the kind of work they did. Most of their students, it seemed, were teachers of English as a foreign language, most of them from overseas but some from Britain. Tim Wright, for instance. Didn't he want to get a job in the Department and wouldn't there be one going now that Crouch was dead, asked Healey. Farrell thought him quite bright but he doubted that he would be willing to work hard enough. There would be dozens of applicants if they advertised, and they didn't want to make the same mistake they had with Crouch. Perhaps they could offer him the post for a year and then advertise. But nothing would happen until Rex got back from holiday.

Carter's name came up again, and his passion for work. Healey said that he would never have guessed that Carter was only a year older than Farrell. Farrell shrugged. He said that he thought of Carter as a 'monstruo de la naturaleza', a monster of nature, and explained that this is what Cervantes of Don Quijote fame had called Lope de Vega, the Spanish writer of the sixteenth and seventeenth centuries, whose literary production had been enormous. He'd been married twice and had several children, some of them illegitimate.

Farrell explained that he had come across Lope de Vega when he had been doing his first degree, which had been in Spanish studies. He had intended to stick with Spanish and had actually registered for a PhD and gone to Madrid, with his wife and their recently born first child, to do research. Short of money, he had started teaching English there – you didn't have to know anything about teaching, just be a native speaker. 'And that,' he said, 'is how I got into this business. I did an MA at Bangor, Rex was the external examiner, he liked my dissertation, and offered me a job here. That's *my* life story. What about yours?'

Healey told him about how he'd come to join the police. 'In spite of what my grandmother told me.'

'What was that?'

'That when you join the police, you're no longer a man.'

'What did she mean by that?'

'I think she meant that you aren't free to do what you personally think is right, you have to follow the rules. I *think* that's what she meant. I remember one of the stories she told us as kids was of her sister's husband, who was in the police. He set fire to his chimney – probably just to clean it, my father always did – and his brother, who was also in the police, reported him. Who to, I don't know, but she thought this wasn't the way to behave.

'There was another story my grandmother told us, about her husband walking home in the evening – he was a shop manager – and coming across two policemen giving someone a beating in a dark alley. 'Leave that man alone,' he said, or some such thing. They did, but they must have found out who he was, because from then on police kept coming to the shop where he worked and asking to see him. Just to cause trouble for him.' Healey paused. 'That was Liverpool. She wasn't the only one who didn't hold the police in high regard.'

'No,' agreed Farrell.

They walked on a little way, stopping under a streetlamp, leaning against the low wall of one of the large red brick houses that lined the pavement side of Wilderness Road. On the other side was the Wilderness itself, a wooded area that was part of the old university campus and enclosed by a tall chain-link fence.

'But getting back to you,' said Healey, 'what do you teach? English?'

'Not so much English. Chris does that. Well he doesn't teach English exactly; he teaches *about* it. You know, the grammar, pronunciation. No, what I teach is *how* to teach English. Different methods, different theories of learning, and so on. And also how to test people's English. That's my speciality in fact.'

Healey passed no comment.

'What I'm really interested in, though,' continued Farrell, 'is the way children learn their first language. I've been making recordings of our youngest since she was a few months old. I've transcribed a lot of it. Just need to analyse it now.'

'How many children have you got?'

'Three. All girls. Thirteen, twelve and three.' He responded to the widening of Healey's eyes. 'Yes, the last one was a surprise, but a welcome one. How about you?'

'Just two. A girl thirteen and a boy eight.'

'So we've both got thirteen-year-old girls. Perhaps they should meet.'

'Probably they already have. Meg's at Maiden Erlegh.'

'Molly's at Kendrick.'

'Ah.' Healey's daughter hadn't wanted to take the entrance exam for the grammar school, and he hadn't tried to make her. He didn't regret it, though he thought *she* might one day. 'Well, yes, perhaps they *should* meet.' It would be interesting, he thought, since Meg insisted that they were all snobs at Kendrick.

An upstairs window above them closed with a bang and there was a rustling in the undergrowth opposite. 'Fox,' said Healey. They walked on.

Somehow or other they got to talking about football. Since childhood Healey had supported Liverpool, who had just won the league for the second year in succession. Once he learned that Farrell's team was Everton, who had come seventh, he became almost apologetic about his own team's success. It was years since Healey had been to Anfield but Farrell managed to get to Goodison four or five times a year, he said. Forgetting momentarily the need for tact, Healey recalled the letter to the Liverpool Echo in which an Everton supporter said that he had noticed that the team's centre forward always wore sweatbands. He had a question: why? The implication being that the player was so lazy that he never broke sweat. Healey chuckled at the memory but Farrell seemed unamused, so Healey quickly changed the subject to the common enemy, Manchester United, who, they both agreed, would never win the league while Atkinson was manager.

They moved on to politics. Healey wasn't surprised when Farrell said he had always voted Labour. Healey couldn't say the same; he had voted for the Liberal Alliance in June, when the Conservatives had won an unexpected landslide victory, something which they both thought was as much to do with the Falklands War as anything else. They had both been against the war. Farrell had taken part in demonstrations, while Healey admitted that, to his shame, he had kept his head down and said nothing about it to his fellow officers.

They had almost reached Beech Lane when Farrell mentioned the part-time course brochures, which Healey had been carrying with him since they left Farrell's house. 'I know you haven't had a chance to look at them, but when you do, if there's anything you want to know, feel free to ask. Give me a call, or whatever. I suppose there's every likelihood we'll be meeting up again soon, as long as you're working on the case.' Before Healey was able to respond, Farrell continued, 'No, don't worry, I'm not going to ask you about it.'

'That's all right. And since you've mentioned the case, I hope you don't mind me mentioning the form you were going to get from Wright.'

'Christ, sorry, yes. I forgot. I saw him but completely forgot. I'll get it from him first thing, before they go to Stratford. Where will you be?'

'I can't be sure. Could you leave it with one of the officers at the Hall?'

'I'll do that.'

'And thanks for this.' Healey held up the booklets. 'If nothing else, they may help me think a bit more clearly about what I want to do.'

They were now standing outside Healey's house. He gestured towards it. 'I'd like to invite you in but I think I'd better get to bed. It's going to be an early start tomorrow.'

'For me too. And the first thing I have to do is get you that form.'

'Thanks. Next time, though, you must come in for a drink.'

'Look forward to it.'

As he watched Farrell make his way up the road, Healey fumbled in his pocket for his keys. Pulling them out, he advanced on the door and, after a couple of failed attempts, fitted the key in the lock and turned it. Inside, switching the hall light on, he looked at his face in the mirror. 'You drink too much,' he said.

In the kitchen he filled a half-pint glass with water from the tap and drank it down. He did the same with a second. Then he walked through to his study, pulled a book from a shelf and sat heavily in his chair. He had got a free copy of Chambers Biographical Dictionary from a book club. In it he found LOPE (DE VEGA) and was directed to VEGA CARPIO. He read that 'the mere list of Lope's works presents a picture of unparalleled mental activity.' Chris Carter all right. But was it true of Carter, as the entry said of de Vega, that 'imagination and creative power were not amongst his gifts?' Healey wondered too whether Carter would die poor, 'after giving almost all his income to charities and the church.' 'Somehow I don't think so,' he said aloud. He made to stand but sank back heavily into the chair. He was only able to get up after he had placed his hands on the arms of the chair and pushed slowly upwards. As he passed the mirror in the living room, he looked at himself again. 'And you're getting old,' he said.

He went into the front room and switched on the television. The cricket highlights were just finishing. And England were just about finished too. New Zealand only needed 101 to win, which they duly obtained. The Australian presenter was there again, praising the New Zealanders on their first victory in a test match in England, lamenting England's performance, excusing only Gower, who had made a century and Willis who had taken five wickets for very few runs in the second innings. 'Bugger off,' said Healey, switched off the television and made his way upstairs to bed.

His daughter's bedroom door was half-open. Creeping in, he stood by the bed. Her face was lit by the light from the landing. He bent down and kissed her forehead. She stirred slightly but did not wake. Turning, he went out and then into his son's room. Kissing him, he said, 'Won't be long before you're coming back from the pub drunk too.'

In bed, Healey lay on his back, with his eyes open, for several minutes. Eventually he turned towards his wife, who hadn't woken when he came in. 'Things are going to get better,' he whispered, and leaned across her to turn off the light.

* * *

no idea
they've got no bloody idea
no way they can get me
not unless …
but no, that won't happen

TUESDAY

Healey woke at six, feeling fit and well, despite the previous night's drinking. This was going to be a good day. He swung straight out of bed, went downstairs, put on the kettle and went out into the garden. A blackbird that had been searching the earth beneath the rose bushes called in alarm as it made its escape, flying just above the ground until it reached the gap in the pines, then up and over the shed. 'You fool,' said Healey, 'as if I'd hurt you.' He bent down and sniffed a yellow rose that he'd bought on the way to Oxford the previous year; whisky something, he seemed to remember it being called. Straightening up, and wincing as much out of habit as because of the twinge of pain this gave him, he walked to the bottom of the garden and looked back up to the house. The children's bedroom windows were all open and so too were the French windows from the living room, something which he hadn't noticed when he passed through the room the night before.

He went back to the kitchen, and poured boiling water onto a teabag in his favourite mug, one with a picture of Liverpool Cathedral on its side, which his children had bought him when the family had made a day trip to that city. While he waited for this to brew, he collected his notepad and a pen, and began to go through the notes he had made the previous afternoon. Twenty minutes and a second mug of tea later, sitting at the table on the terrace, he made a neat copy of his numbered list of things to do. Before getting up and setting

off to the Hall on foot, he added one more point, at the top:
0 – Teague!

Arriving at the Hall just before 7.30, Healey went straight to the incident room. He took the folder with his name on it from the wire basket on the central table and started to go through its contents. The top sheet recorded a telephone message for him to meet with the Super at three o'clock the previous afternoon, which was dated Monday and timed at 12.11 pm. He had phoned and sorted that out with the Super. When asked where he'd been at three – they'd been unable to reach him anywhere – he invented a visit to the University, where he couldn't find any of the people he wanted to speak to. The purpose of the meeting with the Super had only been to report on progress so far, which he'd done over the phone, apparently to the Super's satisfaction. It was made clear to Healey, however, that the Chief Constable, seemingly a friend of the University Rector, was taking an interest. 'So keep me informed,' had been the Super's last words.

Flipping through the other papers in the file, Healey stopped at the report on the body. He was already familiar with its contents: essentially that Crouch had suffered multiple fractures but had died from the massive insult his brain received when his head hit the ground. The report also noted that there was evidence of another distinct and substantial blow to the left temple which had been inflicted by some blunt object before impact with the ground. Unlikely to be after, thought Healey, grimly. And not while he's falling. He took out a pen and made a note to find out if the earlier blow was sufficient to cause unconsciousness.

The scene of crime officer's report, which he read next, was remarkable for the lack of information it provided. There were no fingerprints other than Crouch's. There was no evidence of a struggle of any kind. Healey was pondering this when he heard the door squeak open behind him. 'Morning, sir,' he heard. It was Teague's cheery voice.

'Good morning, Teague,' he responded in as friendly a manner as he could muster. 'Come and sit down.' Now that the time had come, he wanted to postpone it but he knew he couldn't. 'Look … erm … I realise I've been a bit difficult this last couple of days.'

'No, you haven't, sir.' Teague stood beside him.

'… been a bit off hand … haven't kept you abreast of things … so I thought we should just sit down and go through everything together.'

Teague, managing to look both baffled and pleased, pulled up a chair and sat down. Healey took out his list. 'First, we agreed that we're dealing with murder, not suicide?'

'Even though there was that note that threatened to expose something he'd done?'

'Well, let's come back to the note later. By the way, have we had anything back on the comparison between that and the notice I gave you?' Healey started to look through his folder.

'No, I'll get on to them right away, as soon as we've finished,' said Teague.

'Right. No, the key thing is the blow to the head before he fell.'

'But nothing in the room he could have been hit with.'

'No, but something missing from the room that you'd expect to be there.'

'What's that, sir?'

'His bat. He'd been playing cricket. He uses his own bat. The rest of his kit is in the room. But no bat.'

'Ah.' Teague looked suitably impressed.

'And while we're talking about things missing from the room, where's his diary? Look at everything that Crouch has to do with and you see he's a methodical person. His books, his files, his tape recordings, all of them neatly organised. So he must have a diary. It isn't in his briefcase, not in the clothes he had at the Hall, not in his office at the University.'

'What about his house?'

'I looked there too.'

'So you're saying someone took it.'

'And why would they take it?'

'There's something incriminating in it?'

'Such as?'

Teague was silent for a few moments. 'Their name? Maybe an appointment. An appointment that night. He was expecting someone and he had them down in his diary.'

'Spot on. At least that's what I think. It would explain why he told his wife he was staying late in the Hall. And that would also suggest that it was someone he knew well, to arrange to see them around midnight or later.'

'So find the diary.'

'Or find the bat. Though there's every chance that they've been disposed of by now. But, yes, we should be looking for them. Can you organise a search of university grounds, any wasteland and the front gardens of the houses around the Hall?'

'Yes, I'll do that, sir. Pity we didn't …'

'Didn't what?'

Teague looked embarrassed and said nothing. Healey, who knew perfectly well what Teague was suggesting, that they should have searched for the bat and diary days ago, didn't press the matter but simply said, 'And can you see what you can find out about the bat. What make. What colour the handle is. His wife isn't likely to know, but ask her. And ask Wright. They played together on Friday. If you don't get any joy there, ask other people in the side. University staff, they were.'

Healey fell silent and appeared distracted. In fact he was

thinking of what he had seen in Farrell's garden the previous evening. A piece of what might have been red rubber. Could it have come from a bat handle? It seemed highly unlikely. But then, they were burning something that had smelled like wood. If he could get that piece of rubber and a sample of the ash. Did they still make cricket bats out of willow, he wondered. As he thought of these possibilities, he realised that, despite his new resolution, he didn't particularly want to talk about them to Teague.

'Is that OK then?' he asked. Teague, who was making notes, nodded.

Healey stood up and felt inside his jacket pocket. 'Another thing I'd like you to do,' he said, as he pulled the computer disk from his jacket pocket, 'is see what you can do with this. There was a file on Crouch's computer at home that was protected by a password so I copied it onto this. It may be nothing but I think it's worth checking out. I was going to try and get into it myself but I'm sure you'll be better at it than me. Would you mind having a shot?'

'Of course not, sir.'

'Thanks. Something else. Did you send that little tape recorder I gave you on Saturday to Forensics?'

Teague looked uneasy. 'Actually, no, sir. Didn't seem much point, what with our fingerprints all over it.'

'I suppose you're right. Anyhow, it was in his briefcase. There was no cassette in it. Why not? Crouch doesn't seem to me to have been the kind of man to go around with a tape recorder that he wasn't going to be able to use.'

'So somebody might of took the cassette?'

Healey ignored this double lapse from standard English, tempted though he was to draw it to his sergeant's attention. 'They might, yes.'

'For the same reason as they took the diary.'

'It's possible. Get them to look for that too when they're

searching. But something that has struck me though is that I saw a lot of tape cassettes in Crouch's house but they were all the standard size. I didn't see any that would fit this. I think I'm going to go back to the house and look again. It will be a chance to see if Mrs Crouch has anything new to say. I can ask her about the bat.' Healey thought he saw the beginning of a smile on Teague's face. If there was one, it was quickly extinguished.

'About the search, sir.'

'Yes.'

'How far should it extend, do you think?'

'I'll leave that to your judgement, Teague,' said Healey, uncertain himself as to how far it would be reasonable to search. Teague went off slowly, apparently deep in thought.

Healey was consulting his notes again when he heard his name spoken. He looked round to see the Hall Warden striding towards him. 'Good morning, Chief Inspector,' she said. She gave Healey the benefit of a wide, yellow toothed, humourless smile. 'I have someone in my office who is anxious to speak to you.'

'And that is?'

'Miss Woods.'

After he had said hello to Enid the secretary and Daisy the dog, Healey was ushered into her office by the Warden, who closed the door behind him. Miss Woods was sitting with her back to him, facing the Warden's desk, which was again covered with papers. Healey put his hand on the back of her chair. 'Miss Woods,' he said, 'you wanted to see me.'

She turned towards him. 'Yes, you see I've remembered something. But why don't you sit down.' She pointed to the Warden's chair. 'I can't talk with you standing over me like that.' Healey did as he was told.

Miss Woods continued. 'Yes, I've remembered that I did see someone when I was walking Daisy on Friday night. It was a man …'

'Can you describe this man?'

'If you give me a chance, I can. He was quite tall, he had a limp, and he was wearing a raincoat.'

Healey smiled and almost laughed out loud.

'Is there something wrong, Chief Inspector?'

Healey was impressed that she had remembered his title. 'No, nothing wrong, Miss Woods, but I wonder why anyone would be wearing a raincoat on such a warm night when there had been no rain for weeks and no sign of it then.'

'I don't know *why* he was wearing a raincoat. I'm just saying that he was.'

'Can you say anything more about his appearance? Colour of hair? His build? His age?'

Miss Woods hardly hesitated. 'Dark. Medium build. Young.'

'How young?'

'I couldn't say.'

'A teenager?'

'No.'

'In his twenties?'

'He could have been.'

'Thirties?'

'Possibly.'

'Forties?'

'I said young.'

'Where exactly did you see this man?'

'At the corner of Marlborough Avenue and Elmhurst Road.'

'What direction was he going in?'

'He was coming from Marlborough Avenue and going towards the playing fields.'

'Did he go into the playing fields?'

'I think he did, yes.'

'Did he pass close to you?'

'Yes, we passed on the corner.'

'Did you stop after he passed you?'

'No. Why should I?'

'No reason. Well thank you Miss Woods.' Healey stood up.

'Don't you need to write this down and get me to sign it?'

'Not for the moment, thank you.' Healey went to the door, opened it and found the Warden standing outside.

'Finished already?' she asked.

As Healey went down the corridor, he thought he heard Miss Woods say, 'I don't think he believed me.'

As he headed back to the incident room, Healey passed through reception, where he met a group of what he took to be course participants, twenty or more of them milling around and carrying cardboard lunch boxes. Presumably they were about to leave for Stratford. He felt a hand on his arm and looked round. It was the Italian woman, Silvia, smiling at him sweetly. 'Hello,' he said. 'Off to Stratford?'

She continued to smile at him, and hold his arm. 'Why don't you come with us?'

'I only wish I could.'

Slowly she released her grip. With a nod and a smile, Healey, looking decidedly flushed, left her and edged his way slowly through the throng. From behind the reception desk, Bird raised his hand to him but Healey wasn't looking.

Back with Teague, Healey told him briefly what Miss Woods had said. 'It's not only the fact she said he was wearing a raincoat, but from where she was, she couldn't possibly have seen anyone going into the playing fields.' He shook his head. 'Poor old thing. She even seems to have forgotten she's got Alzheimer's.' Teague's chortling at this not very clever remark made Healey wish he hadn't made it. Still, this was his be nice to Teague day and it wasn't nine o'clock yet. He'd have to try harder.

He looked at his notes. Opportunity. Actually, even with all the statements and apparent corroborations, any number of people could have got to Crouch at the time he died. Especially if there were two people involved and they gave each other alibis.

'What I'd like you to do, though, Teague, is get someone to make a matrix with all the names down the left hand side, and all the names across the top. Including Crouch. Got me?' Teague nodded, a little uncertainly, and Healey continued, 'and then mark the cells to show who was accounted for by whom. Look.' He quickly drew a matrix of eight cells and wrote the letters A to D, one letter at the top of each column, then wrote them again, one against each row. 'So B accounts for D, say. Find B on the left and D along the top. And in the cell where they meet, write in the place, time and date. Is that okay?'

'I think so.'

'Good. That will give us a quick overview. And we'll see what patterns there are. In the meantime, though, we've got Wright and Reyes to think of. Wright because of his dodgy alibi, Reyes because of his going missing, and both of them because of the Philippines connection. Have you got any thoughts?'

'I agree with what you said about Wright, him not being likely to have done it. He doesn't look as if he's got it in him. He'd have to give Crouch a bang on the head, with the bat if you're right, and then heave him out of the window. I can't picture him doing that. But he's got something to do with it, I'm sure.'

'And Reyes?'

'He might be a kung fu champion for all we know. Did you find out anything about him, sir?'

'Not yet. The British Council is supposed to be getting back to me. And Peter Farrell is getting his form from Wright. What about motive?'

'There's that letter again. If we knew who wrote that.'

'Okay.'

'Could be something personal, his wife maybe, had enough of him, got somebody else to do it, Wright for instance …'

'But you said you couldn't see Wright doing it. Sorry! Carry on.'

'Or one of his colleagues, something to do with his work, I was thinking.'

'That's possible, yes, though I haven't uncovered any animosity between him and anyone else. So far, at least.'

'Then there's those payments into the Isle of Man bank. Could be he's been paid for doing something a bit naughty, do you think, and decided that he wanted more. The amounts did go up, didn't they?'

'They did, yes, but they weren't very large amounts, even at the end. It wouldn't seem that he was into anything very big.'

'No, sir, but he could have *known* about something big. He might have been asking for more just to keep quiet.'

'That's true. And what could the big thing be?'

'Drugs. The more I think about it … the Philippines, of course. Drugs do come in from there, don't they?'

'I'm not sure. Do they?'

'Yes they do. I was reading about it the other week. Supposed to be on the increase. I think we're onto something, sir.'

Healey found himself reluctant to agree. But this was Teague's day. 'You could be right, Teague,' he said. 'Why don't you find out the latest on that, anything known to be going on at the moment. As well as everything else I've asked you to do.' He smiled and patted Teague on the shoulder. 'Don't 'forget this,' he added, picking up the computer disk that he had already handed to his sergeant.

'Oh no, sir,' said Teague, taking it from him and looking inordinately pleased with himself. 'I'll have that file for you in no time.'

Oh will you? thought Healey, but nodded as if in appreciation. Beaming, Teague turned on his heels and strutted to the door and out into the corridor. A busy man with important things to do.

Going through the contents of his file again, Healey came across the bank statements that Teague must have put there after Farrell had interrupted their discussion of them at the pub the previous day. He put them into his pocket. He also found a paper that he had missed when he was looking earlier. Teague must have missed it too, or not looked at the file since the paper had been added.

It was a report on the letter and the notice that he had taken from Crouch's door. It had struck him when he saw the notice that the print or whatever it was called, looked similar to that of the letter. The report seemed to confirm this. In both cases, it said, the font was Courier 10 point and a dot matrix printer had been used. It went on to say that the same printer might have been used for both the letter and the notice, though it was impossible to say for certain, as it would have been if a typewriter with damage to particular keys had been used. It certainly wasn't possible to say whether it had been written on the same computer. Thinking about this and a possible change in his plans for the day, Healey became aware of Peter Farrell approaching him, looking rather sheepish. 'You won't believe it,' he said, 'but Tim has mislaid that form. Can't find it anywhere.'

'What! Where is he?'

'He's just left on the coach to Stratford.'

'That's handy.'

'I'm sorry. How important is it to have the form? Is it urgent? Perhaps we could get a copy from the British Council.'

'They say they haven't got one. They were supposed to be getting back to me about Reyes anyhow. I'd better call them again.' The room was stuffy, Healey was sweating, and he began to wonder if it was going to be such a good day after all. He picked up the phone and dialled the British Council, ignoring Farrell who stood behind him looking at a loss.

'Yes,' said Healey into the phone, 'someone was supposed to call me about a participant on the Reading summer school, name of Reyes, from Manila.'

* * *

Healey found a shady spot in the University of Berkshire car park, rolled down his window, and thought about what he had learned just a few minutes before. The British Council had told him that Reyes was in Manila. What is more, he had never left there. He hadn't gone to Reading. By chance a member of the British Council staff had met him in the street only a couple of days before and asked him why he was still there when the course had already started. Apparently he had looked somewhat shamefaced but explained that a death in the family had prevented him leaving. He had been going to let the Council know, but what with the death and all that entailed (there was property to be shared amongst various members of the extended family and it was his responsibility to deal with the lawyers) he hadn't got round to it yet.

This news raised the interesting question as to who it was that was presenting himself as Reyes on the course, if indeed there was any such person. But of course there was. He had been interviewed. And Wright had spoken about him. Yes,

Wright had certainly spoken about him. But Wright knew Reyes – at least he said he did – so why hadn't he exposed the man as an impostor? When Healey's call to the British Council had ended, Farrell had still been standing beside him. Healey immediately asked him to tell him anything he could about Reyes, what he looked like, how good his English was (Healey had in mind the letter to Crouch), but Farrell was unable to tell him anything. It was slowly dawning on Healey that Farrell, pleasant and willing as he seemed, wasn't very much concerned with the day-to-day running of the course of which he was director. He couldn't imagine having such a hands-off approach to the job himself.

Now, sitting in his car, he realised that it was going to be a long day. They wouldn't be getting back from Stratford until one in the morning and he would have to wait until then to talk to Wright. He certainly wasn't going to give him the opportunity of finding out that he knew about Reyes and possibly taking off before he could question him. No, he'd be waiting for him when the coach arrived.

As he got out of the car, it occurred to him that if Peter Farrell had told him a bit sooner about Wright not having the form, he could have asked him to stay behind and find it. Why hadn't Farrell asked him to stay anyhow? What the hell was Wright doing swanning about Stratford when he should be here helping with a murder enquiry? Swanning around. Sitting in a pub, the Dirty Duck perhaps.

Carter wasn't in his office when Healey knocked but he appeared a moment later with a mug that smelled of strong coffee. He greeted Healey, sat down at his desk, and proceeded to put several teaspoonfuls of sugar into the mug. 'Bags of energy,' he said. 'Know the reference?' Healey admitted he didn't.

'The L-Shaped Room. Lynn Reid Banks,' went on Carter. 'She used to do news reports on ITV. Don't you remember?'

Healey said he did vaguely, before saying, 'Look, I want to print something out on the printers in the Department. Is that possible?'

'But of course. Let me have it and I'll do it for you.'

'I don't have it yet, I'm afraid. It'll have to be word processed first.'

'No problem.' Taking a quick sip from his mug, Carter went over to his computer. 'Fire away,' he said.

From his pocket, Healey pulled the copy he had made of the letter that had been in Crouch's room in the Hall and handed it to Carter. 'Good God,' said Carter. 'Is this for real?'

'Real enough,' replied Healey.

Carter set about the task, pausing only to confirm that he should copy it exactly as it was. 'That's it,' he said, in what seemed no time at all. 'Do you want me to print it?'

'Please.'

'On my printer?'

'Could I see it on that first, if you don't mind.'

Carter printed it out and handed the page to Healey. It looked very similar to the original. 'What font is this?' he asked.

'Courier ten point.'

'And the printer is called a dot matrix, is that right?'

'Yes.'

'Who else in the Department has a printer of this kind?'

'Just me and ... Neville ... did. Because he was the Departmental Administrator.'

'And you?'

'Because I bought it myself.'

'That seems a bit hard. Having to buy your own printer.'

Carter shrugged. 'Not much money around this department. It was worth buying it not to have to wait for something to be printed by the secretary.'

'Her printer is different?'

'It's a laser.'

Healey asked if they could print the letter on Crouch's printer.

'I don't see why not. I'll just copy it onto a floppy and then get the key to his room.'

Five minutes later, while Carter was printing the letter, Healey noticed that the child's drawing that had been pinned to the notice board the day before was no longer there. 'Has anyone been in this room since I was here yesterday?' he asked.

'Not to my knowledge. But why don't we ask Hannah.'

'Hannah?'

'Our secretary.'

But the secretary didn't know of anyone who had been in the room. 'Could have been one of the cleaners, of course,' she said.

* * *

There was no sign of life in the Crouches' house but behind the frosted glass of the door of the house next door, Healey thought he saw a movement. By the time he reached the door, he could make out a human form just a few feet from him, on the other side of the glass. He rang the bell, the form immediately grew larger and the door opened. He found himself face to face with the Crouches' observant neighbour. Her dyed blond hair, grey at the roots, was pinned on top of her head. Her large bust was covered only by a lime green singlet through which her nipples protruded. She was sweating.

'Oh, hello,' she said, brushing back wisps of hair that had escaped the pins and fallen onto her forehead. 'I was expecting someone else.'

'Good morning,' said Healey. He produced his warrant card.

'Yes, I know. Teresa told me.'

'Could I ask you a couple of questions?'

'Please do.'

'Last Friday evening. Can you remember where you were between nine o'clock and eleven?'

The lady pouted and frowned, as if to indicate intense concentration. 'Yes, I can, actually. I was watching television until the news came on at nine, and then I came out into the garden.'

'This garden? The front?'

'Yes. And I stayed out until it went dark. I was weeding.' She gestured towards the beds that edged the tiny lawn, which did indeed seem to be weed free.

'While you were here, did anyone come to Mrs Crouch's house?'

'No.' The reply was instant and unequivocal.

'You're sure?'

'Absolutely. And after that I was in the front room watching telly again. Nobody would have got in without me seeing them.'

'And the next morning, did you see anyone other than Mrs Crouch and her daughter leave the house?'

'No, but that doesn't mean they didn't. I always go to Waitrose on Saturday mornings. Somebody could have left while I was out.'

Healey nodded sagely. 'Thank you, erm, Mrs …'

'Parker. Miss.'

Healey couldn't resist the urge to ask for an initial, just to see if it might possibly be N. It wasn't, but it was close. It was M. 'For Mildred.'

'Well, thank you, Miss Parker. That's all I wanted to know.'

'If there's anything else,' she offered.

'If there is, I'll be in touch.' Healey made his way to Miss Parker's gate, closing it carefully behind him, then down the

Crouches' path to the door. As he rang the bell, Miss Parker, arms folded, watched with undisguised interest. She saw the door open and Healey disappear inside.

Except for the moment when he had told her that her husband was dead, Healey seemed never to hold the initiative with Teresa Crouch. This time, he had no sooner entered the house than she said that he looked hot and needed a cup of tea. Watching her go into the kitchen, barefoot and dressed in just a pale blue T-shirt and cut-off jeans, he thought she looked smaller and younger than she had before. But she was still beautiful. He wondered how old she was.

A few minutes later, perched on the edge of an armchair, holding a cup of tea too hot to drink, he found himself answering her questions, mostly about the inquest, which she had learned was to be held on Friday. Healey explained that he would be asking for an adjournment, which the coroner would certainly grant, and that he would oppose any request she made for Neville's body to be released for burial. He also admitted that they were now treating his death as murder.

Eventually, as the tea grew cooler and Teresa had no more questions for him, he asked about her husband's friends. She said that his only friends were in the Department: Peter Farrell and Chris Carter. Without pressing her on this, Healey then asked her if she was able to tell him about money her husband earned other than his salary. She could only think of the royalties which he received from the book he had written with Carter and which amounted to no more than about a thousand pounds a year. These were paid into their joint current account and went immediately towards paying off their credit card balance, which tended to accumulate between royalty payments.

When Healey asked about other bank accounts that she

and her husband held, singly or jointly, she said there was only one, their deposit account, in which they had tried in vain to save money. Its present balance, she thought, was less than a hundred pounds. 'Lecturers are not well paid,' she informed Healey.

'Then what do you think about these?' he asked, leaning forward and handing her the statements he had found in the filing cabinet.

She looked at the first statement and appeared dumbfounded. 'I have no idea,' she responded at last, as she turned to the second statement. 'Where did you find them?'

'In your husband's office.' He watched her as she looked at each of the statements in turn, slowly shaking her head. 'You see they go back more than five years. Can you remember anything happening at that time, anything unusual? Did your husband travel anywhere, for example?'

She shook her head.

Healey continued, 'As far as you are aware, after you left the Philippines, did he have any dealings with people out there? Of any kind at all.'

Again she shook her head.

'Please think carefully, Mrs Crouch. This could be important.'

When she still said nothing, Healey asked if the name Reyes meant anything to her.

'I know a family with that name, yes. In Manila.'

'And Ricardo Reyes?'

'If you mean the teacher Neville worked with in Manila, yes.'

'That's who I mean. Is he a member of the family you mentioned?'

'Yes.'

'Can you tell me something about the family?'

'It's a large family, well known. They are rich. They own

land. They have a business, import-export. I'm not sure what you want to know.'

'That's enough for now.' Healey looked her directly in the eyes. 'So, Ricardo Reyes, when is the last time you saw him?'

'I haven't seen him since we left the Philippines.'

'You're sure?'

'Yes.'

'You haven't been back since you came to England?'

'I've been back twice but I didn't see Ricardo.'

'Did your husband go with you on either occasion?'

'No. We couldn't afford for us both to go. The second time I went with Gia.'

'Has your husband been back at all?'

'No.'

'So, as far as you know, your husband has had no contact with Ricardo Reyes.'

'I didn't say that.'

'You said he had no dealings with anyone in the Philippines.'

'He didn't have *dealings* with Ricardo.'

'What then?'

'Ricardo wrote to say that he was coming to the summer school.'

'So he's here now?'

Mrs Crouch hesitated before answering. 'No, in the end he didn't come.'

'Do you know why?'

'No.'

'Did anyone come in his place?'

'I don't know.'

Healey closed the notebook in which he had in fact written no more than half a dozen words while Mrs Crouch had been talking. From his pocket he took the tiny tape recorder he had found in Crouch's room in the Hall and which he had brought with him from the incident room. 'Do you recognise this?' he asked.

She took it from him and turned it over in her hand. 'Where was it?' she asked.

'In your husband's briefcase in the Hall.' To his alarm, Healey saw tears begin to form in her eyes.

'It was a present. I gave it to him for his birthday.' Tears now rolled down her cheeks.

Healey swallowed hard. Now he had the advantage, he would press on. 'So this was some time ago?'

'Some time ago?' she repeated.

'Before he began to be violent with you.'

Her eyes flashed at him in anger. Without a word, she stood up and walked out of the room. A minute later she returned, dabbing her cheeks with what looked like a piece of screwed up kitchen roll. 'Is there anything else you want?' she asked.

'Yes, there is actually. Do you know where your husband kept the recordings he made with that tape recorder?'

* * *

That evening, after supper, Healey sat at his desk at home, browsing through the part-time course information that Farrell had given him. He looked first at the brochure for Farrell's own department. The modules they offered included some, such as grammatical theory and semantics, that made more or less sense to him, and others, like psycholinguistics and semiotics, that, despite the simple descriptions provided, seemed more mysterious and rather forbidding. Sociolinguistics, which 'explores the relationship between linguistic variation and social variation (class, age, etc)' was more attractive to him.

Turning the pages, he came to brief pen portraits of the

staff, amongst whom he recognised Farrell, Carter and, of course, Crouch. Seeing the name 'El Alaoui-Carter' made him realise that he had not seen Carter's wife and knew nothing about her except that she had been a student in the Department. He read now that she specialised in Arabic-English contrastive studies and had recently published a book 'comparing the expression of modality in the two languages'. Modality, what could that mean, he wondered, and reached for his dictionary. The most relevant definition he found there was 'classification of propositions as to whether true, false, necessary, possible or impossible'. Sounded a lot like what he did for a living.

Putting aside the Communications Department brochure, he began to look at others: English literature, History, Philosophy, Classics. As he did so, however, his mind went back to thoughts of Mrs Carter. He wondered what kind of woman she was that would choose to live with – what had Farrell called him? – a monster of nature. An intellectual, presumably. But after that, what was she like? What did she look like? These questions, and imaginings about the lady led Healey imperceptibly to thoughts about another departmental wife. Departmental widow rather.

* * *

That morning, after her brief but obvious show of anger, Teresa Crouch had been polite but distant. She had taken him again to her husband's study, where she had remained standing in the doorway, as he looked through the desk, on shelves, and in various cardboard boxes on the floor, which turned out to contain only stationery. Healey took his time and was, for him, very thorough. The cassettes were small, and one of them by itself could easily be overlooked, especially if it had been deliberately put somewhere where it would be unlikely to be found by accident. Eventually, Healey had to conclude that there were no cassettes in the room except the more normal-sized ones that were lined up on a shelf. 'Where else do you think they might be?' he asked.

She had shrugged and turned away from the door. Healey followed her out onto the landing, where she stopped and stood against the banister opposite a bedroom door. 'You can look in there,' she said. Healey went in, uncomfortably aware of the dirt he was probably depositing on the cream-coloured fitted carpet. This was not the time, though, or the place, he thought, to offer to take off his shoes. The room was south-facing and oppressively hot. Loosening his tie and undoing the top button of his shirt, Healey moved to the window and glanced down to the road below. A van was parked outside Miss Parker's and she was in the garden talking animatedly to a man, presumably the driver. The man turned and looked up at the window where Healey was standing, then turned quickly away again.

Healey himself turned to survey the room. All the furniture was pine. On the dressing-table was a black and white photograph of Crouch in whites, cricket pads on, gloves in one hand and a bat in the other. Healey looked back to where Teresa was standing in the doorway.

'I don't suppose you know what colour the handle of your husband's bat was, do you?'

She shook her head. 'No, unless it was red.' She paused. 'Or maybe it was black.'

Healey continued to look around the room. There was a double bed, a dressing table, a chest of drawers, a wardrobe, and, at each side of the bed, a small cupboard. 'Which side …' he began. Before he could finish, with a single finger she indicated the side of the bed farthest from her. Healey went there and knelt down in front of the cupboard and opened it.

Inside, in neat piles, were perhaps thirty or more of the

mini-cassettes in their cases. Still on his knees, he looked across at Mrs Crouch in the doorway. 'They're here,' he said. She didn't seem surprised. He took them out of the cupboard and put them on the bed. He was about to ask her if she could give him something to put them in when he realised she was no longer there. A moment later she was back with a plastic shopping bag. She stood beside him and held the bag open while he put in the cassettes.

As she gave him the bag, her hand brushed against his. Healey felt sure it was deliberate but before he could even think of responding in any way, she was already walking to the door. When he got downstairs, the front door was open and she was standing outside, waiting for him to leave. He thanked her as he passed her. She said nothing. By the time he had got in his car and fastened his seat belt, she had already gone inside and closed the door. Driving away, looking in his mirror, Healey saw Miss Parker and her visitor come out of her house and stand in the garden.

* * *

Healey woke with a start and looked around him. It was still light. As he got slowly from his chair, the brochure that he'd been looking at when he fell asleep dropped to the floor. He bent to pick it up, groaned at the twinge in his back, then saw his wife standing in the door, smiling. 'Poor old man,' she said. 'Did you hear me call?'

'No.'

'I just wondered if you wanted me to make coffee. Were you asleep?'

He nodded and yawned.

'So you do?'

'Please.'

They drank their coffee at the table on the terrace. 'Gosh,' said his wife, 'isn't the mock orange strong? Did I tell you, you know how it's planted on next-door's side of the fence, even though all the blossom is on our side. I was talking to Christina, yesterday I think it was, and mentioned it and she didn't even know it existed. It was so funny.' Christina was their next-door neighbour.

'It won't be so funny if that husband of hers decides to cut it down. You know what an idiot he is.'

'Oh I'm sure he won't. Don't worry about it. I told you just because I thought it was funny that we have this beautiful plant which is theirs really and they didn't know about it.' She came round the table, put her hand on his shoulder and gave him a kiss on the cheek. 'What are those?' she asked.

Healey had brought the brochures out with him. He told her that he wanted to find out what possibilities there were for him to take a degree.

'I think you should. You need something like that to stretch you. The police has become your whole life and it's not enough.' Healey smiled.

'Really, Dick, I'm being serious. If you found something completely different to do, you'd be happier. Less cynical. Even if you stayed in the police.'

'Less cynical? I don't think you can blame the police for that. The first time you met me you called me a cynic.'

'But I was joking then.'

Before Healey could respond, there was a banging at the French window. 'Dad,' shouted Jamie, 'there's someone at the front door.'

The person at the door was Peter Farrell. He was persuaded to come and join them on the terrace for coffee, even though he had at first protested that he only wanted a quick word with Healey. While Jill made more coffee, Farrell explained to Healey that he felt bad about what happened that morning. 'I know I shouldn't have let Tim go off like that. But it wasn't that I wasn't taking your case seriously, I just wasn't thinking. I've got a lot on my mind at the moment. I even got mixed up about that lecture I said I had to prepare for yesterday morning. Turned out I didn't have to at all. We swapped it for one on Othello but I hadn't changed it in my diary.' He paused.

'You see, I've got the chance of going to Spain for two years, to work on a child language project there, in Madrid. Looking at children brought up bilingually. Spanish and English. I'd jump at it, it's just the kind of work I want to do, and I need to get away from Reading for a bit. Trouble is, Pam doesn't like the idea. She'd have to give up her job at the hospital with no certainty of getting it back again. And she thinks it would be bad for the kids' education. I think the opposite. It would do them the world of good to live in a different culture for two years. I've actually applied for a grant. Oh, thanks.' Healey's wife had put down a mug of coffee in front of him.

The three of them talked at length about the narrowness of a British education system which seemed likely to grow narrower if the present government had its way. Eventually, Farrell stood up, saying he had jobs to do, but if Healey was going over to the Hall to meet the coach when it got back from Stratford, he would come along with him, if that was all right. It was, said Healey and they agreed to leave at twelve in Healey's car. As Healey stood in the door and watched Farrell walk up the road back to his house, he thought that the story about the lecture didn't ring true. He wondered why Farrell had gone to the Hall so early. He also wondered whether Farrell had a reason to keep the Reyes form from him.

* * *

As they walked into reception, they were greeted by Mr Bird from behind his desk. 'Good evening, Dr Farrell. Good evening, Chief Inspector. Or should I say good morning?' He raised his arm, turned his wrist and studied his watch, now in front of his nose. 'I've been here exactly twelve hours, seventeen minutes, and forty-five seconds, and I still don't know when I'm going to finish. That bloody Welshman didn't turn up, did he?' Seeing Healey's obvious incomprehension, he added, 'Flynn, he's the night porter. So the Warden says, Oh I'll see you right, Mr Bird. See me to my grave most like.' Farrell touched Healey's arm and made off, leaving him in the company of Mr Bird.

Waiting until Farrell had disappeared down the corridor, Bird leaned forward over the desk and gestured with his head that Healey should come closer. 'I don't know how interesting this is to you, but there's been a lot of funny things going on here these last couple of weeks, during this course sort of thing, I mean. Drugs, for example.'

'Drugs?'

'Ask the cleaners. My wife's one of them, you know?'

'Not ...' Healey searched for the name. 'Rita?'

'*Not* Rita, thank you very much. No, my wife says the very first morning, there's a lot of drugs about, Ernie. Every other bloody room, if you ask me. Marijuana and that sort of stuff. She smelt it, didn't she? And the others did.' Bird paused to let this sink in. 'There's a lot more going on than meets the eye here. I mean, what with the hanky-panky between the staff and the students. Students! I wouldn't call them students. Some of them are older than me. Supposed to be teachers. Teachers of what, I'd like to know. English? Ha! Can't even ask the time, some of them. At least one of them, that Filipino. Flippin' Eeno, I call him.'

Before Healey could ask about the Filipino, presumably the one passing himself off as Reyes, Bird went back to his earlier theme. 'You don't know who's sleeping with who. Well I do, cos my wife tells me. And *he's* ...' Bird gestured towards the door by which Farrell had left, 'he's not above ...' Bird suddenly stopped talking and picked up a clipboard, ran his finger down a list of names, and began to whistle tunelessly. Farrell was standing in the door.

'Should we wait outside?' he asked. 'It'll be more pleasant there. A bit cooler.'

As he waited for the coach to arrive, Healey wished he'd asked Teague to be there too. It wasn't just that he wanted him to feel more involved. It was often better to have two of you interviewing, one picking up things that the other missed. It wasn't always so. Talking to just one of you, people frequently became more confiding and said things they wouldn't otherwise have done. Getting people to confide in him was one of his strengths, Healey knew, but perhaps it was becoming too much of a habit. There was the danger of becoming too involved oneself, not being detached enough to judge the truth or the importance of what was being said. The modality, he said to himself, remembering what he had learned earlier.

It was almost one o'clock when the coach arrived. Yawning, bleary-eyed participants stumbled down the steps of the coach and onto the pavement. Healey felt a rush of excitement as the Italian woman appeared in the door of the coach but she didn't seem to see him. She climbed down and walked off towards the Hall. Eventually the flow of people stopped. To the surprise of the driver, Healey climbed up into the coach and walked to the back looking left and right at every pair of seats. There was no one there. Wright had not come back on the coach.

* * *

Farrell sniffed appreciatively at the Laphroaig that Healey had poured him. 'Mmm, smell the peat,' he said. 'It's like iodine. Bit different from Teacher's.'

'Something of an acquired taste,' said Healey. 'Can I get you something else?'

'No, this is fine.' Farrell took a sip. 'In fact I think it's a taste I'd like to acquire.'

Healey grinned. 'It's one Jill wishes I never had.'

'Really?'

'No, not seriously. But she does go on about my drinking sometimes. No harm in that.'

'You don't give the impression of drinking too much.'

'Depends what you mean by too much. And how much the person getting the impression drinks himself.'

Farrell acknowledged this with a smile. 'Did you have a chance to look at those brochures yet?' he asked.

'I did, thanks.'

'And?'

'I'm pretty sure I'd like to do something, but I'm not sure what.'

'Fair enough. I'm not trying to push you, but if you were to think of starting this October, you'd have to get an application in pretty sharpish. Once you get into August, most people are away and nothing much happens.'

'I'll bear that in mind. Thanks.'

When Healey had invited him in on their return from the Hall, Farrell had said it would have to be a quick one, and now he got up to leave. 'So you won't have every police force in Britain on the lookout for Tim, then?' he asked.

'No. Couldn't possibly justify it.' Healey was about to say more but decided not to. He followed Farrell out to the door and watched him walk down the drive and set off along the road. Closing the door, he nodded at himself in the mirror before climbing the stairs to bed. Despite everything, it hadn't been too bad a day.

That night he dreamed he was following a woman in cut-off jeans along a river bank, in some exotic place. He was sure it was Teresa Crouch. But when he caught up with her and spoke her name, and she turned round, he found himself looking into the face of his wife.

WEDNESDAY

It was eight o'clock and already warm when Healey parked his car in the road outside the Hall. Walking into reception, he found Teague deep in conversation with Bird, the porter. Bird must have said something because Teague, who had his back to Healey, turned round sharply and started towards him. 'Good morning, sir,' he said brightly. 'I've got something interesting for you.'

Teague it seemed had been up late the night before, trying to discover the password to the file that Healey had copied onto the disk. He had begun by collecting all the documentation he could on Crouch and the Department that he worked in, including copies of any statements they had taken which might include anything directly relevant to Crouch. He had then gone through these, systematically trying any word that Crouch might have used as a password. These included the names of colleagues, of his wife, and of roads around the University and Falstaff Avenue, Philippines connections, including Reyes and Ricardo, titles of courses in the University handbook. But he reached the end without success. He was about to give up and go to bed, when he suddenly realised that none of the documents included the name of Crouch's daughter. It was too late to call Mrs Crouch but he seemed to recall hearing her speaking the child's name when he was at Falstaff Avenue. For the life of him, though, he couldn't remember what it was. He had gone through the alphabet in his mind, finding several names for each letter, but none that rang a bell. He felt closest to it when he tried names that began with J. Then he had a thought. Didn't the missus buy a book of names when their little one was due? He had actually woken her up, and she wasn't best pleased, as you can imagine, and asked her if she still had it. Well, she did still have it and it was in the spare room. He had gone straight to names beginning with J but none of them seemed right. The nearest, he thought, was Jemma. Then it struck him that he would have spelled that name with a G, which made him look at those beginning with G.

Healey listened to all of this with mounting impatience but did not interrupt. Teague went on to explain that he had found the name Gina, which he thought might be it. He entered it as the password but no joy. Then he thought, didn't one of the wife's friends have a kid with a name just like Gina, but different. So, since she was already awake, he asked his wife and she said right away, yes, Lucie's daughter is called Gia. That was the name, he was sure. He tried it and, hey presto, he was able to open the file.

'Well done,' said Healey, 'I'm impressed,' though he could not bring himself to look into Teague's face. He did, however, stop himself from telling Teague that he could have saved himself a lot of trouble by phoning him for the name of Crouch's daughter. 'And what did you find in the file?'

Teague took from under his arm a small brown document case, unzipped it and produced with a flourish an A4 sheet of paper, which he handed to Healey.

At the top were the letters PF. Below these, on either side of the page, were two headings: IOM and BJ. Under each of the headings was a vertical list of dates and sums of money.

Healey looked at it briefly. 'How does it match the bank statements we found?'

'Exactly. I mean, all the IOM dates and amounts are the

same. I suppose BJ could be another bank, do you think, sir?'

'Could well be, yes.'

'And what do you make of the PF, at the top?'

Healey had immediately thought of Peter Farrell. 'What do *you* think?' he asked.

'Farrell. It is *Peter* Farrell, isn't it?'

'Yes. But … yes, it's a possibility.'

'Could be more than that, sir.' Teague was clearly excited; his lips were moist. 'I was just talking to Ernie now and …'

'Ernie?'

'Sorry. Bird. He was telling me that he'd seen Farrell and Crouch having a row, a real up and downer, he said. Before the course began, when they came over to look at the Hall.'

'Did he say what they were arguing about?'

'He couldn't hear properly. He was in a storeroom and they were at the other end of the corridor, and he couldn't come out or they would have seen him. But it was something to do with money. Crouch was asking for it and Farrell was saying no, there was no chance. At least that's what Bird thinks he heard.'

'How did Bird come to volunteer this information? Did you ask him about Farrell?'

'Not directly. Just about the staff on the course. Had he seen any aggro between Crouch and anyone.'

'Did he mention anyone else?'

'No, sir.'

'He hasn't said any of this before.'

'Well, we didn't ask him before, really, did we? And he told me he didn't want to say anything out of turn, didn't want to stir things up, cause trouble for anybody.'

'Cause trouble? Doesn't he know we're investigating a murder, for God's sake?'

'Well you know how it is, sir. People do worry about what will happen if they say something, but I think Bird is beginning to loosen up. I've been dropping by the Hall the last couple of days and chatting to him, bought him a pint. I reckon he knows as much as anybody about what's been going on.'

'You may be right.'

'So what about PF, Farrell?'

'I think we ask him about it directly, don't you? And we should do it together. In fact, I want you to stay with me today.'

'Yes, sir.' Teague seemed pleased.

'Oh, there is one thing, though.' Healey picked up the plastic bag he'd put on the table when he arrived and passed it to Teague. 'I found these tapes. They were in Crouch's bedroom. As soon as you get the chance, I'd like you to go through them. You'll need this too.' He handed over the miniature tape recorder.'

Teague peered inside the bag. 'How many are there?'

'About thirty.'

'So how long will that take? One hour each? Thirty hours?'

'I suppose so. But I can't trust anyone else to do it. They wouldn't know what to listen for.'

'What should I be listening for?'

'Anything that's relevant.'

'Right.' Teague was less bubbly now.

'I meant to ask you, how did the search go? I assume you didn't find anything.'

'Sorry, I should have told you, sir. No bat, no diary, no cassette. We could extend the search, I suppose. We did a quarter of a mile round the Hall.'

'No, I don't think so.'

Healey put his hand on Teague's shoulder. 'Come on, let's see if we can find Farrell.'

Farrell wasn't to be found in his room or anywhere else in the Hall, so Healey and Teague drove over to the building on the campus where the course lectures were given. On their way Teague glanced through the playing-fields entrance and caught sight of Miss Woods and Daisy standing near the pavilion. 'You know how we thought that Miss Woods must have imagined someone wearing a mac on Friday night,' he said. 'I've been thinking. What if it was somebody hiding something under the mac, like a …'

'Cricket bat.'

'Yes, and …'

'And that could make them walk awkwardly and look as if they were limping.'

'That's what I was thinking,' said Teague, looking hurt that he hadn't been given the chance to say it all himself.

'Good thinking, Teague. Though it doesn't explain how she saw the man go into the sports field from a position where she couldn't possibly have seen him do that.'

'No, but she could have been confused about that.'

'She could have been confused about all of it. After all, she does have Alzheimer's. Or at least she says she does.'

* * *

Healey eased open the door at the front of the lecture hall and saw Farrell sitting in the front row. Sitting next to him was Mary Walters, who, seeing Healey, nudged Farrell and gestured towards the door. Farrell got up and came out. 'I'm sorry to bother you,' said Healey, 'but we need to talk to you. This is Sergeant Teague, by the way.'

'Yes, we *have* met,' responded Farrell, as Teague gave him a brief nod.

They went to a nearby classroom and sat around a desk beneath a green wallboard on which was written 'May – might – must Epistemic Truth'. Motes of dust swirled in the air, lit by the rays of sunlight that entered the room through gaps in the blinds. 'I'll let Sergeant Teague ask the questions,' said Healey.

Farrell turned towards Teague, who coughed, his hand to his mouth, before beginning. 'Dr Farrell, what can you tell us about your relationship with Neville Crouch?'

Farrell looked towards Healey, who appeared to be studying the far corner of the ceiling. He did not see, or chose to ignore, Farrell's glance.

'With Neville?' said Farrell. 'We were colleagues, of course. Otherwise we had very little to do with each other. He kept very much to himself.'

'Would you say there was any rivalry between you?'

'What? No, not at all.'

'Not at all? Not even the slightest?' Teague's eyes and tone of voice expressed disbelief.

'Well, no more than between any two people in a department.'

'So what form did this rivalry take?'

'Wait a minute, I just told you there wasn't any rivalry.'

'And then you said 'no more than any two people in a department'.' Teague paused, as if to give his point its full weight, before going on. 'So can I ask you again, what form did your rivalry with Neville Crouch take?'

Farrell turned again towards Healey, who continued to look at the ceiling. 'I suppose …' he began, 'I suppose that we both wanted to do well, and our areas of expertise overlapped somewhat, but in the end you just do things as well as you can and hope that it's recognised.' He stopped but Teague said nothing and continued to look at him. 'Look …' began Farrell.

'Yes?'

'There may have been some rivalry, yes, but no animosity. We got on pretty well.'

'At work.'

'Yes.'

'And what about outside of work?'

'As I said, he kept himself to himself. We didn't see each other outside work.'

'You weren't involved in any kind of business together?'

'No.'

'So there was nothing for you to fall out about?'

'No.'

'Women?'

'What?'

'Women. They're often the cause of er … difficulties between men, especially if they're attractive. Like Mrs Crouch, for instance.'

'You're suggesting that there was something between me and Mrs Crouch?'

'Was there?'

'No there wasn't. And there was nothing between me and Neville.'

'So you and Dr Crouch never had any kind of what you might call a row?'

'I can't think of any.'

'No?'

'No.'

'What about the twelfth of July? Didn't you have a row with him then?'

'The twelfth. When was that?'

'The Thursday before the course began.'

Farrell went still and looked into the distance, as if concentrating. Eventually he focused his gaze on Teague and said, 'I can't think of anything.'

'Really? We've been told that you did. When you and Dr Crouch went to the Hall together.'

Again Farrell seemed to concentrate. Then he shook his head. 'No, I can't think of anything.'

'Very well, sir.' From his document case Teague took the printout of the file he had managed to open. 'Can I ask if you had any kind of financial dealings with Dr Crouch?'

'None at all.'

Teague passed the printout to Farrell. 'Then perhaps you'd be good enough to tell me what we should make of this.'

Farrell looked at the document for a few seconds, then handed it back. 'I've no idea what you should make of it. But I can tell you it's got nothing to do with me.'

'Despite the fact that your initials are at the top of the page.'

'The letters P and F are at the top of the page. Why should they be my initials? They could stand for a thousand different things.'

'Such as?'

'I think that's your problem. It's certainly not mine.'

'So you are saying that the amounts of money on that page mean nothing to you.'

'Nothing at all. And if you don't mind, I need to go now. The lecture will be over in a minute and I have some announcements to make.' He looked to Healey, who gave him a small, grim, almost apologetic smile. No one spoke. Farrell stood up and walked slowly to the door and out. Once he had gone, Teague turned to Healey. 'Was that all right, sir?'

'That was fine, Teague.'

As they got up, Healey caught a glimpse of a figure passing the door that Farrell had left open. 'Mr Wright,' he called out. As Wright reappeared in the doorway, Healey added, 'Can we have a word with you?'

* * *

Healey and Teague came out of the building where they had spoken to Farrell and Wright. Sitting in the car, they discussed the morning's events so far. After initially protesting that he couldn't possibly talk to them then, Wright had gone to his group to 'get them started' and then returned to sit in the seat that Farrell had so recently vacated. Ignoring the no smoking sign over the door, he busied himself with rolling a cigarette. He drew deeply on it and looked at Healey as if to say that now he was ready. Healey nodded to Teague who began the questioning.

In reply to Teague's questions, Wright told him that he had missed the coach back from Stratford because he had been with two friends from Oxford, going from pub to pub, and hadn't noticed the time. No, he hadn't been to the play, and he hadn't intended to. He had arranged to meet the friends there. No, he didn't think it odd that they should have met in Stratford when he could easily have driven to Oxford. Stratford was a pleasant place and they had a picnic lunch and rowed on the river in the afternoon. Yes, he had seen course participants in various places during the day but he wasn't sure that they had seen him; they probably wouldn't have noticed him with his friends. He hadn't talked to any of them.

How had he got back? His friends drove him to Oxford and he got a taxi from there, which cost a fortune. What time did he reach the Hall? About two, he thought, perhaps a bit later. No, there hadn't been anyone in Reception when he got back. He didn't have a receipt for the taxi fare; what would have been the point of that? And no he didn't get a card from the taxi driver. His friends had phoned for the taxi so he couldn't say what the name of the taxi firm was. Yes, he could give them the names of his friends, their address and telephone number (which he later did) but they wouldn't be able to contact them immediately because they had left early that morning for France, where they would be spending the next four or five weeks, touring about.

When Teague asked whether these friends were from the

Philippines, Wright said no, why should they be, they were English, people he'd been at university with, if that was of interest.

Wright was wearing a pink silk shirt, the same dark pink trousers as when Healey had interviewed him in his room, dark grey silk socks, and light grey suede shoes. As he answered Teague's questions, his hands folded behind his neck, he rocked backwards and forwards, balancing his seat on its two back legs. Occasionally he would stop rocking and concentrate on relighting a cigarette that had gone out, or slowly set about rolling another.

His behaviour, it was clear to Healey, was calculated to show unconcern at the questions and disdain for the questioner. So far, he was saying in effect that he was happy to tell a pack of lies, knowing that it would take a lot of trouble and a long time to show them as such, and that, anyhow, he hadn't done anything wrong. Healey didn't like Wright at all but his performance this morning only confirmed his belief that he couldn't have murdered Crouch. Still, he was going to test him a bit further.

When Teague's questioning came to an end, Wright picked up his bag of tobacco and packet of cigarette papers from the table and made as if to get up.

'We haven't finished,' said Healey abruptly. For the first time Wright seemed a little disconcerted. 'No,' continued Healey, 'we're by no means finished.' He looked directly at Wright, who had become very still, his left hand holding the tobacco and papers. Healey went on, 'Mr Wright, you have been lying to us.' He ignored Wright's attempt to protest. 'You may or may not have lied to us today but you most certainly lied to me two days ago. I asked you then about Ricardo Reyes. You told me that he had been to classes on this course. Isn't that so?'

Wright remained still and did not answer. Healey continued,

'But Mr Reyes never came to Reading, did he? He never left Manila. You were lying and now you had better start telling us the truth, or you'll find yourself in serious trouble, Mr Wright. Obstructing the police in the investigation of a murder is a serious offence.' He gave time for this to sink in. 'To start with, tell me, who is the person that has been passing himself off as Reyes?'

Wright stiffened for a moment then visibly relaxed. He gave Healey a toothy grin. 'The person passing himself off as Reyes, as you put it, is Reyes.' He paused. 'You asked me about Reyes and I told you about Reyes. The only difference is that we were thinking about different Reyeses.'

'I asked you about Ricardo Reyes.'

'I think you'll find, Chief Inspector, that you were not so specific. You referred simply to a Mr Reyes and naturally I thought you meant the one on the course. I'm sure your record of our conversation will confirm that, if you kept one, that is. I'm sorry that there has been this misunderstanding but I can assure you it was entirely accidental. I would never dream of obstructing the police.' He grinned again.

You little bastard, thought Healey, You know I didn't take notes and now I can't be sure I did say Ricardo Reyes. To Wright he said, 'You know perfectly well that I said Ricardo Reyes, but putting that aside for the moment, who is the Reyes on the course, if, as you say, his name really is Reyes?'

'Ricardo's brother, Roberto.'

'Is he an English teacher too?'

'No.'

'Then why is he on the course?'

'He couldn't get a visa any other way. He used his brother's. And the passport it was in, of course.' When Healey looked sceptical, Wright added, 'They look very like each other. You'd think they were twins.'

'But why does he want to be here at all?' asked Healey.

'He's looking for people to import stuff he makes in his factory.'

'And what stuff is *that?*'

'Stuff made from shells. Jewellery, lampshades, decorations, that sort of thing.'

'I don't see why he wouldn't get a visa to do that.'

'Nor do I, but that's what he told me.'

'And why didn't you say anything about this to anyone? Dr Farrell, for instance.'

'I didn't think it was for me to do that. And I didn't want to cause trouble. If I *had* said anything, what would have happened? He might have been sent back. But nobody would have been better off. Just one less person on the course.'

Fewer, thought Healey, but asked, 'Trouble for whom?'

'For Roberto, for Ricardo and possibly for me. If I go back to Manila, and that's quite likely, I wouldn't want the Reyes family as my enemy.'

'Why?' asked Healey. 'What would happen? What sort of family are they that you'd be so worried?'

'They've got money. And connections. It just isn't wise to get on the wrong side of people like that in the Philippines.'

Healey sensed that for Wright a moment of danger had passed and that he was beginning to enjoy himself. Then a thought struck him. 'You told me that Reyes was actually attending classes. Am I right?'

'Yes. Well, at least some.'

'Which meant that he was around the Hall or the University a lot of the time during the first two weeks of the course.'

'I suppose so.'

'Don't you find that strange for someone who is trying to make business contacts?'

'I imagine that he didn't want to make it obvious that he wasn't here for the course. I don't know.'

Then Healey had another thought. 'Dr Crouch must have realised that it wasn't the Reyes who was supposed to be here.'

'Yes.'

'What did he think about it?'

'I don't know. We didn't really talk about it.'

'What? You didn't talk about it?'

'I mean, we both knew it was Roberto and why he was here, and that was it really.'

'Why didn't Dr Crouch tell anyone?'

'I don't know.'

'Presumably not for the same reason as you?'

'It could have been. He might have intended to go back to the Philippines again sometime. I don't know.'

'When did you last see Mr Reyes?'

'Roberto?'

'The Reyes that was here.'

'When?' Wright appeared to ponder.

'Was it yesterday? Is that what you were really doing?'

'No. I was with friends, as I told you. The last time I saw Roberto was on Friday morning.'

'In your class?'

'Yes.'

'And you don't know where he went?'

'No.'

'And you don't know where he is now?'

'No.'

'Well thank you, Mr Wright. We shall be checking everything that you have told us so far. If in the meantime you'd like to make any changes to what you have said, or add to it, just let us know. You can tell one of the constables in the Hall if you do.'

Wright smiled. 'I won't need to add or change anything.'

As Wright got up to go, Teague asked, 'One last thing, Mr

Wright, if you wouldn't mind. Do you happen to know the colour of the handle of Dr Crouch's cricket bat?'

Wright laughed. 'I haven't the foggiest idea,' he said. 'Can I go now?'

Now in the car, after they had kept Wright a further ten minutes while they took details of his friends and of his supposed movements of the previous day, Teague expressed the view that they had been talking to a pair of lying bastards and if the education of the nation's brightest children was in the hands of such people, what hope was there for the future. Without much enthusiasm, Healey pointed out that there could well be a difference between an academic's attitude to truth in their work and in their private lives, especially if the latter were under attack in some way. Teague, showing more perseverance than usual in discussions with Healey, asked whether, say, marking students' essays was work; couldn't it also be private? What if they were having it away with a student, like Bird said they were, wouldn't that affect the marks they gave? Healey, feeling as he did, closer to some at least of the academics than he did to Teague, said that he didn't know.

What the two men found easy to agree on was that there were two main areas to explore in relation to Crouch: any enmity between him and other academics; and the source or sources of the substantial sums of money that he had managed to salt away over the previous few years. Farrell was a candidate for investigation on both counts, as Wright might be too. Reyes, presumably Roberto Reyes, was a possible link with the money; the sooner they could get hold of him, the better. Bird had said that he would look out for him and regularly check his room, and let Teague know as soon as he put in an appearance.

Teague persisted somewhat with his notion that a woman

might be involved (Cherchez la femme, he said again). When pressed by Healey to say which woman and what role she might play, he could only suggest that there could well be more to Mrs Crouch than met the eye. Thinking that there was already quite a lot of Mrs Crouch that met the eye, Healey said that, yes, she might be involved but that it would be helpful if they could think of the role she might have played, in order to have an angle from which to approach her. He suspected that going over the same ground with her, however carefully, was unlikely to reveal anything significant. But that was true for the other two as well.

In the meantime, said Healey, it might be a good idea to go back to Chris Carter. Not only did Healey feel that he hadn't learned as much as he might from Carter, but, remembering the tapes, it would also be an opportunity for Teague to listen for the first time to someone who might feature in the recordings.

They were driving to the University of Berkshire. As they passed the Huntley and Palmer building, Teague gave a nervous cough before saying, 'I've been thinking, sir, about those tapes. Wouldn't it be more efficient to get a couple of typists at HQ to listen to them and type them out? Then we'll be able to read them through quickly and decide if there's anything relevant. And besides, we'll have to get them typed out sometime if we're going to use them as evidence, won't we?'

Healey had already thought of this possibility. 'Two problems with that, Teague. First, it will take a lot longer to transcribe the tapes than to listen to them, so we lose time. Second, the typists may not be accurate. I mean, they may not be able to type exactly what is said or even to hear it. Somebody who knows what they're listening for has to do it, I'm afraid. I don't think there's any way round it. I tell you what, though, I'll take some of them myself. Why don't we take half each? I know we've only got one recorder at the moment but if you could give me that one back and pick one up at HQ after we've talked to Carter … Oh, by the way, while I think of it, did you finish that matrix I asked you to construct?'

Teague seemed confused. 'Matrix?'

'The names, who saw who and when.'

'I gave that job to Gifford.'

'And?'

'He said there would be more than 2500 cells, as you called them. It was going to take a long time. I'll have to check.'

'Please do that. And about the 2500 cells, that's bollocks. It's the number of positive entries that matters. Anyhow, let's not worry about that now.' Healey pulled off King's Road into the car park and stopped. 'Let's see what Carter can tell us.'

They found Chris Carter sitting in semi-darkness. The little light there was entered through cracks in the blinds that hung down behind him and which, though the windows and door were open presumably to create a draught, made no perceptible movement. He looked up from his computer and greeted Healey, who introduced Teague.

Healey apologised for the interruption but explained that there were certain matters they needed to go over again. What they were looking for, to put it bluntly, was a motive for Neville Crouch's murder. They were pursuing other possibilities outside the Department but for the time being at least they had to consider that the murderer might have been a colleague.

Carter frowned. He began by saying that effectively they were talking about him and Farrell, as all the other members of the Department were away on holiday at the time of

Neville's death. Healey pointed out that this was not necessarily the case, as a clever person might use a supposed, or indeed a real holiday as an alibi. So, could Carter go through the various members of the Department please and try to remember anything between them and Dr Crouch.

Carter took out a sheet of paper and wrote down five sets of initials, a sixth, his own, added as an afterthought at the bottom, and then proceeded to discuss their owners, each in turn.

RBL was the Head of Department, Rex Bradshaw-Lewis. To think of him as a murderer was inconceivable, said Carter. Rex might have liked to get rid of Neville from the Department, given his poor publishing record, but murder would have been excessive. Rex was a kindly man, a devout Christian, a regular churchgoer. (Healey was reminded of Wright saying something similar about Reyes, the Reyes who hadn't come to Reading.) Yes, Rex lived for his family, his research and his garden. He wouldn't hurt a fly – except greenfly, Carter added, smiling thinly.

Next there was ML, Monty Lightfoot. Something of a hermit who had little time for his fellow men. As soon as term was over, he disappeared to his sister's cottage in Somerset and wasn't seen again until the beginning of the next term. There had been a bit of trouble between him and Crouch, Carter recalled, all to do with secret recordings that Crouch had made of his colleagues. Most people hadn't minded, or at least not much, but Monty had huffed and puffed, claimed it was unethical, uncolleaguial behaviour, and insisted that all the tapes should be destroyed. Healey asked if they had been and Carter replied that they hadn't. Rex had taken Monty aside and told him not to be so silly. And nothing more was said. That was years ago and was over and done with. Besides, Monty had been in the States on sabbatical since January and wasn't due back until September. When

Healey asked if the recordings that Lightfoot had objected to were made with a miniature hand-held recorder, Carter replied that he wasn't sure but that they could well have been.

XL, Xiao Lim, was a gifted young Chinese who had done postgraduate work at Oxford, at the end of which, desperate not to return home, he had applied for, been offered, and to everyone's surprise, accepted a post in the Department. That had only been a year ago and he was unlikely to stay long, Carter confided, but it was a welcome change to have someone as bright and active around. He too was in the States, giving a paper at a conference. Teague asked if Carter knew whether Lim practised martial arts. Carter didn't know but suggested that it would have to be a very special form of martial arts if it were to be effective over several thousand miles, if that was what Teague had in mind. Teague blushed but said nothing.

Carter looked down at his list of initials. 'Then of course there's PF whom you already know,' he said, addressing himself to Healey and ignoring Teague. 'I assume you don't need me to say anything about him.'

'I'd appreciate it if you would. I realise that he is a friend of yours as well as a colleague but we need to find out as much as we can, that's relevant of course, about anyone who was involved with Dr Crouch.'

'I understand. Well, putting aside the fact that Peter was with me at the time that I take it the murder was committed, I can't think of anything between him and Neville that would be of interest to you.'

'What about the recordings?' put in Teague. 'Was Dr Farrell happy about that?'

Carter didn't look at Teague as he replied. 'I wouldn't say he was happy, but he wasn't particularly unhappy either. He didn't think it was worth getting upset about.'

'And what about you, sir?' asked Teague. 'Were *you* upset by it?'

'Me? Certainly not. How else are you going to collect data on how people actually speak? If they know they are being recorded, then of course this affects what they say.'

'And how they say it,' added Healey.

'Precisely.'

Healey felt pleased with himself and would have liked to pursue this further but knew he had to concentrate on the task in hand. 'Getting back to Dr Farrell,' he said, 'do you know of any business that they might both be involved in? Anything that might involve money passing from one of them to the other?'

'I don't think so. Though, come to think of it, they did talk at one time of setting up a language school together, but nothing came of it, as far as I know. Nothing much came of anything that Neville was involved in, I'm afraid.'

'There was the book,' said Healey.

'But only because I wrote it.'

'Where was the language school going to be?' asked Healey. 'In Reading?'

'No, Manila. Apparently they're queuing up to learn English there and the schools that exist aren't very good. Peter went out a couple of times to talk to people there. Once with Teresa. Mrs Crouch. She had useful connections, apparently.'

'You wouldn't know the names of any of the people there, would you?'

'No, this is years ago, soon after Peter joined the Department.'

'Does the name Reyes mean anything to you?'

'Reyes.' Carter scratched his beard as he repeated the name. 'Reyes. That does ring a bell. I remember thinking that it meant Kings and wondered what the significance was. Never did find out. But, yes, Reyes. It could well have been to do with the business of the school.'

'And when Dr Farrell travelled to Manila with Mrs Crouch, did Dr Crouch stay in Reading?' asked Teague.

'Yes.' This time Carter did look at Teague.

'To look after the daughter, I suppose?'

'No. They didn't have a child then. No, I think it was just to save money.'

'As a matter of interest,' said Teague, 'when was the Crouches' daughter born?'

'I can't give you a date. But I suppose it must have been about a year after the school business. After Gia was born, they lost any remaining interest they may have had. The Crouches, that is.'

'And Dr Farrell?' asked Healey.

'You should ask him, but I think he was well out of it.'

'Did he harbour any resentment, do you think?'

'He was a bit pissed off, of course. After all, he'd spent quite a lot of money just travelling and it was all down the Swanee. But Peter isn't one to harbour grudges. He still got on all right with Neville.'

'Do you know of any other business ventures that Dr Crouch may have undertaken?' asked Healey.

'No. He was always hinting that he was onto something big, either in his research or in some venture, as you put it, but I doubt if anything ever came of it. That was Neville. A lot of talk, and no action.'

'Who's next?' asked Healey.

'LEC,' replied Carter. 'Leila El Alaoui-Carter. My wife. I don't know what I can say about her.'

'She was a student here, wasn't she?' asked Healey.

'Yes. She did the MA in ELT and then her PhD.'

'When did you get married?'

'About a year after she came back to do her PhD.'

Healey nodded and was going to ask about her work in the Department, when Teague broke in, 'Can I ask you, Dr

Carter, when your relationship with your present wife commenced?'

'Is that relevant?' Carter looked at Healey, who didn't respond.

'It could be,' said Teague. 'I realise that it is a rather delicate matter, but if you could just tell us.' As Teague pronounced the word 'delicate' with what seemed like pleasure, Healey saw saliva come to his lips.

'I can't see the relevance,' replied Carter, 'but if you must know, it was when she came back to do her PhD.'

'Oh,' said Teague, 'not prior to that?'

'No.'

'But when she was still a student.'

'She was a mature woman with a mind of her own. Look, I don't like the tone of your questions, Sergeant. Nor do I see their relevance.' He turned to Healey, who again did not respond.

'I'm only trying to ascertain the facts, sir,' Teague went on. 'As to their relevance, you have to let us be the judges of that.'

Carter said nothing, remained motionless, and stared at Teague through his glasses.

Teague continued. 'So your relationship commenced when your wife was a student. How long had she been back at Reading when this happened?'

Carter did not answer and it was Healey who spoke. 'All right, Teague, I think we can leave it there. Dr Carter isn't obliged to answer our questions and he clearly doesn't want to. I think we can take it that Mrs Carter wasn't involved.'

Teague made a little pout and snapped his notebook shut. 'If you say so, sir.'

'Right, Dr Carter, who does that leave us with?' asked Healey.

'Just me.'

'And you had no difficulties with Dr Crouch, other than with the book, which you have already told us about.'

'None at all.'

'And no business dealings with him.'

'Certainly not.'

'Well, I think that just about ...' Healey stopped as out of the corner of his eye he became aware of someone in the doorway.

'Let me introduce my wife,' said Carter. 'Leila, this is Chief Inspector Healey. He's investigating Neville's death.'

Healey stood up and turned to Mrs Carter and offered his hand, which she took and held for a moment longer than he would have expected. Another very attractive woman, he thought. Tall, almost as tall as Carter he guessed, with long black hair, olive skin, wide set brown eyes, and a full mouth. She wore pendant earrings of lacy silver studded with coral pink and turquoise stones. The low neckline of a simple, loose-weave black dress revealed a generous bosom.

'Chris, darling,' she said, showing very white and even teeth, 'it's twelve. Time we were off.'

'We were just going,' said Healey. 'Thank you, Dr Carter. You've been very helpful.'

Carter gave him a curt nod. Teague, who had remained seated since their arrival, stood up and followed Healey to the door.

'Nice to meet you, Chief Inspector,' said Mrs Carter, who came up close to Healey and shook his hand again. The perfume she gave off smelled strongly of some exotic plant that Healey couldn't place. It contrasted markedly with Carter's body odour, which had grown stronger during the time they had been with him. Perhaps that's how she deals with it, thought Healey.

* * *

Back in the Hall, while Teague went to headquarters to collect a tape recorder, Healey sat at a table in the incident room and read the report that had arrived on the two printouts of the letter he'd had Carter word process for him. As far as could be told, and the report was very tentative, the one that most resembled the original letter was the one that had been done on Crouch's printer. So what did that mean? Had Crouch written the letter himself? If so, why? Healey was pondering these questions when he realised that Farrell was standing beside him.

'Oh, hello there,' he said. 'Didn't see you come in.'

'You did seem engrossed. Have you got a moment?'

'Yes, sure.'

'About this morning. You asked about a row I was supposed to have had with Neville. Well, I think I know what it must have been that you heard about. It wasn't a row at all. Just a disagreement. You know how we have rooms in hall, even though we live nearby. That's the way the BC, the British Council, set it up. On a lot of their courses tutors do need accommodation and so rooms are booked on all courses as a matter of routine. What Neville wanted was to give up his room and be then paid what the Council saved. He said they were benefiting from him having a house nearby and so shouldn't mind paying him what they'd already budgeted for anyhow. He asked the same question last year and they said no. He wanted me to ask again and I said I wouldn't. They'd only say no again, and I'd just look stupid. He persisted and I suppose I was a bit sharp with him. But that's all there was to it. I didn't think about it this morning, it was such a small thing. I hope that's okay.'

Healey nodded. 'Thanks. I'm sorry if we gave you a bit of a hard time.'

'That's all right. I understand perfectly. You've got a job to do.'

'I've actually got another question for you.'

'Go ahead.'

'Well, you said you'd had no financial dealings with Dr Crouch, didn't you?'

'That's right.'

'What about the language school you were planning to set up with him in Manila?'

'Oh that.' Farrell seemed somewhat taken aback and hesitated before continuing. 'I'm sorry. Perhaps I should have mentioned that. Yes, we did have that idea but it never got anywhere. There were no financial dealings as such.'

'But you went to the Philippines?'

'Yes.'

'That must have cost quite a bit.'

'Yes, but I was able to claim against income tax. And Neville didn't pay anything.'

'Except for Mrs Crouch, of course.'

'Of course.'

Despite Farrell's tan, Healey saw his face redden slightly. Clearly a sensitive matter but not one he would pursue now. 'Have you thought any more about that list with PF at the top that we showed you?' he asked.

'Yes, I have. I don't have an answer, but whatever PF stands for, I can assure you that it doesn't stand for Peter Farrell. That's all I can say.' He looked over Healey's shoulder as if he had noticed someone. 'If you'll excuse me, I have to talk to our course assistant, about a small problem in the toilets, would you believe. Oh, and while I think of it, I wanted to ask you if you would like to come to the end of course party on Friday night. You're very welcome. And your Sergeant, if you like.'

'Thanks. I'll see what's happening nearer the time. Do I need to tell you if I'm coming?'

'No, just turn up. Or don't. I hope you do, though. Should be fun.'

Healey caught sight of a round-faced young woman with a shock of pink and blue hair, wearing a black blouse and mini-skirt, approaching them.

'Oh! Sam,' said Farrell, 'I was just coming to look for you. Let me introduce you. Richard, this is Samantha, our course assistant. Samantha, Chief Inspector Healey, as you probably already know.' Farrell addressed himself to Healey, 'Sam knows everything. She's the person who actually runs this course, not me.' He put his hand on her shoulder. 'To the toilets,' he said, and set off with her down the corridor.

Healey watched her mini-skirted bottom as she clomped along in her Doc Martens until, remembering that his daughter wore a pair too, he felt suddenly guilty.

* * *

Healey sat at his desk at home, in his hand the mini-recorder, containing the first of the cassettes that he planned to listen to. Teague was right; it was going to take a long time, even now that they were sharing the task. To his credit, Teague had noticed miniscule markings on the cassettes, practically invisible to Healey without his reading glasses. Each cassette bore twelve digits without a break between them, which Teague had quickly worked out must refer to dates, the first six digits indicating the starting date of the recordings on the tape and the second six indicating the finishing date. If this was indeed what the numbers meant, and it seemed almost certain that they did despite some discrepancies, then the recordings had been made a few years before and covered a period of eighteen months.

Healey started listening to what turned out to be a conversation between two people whose voices he didn't recognise, talking about what they referred to as pragmatics. From what Carter had told them that morning, he was fairly confident that the speakers were the Head of Department, Rex whatever it was, and the hermit, Monty. What he could be absolutely sure of, however, was that the content of the tape could have nothing to do with Crouch's death. It could well have something to do with me falling asleep very soon, though, thought Healey. He got up, went into the living room and pulled the curtains to.

He was just easing himself onto the sofa when the phone rang. It was his Superintendent, who, having first observed that Healey was at home again in the middle of the afternoon, said he just wanted to know how the case was progressing. As Healey told him, the Super hardly made a comment and Healey sensed that he wasn't really listening.

After Healey had finished his account by explaining that the reason he was at home was to be able to listen to the tapes without any distractions, the Super said 'Fine. Fine. One thing, though. Mind you don't get too close to those academics. Wouldn't want it to cloud your judgement. They can be devious buggers at the best of times. Wouldn't trust them as far as I could throw them myself. Okay? Right. Keep me appraised.'

So that was why he had called, and it could only be because he had been talking to Teague. It must have been when Teague went to get the tape recorder. Healey felt depressed, and no longer sleepy. He went back to his study and, having looked in the dictionary to confirm what he suspected – that what his Super meant to say was 'apprised' and not 'appraised', began to listen to the recording again. As he did so, he had the nagging feeling that there was another word he wanted to check, from something said that morning.

Healey woke with a start, unsure where he was. He felt a hand on his shoulder. 'Dad, wake up.' It was his son, Jamie. 'Dad, wake up. Mum says supper's nearly ready and do you want a cup of tea.'

'Yes, please.' Healey watched his son run through the living room in the direction of the kitchen. He yawned and ran his hand through his hair. He was still at his desk but the tape recorder was no longer in his hand, and nor was it on his desk. He looked down and saw it at his feet. He leaned over to pick it up and felt a spasm in his lower back. He was down on his knees retrieving the recorder when his wife came in with his tea.

'Are you all right, love?' she asked.

'Yes, fine. Just getting this.' He lifted the recorder to show her, and got slowly to his feet.

'Back bad again?'

'It's okay.'

'It's not, is it?'

'It's fine. Don't worry.'

'You should see about it. You can't go on like this.'

'It's all right. Let's not talk about it.'

'I'm the one that will have to look after you if it goes again.'

Healey said nothing. His wife took down a paperback from the shelf, put it on the desk, and placed the mug of tea on it. 'Supper'll be ready in five minutes,' she said.

* * *

After supper Healey went back to his desk and the tape recorder. It took him a while to find the place where he must have been when he fell asleep and when he did and started to listen again, he found it as boring as it had been before. The two speakers were still going on about what seemed to him highly theoretical and extremely subtle differences of interpretation that did not interest him and, to be honest, which he did not fully understand. It occurred to him to fast forward until he found something that might be more relevant to the case but decided not to because there would be no way of knowing whether he had missed something important. So he listened to them droning on, as he put it to himself, for another ten or twelve minutes, becoming increasingly restless, then stopped the machine. This was no good. He had to get out, move about, do something different.

Without thinking about it further, he got up, called out that he was going for a walk, and set off down Beech Lane in the direction of the Wilderness, which was just a couple of hundred yards from his house. When he had crossed Wilderness Road and passed through the narrow pedestrian entrance and was making his way along one of the tracks, it occurred to him that he could have brought Maisie the dog, but he couldn't be bothered going back now.

Emerging from the shade of the trees into still bright sunshine, he passed by some science blocks, came to the main administration building, and then realised that what had seemed an aimless walk was taking him towards the cricket ground and the hall where the summer school was housed. He realised too that what he wanted was for something to happen, something different from the routine of work and family life. He began to walk more quickly, with a mounting feeling of expectancy and a pleasurable sense almost of danger, something he hadn't experienced for a long time.

To his disappointment, when he got there, the Hall seemed deserted. The incident room was locked, there were no participants about, and even Mr Bird was not at his desk. He was about to leave when a voice called out, 'Hello there.' It was the course assistant, Samantha.

'Where is everybody?' Healey asked.

'They've gone to Windsor to see a play. I was supposed to go too but we were so late getting back from Stratford last night that Peter, Dr Farrell, said I could have an early night and he'd go instead.'

'That was nice of him. Do you know what time they get back?'

'I think about eleven, unless they stop off at a pub on the way.'

Healey was on the point of saying goodnight, when instead, out of the blue, he found himself asking an attractive twenty-year-old woman whether she fancied a drink.

'Thanks, but the bar's closed and Mr Bird isn't around to open it.'

'Oh.' Healey hesitated before going on. 'What about the Queen's Head? It's only just round the corner.'

She smiled. 'All right. A quick one then. I want to be safely in my room before they all get back from the play.' She paused. 'Could you wait just a minute. I'll be back.'

When she returned, she was not alone. With her was the Italian woman. 'I hope you don't mind,' said Samantha, 'I met Silvia on the stairs and asked her to come along too.'

'Not at all. The more the merrier,' said Healey and immediately regretted it.

'I'm sorry but you'll have to make do with just the two of us,' said Silvia.

'I didn't mean ...'

'Of course not. Don't be embarrassed,' said Silvia, at which she put her arm around Samantha's waist, pulled her towards her, and kissed her on the cheek. 'We don't want to embarrass you.'

They sat at a wooden table outside the back of the Queen's Head. The women both drank white wine and Healey, somewhat self-consciously, had his usual Guinness. He was struck by the bright blue of Silvia's eyes; her hair, however, shoulder length and straight, was of a colour his wife would have called mousey. His gaze wandered to the tanned skin of her fine-boned arms, against which the hair was bleached pale gold. Needing to distract himself from the thoughts that were coming to his mind, he managed to ask her a question.

'How is it you speak such good English?'

She laughed. 'Because I had an English husband.'

'Had.'

'Yes, he is married to someone else now. A Russian. He likes the exotic.'

'And you?'

'Am I married again or do I like the exotic?'

'Both.'

'No, I'm not married. And no, I don't like the exotic. But I do like Englishmen, strong and silent.' She laughed. 'And what about you … I'm sorry, I don't know what to call you.'

'Richard.'

'What about you, Richard. I think you are married, aren't you?'

'Yes.'

'And do you like the exotic?'

'I suppose I am attracted by it.'

'It? We are talking about women, Richard.' When Healey didn't reply, she went on, 'I'm sorry, I'm embarrassing you again. And I don't think this is a very interesting subject for poor Sam here, is it my sweet? Let's talk about something else. How about the weather? No? How about …' Silvia looked round as if checking that there was no one who could overhear her. 'How about the murder?' she whispered.

'I don't think we should talk about that,' said Healey. 'Not here.'

'Why not? Nobody can hear us. But if you say no, we won't. But we can talk about Dr Crouch, can't we? He was such a kind man. Wasn't he, Sam? Such a terrible thing that he should die like that.'

'He was kind to us students,' agreed Sam. 'He always had time to talk. And if you had a problem with your work, he'd spend ages helping you sort it out.'

Healey wondered whether Crouch had shown such kindness to all his students or just to attractive females like Sam. 'Was he a good teacher?' he asked, thinking it would be interesting to compare a student's view with that of Crouch's colleagues.

'People liked him as a teacher because he told you exactly what you needed to know for exams. If you took good notes at his lectures, you couldn't go wrong. But he was boring. And he said exactly the same things year after year. Didn't change anything. Some people never went to his lectures, just got the handouts, and notes from people of previous years.'

'I don't suppose you know if he was popular with other members of staff?'

'Not really. I think Peter thought he was a bit of a fusspot, from what I've seen on the course. Besides that, I don't know.'

When Healey offered to buy a second round of drinks, Samantha said no, if he didn't mind, she had better get back to the Hall. The coach might get back early and she didn't want to be seen. 'That's the one bad thing about this job,' she said. 'You're always on duty. If they see you anywhere, anytime, they feel that they can ask you to help them do anything. I'm not complaining, it's been a good experience, but just now, after three weeks, I've had enough of them.'

'I'll come back with you,' said Silvia. 'Perhaps we could have a nightcap together. I've got something in my room.'

'Not for me, thanks,' said Samantha.

'How about you, Richard?'

Healey was tempted. Wasn't this just the kind of excitement

he was looking for? He sensed, however, that it was probably unwise. Or was he afraid of what might happen? He wasn't sure, but he said no thanks, he had to get back. As he watched the two women walk off, arm in arm, he felt a sharp pang of regret. 'Home,' he muttered to himself. 'Home.'

Despite telling himself to go home, Healey decided to take a small detour. From Pepper Lane he turned into Falstaff Avenue, and two minutes later stood outside the Crouches' house. The curtains of Crouch's study were drawn but the light was on. As he watched, on the curtains he saw the shadows of two people moving about, first apart then coming together. Two people. Teresa Crouch and who? Wright? No sign of his car. Reyes? It could be. Should he go to the door and ring the bell? He could invent some pretext for the visit. Healey was undecided and for the moment just watched the moving shadows.

* * *

They made love for the first time since that night.
At the climax, there was Crouch again.
Falling, falling, silently falling.

THURSDAY

Healey began to wish that he'd taken the car. Much easier by train, he'd told Teague, who had looked unconvinced, but the one taking them from Reading to Gatwick airport was dirty, uncomfortable, and slow, hardly getting up any speed before slowing down again to stop at some out-of-the-way station where no one got on or off. It was noisy too, after they had opened windows in order to let some air in. Roll on privatisation, he thought. Not that he would have admitted such a thought to his sergeant, whose political views were somewhat to the right of the present Conservative government and who probably believed the whole rail system should be scrapped and the saving in subsidies used to reduce the duty on petrol.

Despite his regret at taking the train, Healey was happy. Things were beginning to take shape and he had the feeling, familiar after so many years as a detective, of moving quickly forwards towards a solution. Everything was about to become clear, he was sure, though he could not say yet, even to himself, who the murderer was.

The previous night he had been standing across from the house in Falstaff Avenue for no more than a quarter of an hour when the light went off in the study and one in the front bedroom went on, only to go off a few minutes later. The house remained dark and Healey set off home, resolving to come back early next morning.

It was just after seven when he arrived at the house. There was no sign of life. He knocked but there was no response. He knocked again and stepped back from the door to look up at the upstairs windows. He was about to knock again when the door opened a crack and a dark brown eye peered at him. The door opened wider. In the same blue dressing-gown that she was wearing when he first saw her, and holding Gia against her shoulder, was Teresa, her face still full of sleep.

'I'm sorry to call so early,' he said. 'Could I come in?'

Without a smile, Teresa turned and walked through into the living room, leaving Healey to follow her, closing the door behind him. He sat down opposite her and the child, who was on her mother's knee and sucking her thumb, watching him closely.

'I'll get directly to the point,' he said. 'I believe that there is someone else in the house. Would you mind telling me who it is?'

Teresa went tense. She didn't reply immediately. Eventually she said, 'What makes you think that there is someone here?'

Healey didn't want to admit that he had been watching her house the previous night. 'Is there?' he asked.

'Is this your business? If I have somebody in my house that is my private affair. Aren't I right? This isn't a police state.'

'No it isn't. And I'm not interested in your affairs as such.' Healey emphasised the word 'affairs'. 'But I'm investigating the murder of your husband and I'm collecting any information that I can that will help me discover who the murderer is. So could you tell me, please, who it is that's here in the house with you?'

'If you must know, it's my cousin.'

'Your cousin?'

'She's here to help me with everything. This isn't an easy time, you know.'

'No, of course. You say 'she'. So it's a female cousin?'

Teresa cast him a scornful look. 'Would you like to see her? Just to make sure that she's female?'

'I would like to speak to her, if you don't mind. If *she* doesn't mind.'

Teresa lifted Gia from her lap, took her by the hand and went upstairs.

The cousin, if that was what she was, came down after a lot of muttering, not in English as far as Healey could tell, some of it appearing to express reluctance on her part. She was younger than Teresa but looked very much like her: quite tall, shapely, with a pretty face. So many lovely women in the world.

She told him that she had arrived from the Philippines only last night and confirmed that she had come to help Teresa while she was sorting out her affairs. Her English, though there was an accent, was faultless. Healey asked her if she would mind showing him her passport, which she went upstairs to get. Teresa, who had said nothing since she had come down with her cousin, went into the kitchen, her child holding her hand, and Healey heard her pour water into the kettle and switch it on.

The name on the passport was Maria Leticia Lopez Reyes. It had a six-month visa for entry into the UK dated a few days previously, against which was a stamp showing yesterday's date, over which were scrawled the initials of the immigration officer who had dealt with her on arrival. 'Your name is Reyes,' said Healey. 'Are you related to Ricardo Reyes?'

The cousin looked surprised and did not answer. 'She is,' responded Teresa, who had come to the kitchen door. 'We all are. It's a big clan.'

'Yes,' agreed the cousin. 'He is my cousin.'

'And Roberto Reyes? Is he your cousin too?'

'Yes, of course. He is Ricardo's brother.'

'And when did you last see these gentlemen?'

The cousin seemed to reflect. 'I saw Ricardo yesterday morning before I left the Philippines. Roberto is in England, I think. I haven't seen him for a long time.' She didn't ask the reason for Healey's questions.

Teresa appeared again at the kitchen door. 'I've made tea, Chief Inspector. Would you like some?'

'No, thank you. But I didn't know you were a Reyes too.'

'I'm not. But I'm related to them. In any case, I don't think you asked me.'

'Perhaps not, but I did ask you about the Reyeses and you could have said that you were related.'

Teresa shrugged her shoulders. 'It's a very big family and I'm not one of the important ones.'

Healey said nothing. He made a note of the cousin's full name and the date and number of the visa, and was on the point of leaving when he asked Teresa if she knew about a drawing in her husband's office at the University, one apparently done by a child.

'Yes, Gia did it.'

'Do you know where that drawing is now?'

'Yes. It's in Gia's room.'

'So did you take it from the office?'

'Yes.'

'How did you get into the office?'

'With my key. Do you want me to give it to you?'

'No, no. That's not necessary.'

As Healey walked towards his car, Teresa watching him motionless in the doorway, he wondered what else she could have done in the office if she had a key. The threatening letter. Could she have written it and printed it there? Not impossible. Still thinking about this possibility, he drove slowly down Falstaff Avenue and turned left into Pepper Lane. Within five minutes he was at the Hall, where he was met by Teague, who strutted towards him with a big smile on his face.

'Guess what, sir. Reyes. He's being held by Customs and Excise. Gatwick Airport. Drugs.'

That was how they came to be sitting opposite each other on this awful train. Teague was doing the crossword. 'Greek island. Six letters, fourth letter b.'

'Lesbos.'

'Lesbos? That isn't where the word ...'

'Yes, it is.'

Healey watched as Teague, chuckling, struggled to hold the paper steady against the shaking of the train as he wrote in the missing letters. He had once spent a lot of time himself doing crosswords, though of the cryptic kind, but one day he had decided that they were a waste of time and hadn't done another since. Now he occasionally did the Quick Crossword in the Guardian, or at least finished the ones his wife had started, but his greatest pleasure, if he was honest, was in demonstrating how easily (usually) he could provide the answers to the clues that baffled Teague.

He had the feeling about this case that he used to have with a difficult crossword. You'd be struggling, then get a couple of clues and suddenly everything fell into place. The drugs, the Reyes family, Crouch's connections with the Philippines. The amounts of money Crouch had stashed away weren't much but there could be more. PF? Peter Farrell or not? Could be a coincidence, though if he were trying to solve a clue in a crossword and he already had two infrequent letters in place, and found a word which fitted and which was somehow connected with the clue, he'd be pretty confident that it was the right one.

The train slowed down and lurched to a stop at Dorking Deepdene. A young blond woman in shorts dragging a large suitcase passed the window, evidently intending to board their carriage. Immediately Teague was up and striding to the door. Through the window, Healey saw him step down from the platform, say something to the woman, take the case from her, and climb back on board, the woman following him. Healey heard the door slam and expected to see the two of them appear but they didn't. They must have passed through into the next carriage. Disappointed, Healey picked up the paper that Teague had abandoned and, after a glance at the half-completed crossword, turned to the sports pages.

* * *

'It's a very simple story, Chief Inspector,' said the Customs Officer, small and neat in his crisp white shirt with a dark blue tie, a Londoner thought Healey from his accent. Healey and Teague sat on the other side of his grey metal desk in an office that was noteworthy most for the fact that it had a window that gave out onto a large baggage area, perhaps twenty feet below, where hundreds of passengers were milling around carousels, or pushing trolleys, some empty, some full, in what seemed like random movements. Healey presumed that any passengers who happened to look up towards the office would not see anything but reflections.

'Yes,' repeated the officer, straightening his already perfectly placed tie, 'a very simple story. We had a tip-off that a consignment of cannabis would be arriving on a flight from the Philippines yesterday. We checked the baggage of everyone coming through but nothing turned up. In the end there are just two cases on the carousel, going round and round. Then we see this man with a trolley standing a distance away, watching them. Can't make up his mind. Then all of a sudden he walks straight over, grabs them, pops them on his trolley, and sets off for the green lane.'

'Where you stopped him,' put in Teague.

The customs officer looked at him in mock surprise. 'Yes, strangely enough, that's just what we did.' He paused to see the effect of his remark but Teague looked straight back at him, as if oblivious of the sarcasm.

The officer continued, 'He denied all knowledge of the contents, said he was collecting the cases as a favour for a friend. A still unnamed friend, I might add. Someone he says he doesn't want to get into trouble.' He laughed. 'Trouble, ha! He's the one in trouble.' His accent was unmistakably London now and Healey half expected him to go on to say 'Cor blimey' or 'Strike a light' in his excitement.

'Is it possible to see his passport?' asked Healey.

The man pulled open the drawer and took from it a green-covered passport similar to the one that Healey had examined earlier that morning and passed it to Healey, who thumbed through it before handing it back.

'I think we can be pretty sure that this isn't his passport,' he said.

'No?' The man didn't seem very surprised.

'Tell me, how would you describe his English?'

'Ropey?'

'Well, Ricardo Reyes is supposed to have excellent English. He teaches for the British Council in Manila. The man you're holding is probably his brother, Roberto Reyes. Said to be a businessman over here to make contacts.'

'He's certainly done that,' said the customs officer. He put his hands on the desk as if to stand, but paused. 'I understand that you want to see him in connection with a murder, is that right?'

'Yes.'

'Then he could be in even more serious trouble.'

Healey made a noncommittal gesture with his head. 'We'll have to see,' he said. 'Can we speak to him now?'

The customs officer stood up. 'This way, gentlemen. Mr Reyes awaits you.'

'Just one thing,' said Healey. 'What was the name on the luggage?'

'Oh, yes. I should have told you. There was no name. No airline tag. Either it was never put on or, more likely, someone took it off for them at the other end.'

'How do you think the cases got on board?'

'Interesting you should ask that. Could have happened in a number of ways. Most likely a passenger. Especially as there is an actual Miss Reyes on the flight list, would you believe? Unfortunately, by the time we had the gentleman's name, she'd already been through immigration and customs. Could be a coincidence but I doubt it somehow.' The customs officer looked at Healey. 'I suppose you're wondering how he managed to get into the baggage hall.' Healey did not demur. 'Well so are we,' the customs officer continued. 'He had a ticket for an earlier flight from Paris on him but he wasn't listed on it. But that isn't of interest to you, is it?'

Before going into the interview room, they watched Reyes on the closed circuit television monitor. He was sitting upright, motionless, his clasped hands resting on the desk in front of him. 'A hard nut,' volunteered the customs man. As Healey and Teague entered, Reyes, smaller than he had appeared on the screen and wearing an open-necked, canary yellow, long sleeve cotton shirt, looked up but otherwise did not move. He must have been about fifty, with thinning swept-back black hair, sallow skin, and hooded amber eyes that reminded Healey of a lizard. There was an ugly dark mole on the left side of his nose.

'Mr Reyes,' Healey began.

The man continued looking at Healey but made no response.

'You are Mr Reyes, aren't you?'

There was a brief nod.

'Can you tell me your full name, please?'

'Ricardo Angel Gomez Reyes.' He enunciated the words slowly, pausing between each.

'Ricardo?'

'Ricardo.'

'Not Roberto?'

Reyes' eyes flickered but there was no other reaction to the question.

'Look, Mr Reyes,' said Healey. 'We know that you are Roberto Reyes and that you travelled to Britain on your brother Ricardo's passport. So let's agree on that, can we? It'll save us a lot of time.'

Reyes blinked but did not protest.

'I'm not interested in what happened last night,' continued Healey. 'I just want to know where you were and what you were doing last Friday night, from nine o'clock onwards.'

Reyes glanced at Teague. 'I already tell this man. When in Reading.'

'And now I want you to tell me.'

Reyes did tell him. Just what he had said in Reading. That he had left Reading for London by train about one in the afternoon, had lunch at a Malay restaurant near Trafalgar Square with some Filipino businessmen he had met during his stay, and then had gone to Heathrow to see them off. He had their business cards, yes, but back at the Hall; nobody had asked him about them before (at this, Healey had to stop himself from looking at Teague). From Heathrow he had gone back into London, spent time (and a lot of money) in a nightclub in Soho, and caught the first train in the morning back to Reading. He thought he might still have the ticket but he wasn't sure. Again, he hadn't been asked for it when he was interviewed in Reading. He said this directly to Healey without looking at Teague. Teague remained silent.

Healey asked about Crouch. Reyes said that he had only met him once or twice, in the Philippines, when there was talk of setting up an English language school. He was really a friend of his brother, not him.

'What?' said Healey. 'Haven't you forgotten that he was a tutor on the course you are on in Reading? Surely you must have talked to him then.'

'We only say hello. He know I must not be there, so he not wanna talk.'

'Really? And what about Tim Wright? You were in his class. Didn't you talk to him either?'

'Only little. Same problem.'

'That's strange. He told me that he talked to you a lot.'

'I don't think so.'

'That's what he told me.'

'I don't think so.'

'So why did he tell me that.'

'I don't know. I don't think he tell you that.'

'What *did* you talk about?'

'About the lesson.'

'What lesson?'

'What we do in class. I don't understand. He tell me what to do.'

'And about Friday night? Why did he go to London with you?'

Reyes paused before replying. 'He did not go to London with me.'

'I think he did.'

Reyes shrugged but said nothing. By this time Healey

realised that Reyes was not a man who was going to be easily wrong-footed. Or panicked. He also realised that he was not going to get any answers to his questions that conflicted with what Reyes had already told Customs. In short, as long as Reyes was held here at Gatwick, Healey knew he wouldn't get anywhere with the man. He was considering what to do next, when Teague spoke.

'Do you practise martial arts, Mr Reyes?'

'Sorry?'

'Martial arts. Karate. Kung fu. Do you …' Teague made an open-handed chopping motion and looked expectant.

'No,' replied Reyes immediately, turning his gaze on Healey. 'I never,' he continued, and made the same chopping motion, and smiled. He was smiling! A man who had been caught handling a large quantity of drugs and now being interrogated as part of a murder investigation, was smiling at their questions. Laughing at them. The customs officers who must be watching and listening to them would probably be laughing at their efforts too. Humiliating. Healey was painfully aware that he hadn't thought through the implications of the man's already having been questioned about his part in the drugs business. He had come here with no clear plan, just with the conviction that Reyes was the key and that by applying the right kind of pressure they would somehow unlock the case. But what grounds did he have for this conviction? Nothing more than a feeling really. Certainly not enough to persuade his superiors to request Reyes' transfer to Reading. He felt foolish. He put his hands on the table to push his seat back and stand up.

As he did so, Teague spoke again. 'You haven't been in Reading for the last four days. Where were you?'

Healey put his hand on Teague's arm. There was no point in asking more questions while Reyes was being held here. However, as Teague turned towards Healey, Reyes answered the question. He was quite effusive. He gave the address of a flat in Hampstead, on Haverstock Hill. He told them that he had rented it for the period of his stay in Britain, and since he left Reading on Monday he had been staying there and meeting various business contacts during the day. He had the keys to the flat with him when he was arrested at the airport. Why didn't they take them and check. The man on the reception desk at the apartment block would confirm what he was he saying.

When Healey and Teague left the interview room, they were met by the same customs officer who had taken them there. He gave them a broad smile. 'How did it go?' he asked.

'I imagine you were watching,' said Healey.

'I heard a bit of it. Yeah. Well most of it, actually.'

'So you know.'

'Not what you made of what he said.'

'Nothing that will help us much. He's not going to say anything to us that will make things more difficult with you. At least not while you're in a position to hear everything he says.'

'I can see that. But nothing we can do. He's hardly going to believe us if we say that we won't listen to what he says and that you won't tell us, is he?'

'Precisely,' said Healey.

Before leaving, Healey asked the customs officer if they had in fact found keys on Reyes. They had indeed. The keys were now with one of their officers, who was watching the flat. Nobody had gone there since they had put it under surveillance but they still thought someone might. When Healey asked him, he said yes, they had made a quick search of the flat but there was nothing of interest. Healey then asked if they would mind if he and Teague had a look at the flat, if they made a detour on their way back to Reading. The customs officer took them into his office, from where he telephoned his superior.

'No problem,' he said, as he put the phone down. 'The keys will be at the reception desk there. If you leave them there when you've finished, if you don't mind.' He sat down at his desk and copied something from a file onto a sheet of blank paper. 'The address,' he said, 'you'll need that.' Healey took the paper and they all moved towards the door. 'Oh,' said the officer, 'I meant to ask you, when you were talking to Reyes you mentioned somebody called Wright. Tom Wright, was it?'

'Tim,' said Healey. 'Why?'

'Nothing. Just wondered if he was somebody we should know about.'

'I don't think so. A former colleague of Reyes' brother. Teaches English.' Healey put out his hand. 'Thanks very much for your help. We appreciate it. And we'll be in touch.' The customs officer seemed as if he might ask a further question but didn't.

As soon as Healey and Teague set off down the corridor, he went to his desk and made another phone call.

The flat in Hampstead, which was in a brick building next door to an Italian restaurant, was large and expensively furnished. 'Thousand a week at least,' said Teague, as he flopped onto a plush blue sofa in the living room. He yawned. 'Nice. Very nice. Very nice indeed.' He yawned again and threw his feet over the arm of the sofa.

Healey walked from room to room, opening and closing drawers and cupboard doors, looking under beds, under pillows, in waste paper baskets. The only time he paused in his search was in the bathroom, where he sniffed repeatedly. Eventually he came back to the living room.

'There's nothing here,' he said. 'No sign of life. Either Reyes didn't use the place or somebody has done a very careful tidy up since he left.'

'Why would they do that?'

Healey didn't answer but went into the hall and turned a switch on the wall. Immediately there was the sound of air coming through the vents just below the ceiling. Healey adjusted a dial and the sound stopped.

'I thought so. About eighteen degrees if this is accurate,' he said. 'The air conditioning must have been on very recently. Otherwise it would have been a lot warmer when we got here. Let's go down and ask the man on the desk.'

The man behind the reception desk was in his thirties and well dressed. Yes, Mr Reyes was staying here but no he hadn't seen him for the previous two days. He had been off sick yesterday. No, as far as he knew, nobody had been in the flat today. A gentleman had left the key at the desk an hour ago, saying that Mr Reyes wanted two associates to be able to stay overnight if they needed to, but he hadn't gone up to the flat. Healey thanked him and left the building with Teague.

'So somebody got in without him seeing them,' said Teague.

'Or he's lying. Let's see if we can find out.'

Healey led Teague to a table outside the restaurant next door, where they asked for draft beer but had to settle for bottled. When their drinks came, Healey took a fiver from his wallet. Before handing it to the waiter, he asked, 'I don't suppose you saw somebody leave that building in the last hour or so?' He gestured towards the door that they had just come through. 'He's a friend of ours, said he'd meet us at his flat but he's not there.'

The waiter eyed the fiver. 'I don't think so,' he said.

'Young man. Medium height, slim build. Long fair hair. Maybe wearing a velvet jacket.'

The waiter looked thoughtful.

'Got a blue sports car. Austin Healey,' added Healey.

The waiter's eyes lit up. 'Oh yes. I didn't notice what he looked like exactly but I saw the car. Must have been half an hour ago. He'd parked it just outside, on the double yellow and they were just giving him a ticket when he came for it. Made a big fuss. I *suppose* that was your friend.'

'It sounds like him,' said Healey. 'Have you seen him around here before?'

'No, I don't think so.'

Healey opened his wallet and slipped the fiver back into it, taking out two pound notes, which he passed to the waiter. 'Keep the change,' he said.

In the taxi back to Paddington, Healey sat with his eyes closed and quickly fell asleep, only waking as they pulled up in the station. On the train, sitting on either side of a table, they unwrapped the sandwiches that they had bought at the station. Teague asked, 'What made you think of Wright back there?'

Healey had bought first class tickets and they had been able to find a place well away from any other passengers. Healey nevertheless looked round before replying. 'Do you think that customs man seemed stupid?'

'Not really. Why?'

'He thinks *we* are. He heard us talk about Wright. He was clearly interested, but he got the name wrong. Tom instead of Tim. Why did he do that? Did he just make a mistake? I don't think so. No, if he was interested, he wouldn't, would he? It can only have been because he wanted us to think he wasn't really that interested. Which means that it was more than casual. And that he thought we were dim.' Healey paused, his eyes glazing over. 'Unless of course he wanted us to think he had a serious interest in Wright and not in something else that we asked Reyes about. But no, it wasn't that.'

'But at the flat?'

'His aftershave or whatever. Didn't you smell it? I mightn't have connected it with Wright if that bugger hadn't asked us about him.' Healey smiled at Teague. 'So something good did come out of making a pig's ear of the ...' Healey looked up as a young woman with two children appeared at the door of their carriage, '... of the interview,' he added quietly.

The journey to Reading took only half an hour. They collected the car from the station car park and set off for the Hall, Healey driving. 'I don't suppose you happen to know what they're doing tonight, do you?' he asked.

Teague pulled himself upright in his seat and took out his copy of the course booklet, his possession of which had failed to impress Healey that first day in Crouch's room. He flicked over the pages briskly. 'Nineteen hundred hours, Canal Trip,' he pronounced. 'Visit country pub.'

'That's good. I'd like you to make an unofficial search of a couple of rooms, if you don't mind?'

'No, sir.'

'Perhaps you could get a pass key from Bird.'

'I shouldn't think that would be a problem. Which rooms do you have in mind?'

'Reyes' and Wright's. We could get a search warrant for Reyes but probably not for Wright. No point in causing problems for ourselves. See if you can find anything of interest.'

'What about Farrell's room? I mean, isn't he our chief suspect? Besides everything else, those initials, PF. He couldn't give us an explanation for them, could he?'

'Well, if they *don't* have anything to do with his name, why should he have any better idea what they mean than anyone else?' Healey might have added 'you idiot' but only said, 'We don't really have a chief suspect.'

Teague was momentarily crestfallen but his face brightened. 'All right, sir, but what are the chances of any two letters coming up at random, so to speak, being the initials of one of the victim's colleagues in a small department?'

Healey was reminded of his own thoughts on this in connection with crossword clues. 'I don't know. I agree that we have to bear it in mind, but more important right now would be to establish a motive. What would Farrell's motive be?'

'I don't know, but what if Crouch was blackmailing him, something to do with drugs. Didn't Farrell go to the Philippines on business? That could have been to do with drugs, nothing to do with setting up a school. And how do we know it came to nothing?' Teague paused. 'Then there's the fact that he went with Crouch's wife, and a baby is born a year or so later. Could have been nine months later, couldn't it?'

'And?'

'Crouch might of found out and got awkward.'

'And?'

'I'm not sure, but they all seem to tie together somehow.'

Healey shook his head. 'Look, Teague, I've got to know Farrell pretty well over the last few days and I just can't see him doing it. But,' he paused, 'I won't stop you looking in his room too, if you want to.'

'Thank you, sir.'

'The boat trip will give you a clear run.'

'If Farrell and Wright go, you mean.'

They were just arriving at the Hall. Healey didn't reply. He was looking for a place to park.

There was no room on the road outside, so he turned into the Hall and parked in the one empty space, the one with the word 'WARDEN' on it, painted in white. 'Feeling brave, sir?' chuckled Teague.

Healey stepped out and slammed the door shut. 'Let's go,' he said.

There was no one in reception. The clock above the desk showed ten past six. As they strode down the corridor they were greeted by the not very pleasant smell of institutional food. School dinners, thought Healey. Was it the gravy that gave off that smell? Swinging open the double doors of the bar, they almost flattened Mr Bird, who had been about to come out.

'Blimey,' he said, staggering back. 'That was a close one. I *thought* I saw you arrive and I was just going to say that it would be best if you didn't park there. The Warden's due back any minute. But …'

'But what?' asked Healey.

Before Bird could reply, Teague cut in. 'Sorry about that, Ernie. There wasn't any space on the road, but I'll find somewhere else.' He held out his hand for the keys, which Healey gave him. 'Bitter shandy for me,' he called back as he went out.

* * *

Holding the tray of drinks level with his chin, his back aching, Healey shuffled down the centre of the converted narrowboat, picking his way between outstretched legs, the backs of chairs, and clusters of standing course members. Even though windows were open, it was hot and sticky in the narrow confined space, which was filled with the chatter of the course participants, making him feel that he was in some kind of human aviary, an aviary with a very low roof.

The back of a large, blond women in a white blouse blocked his way. 'Excuse me,' he said close to her ear, smelling the perfume she had obviously applied liberally in that area.

The woman turned and, on apparently recognising him,

smiled. 'You are Mike's friend,' she said. 'Hello. Good to see you. And where is Mike?' Healey looked into her pale blue eyes, then at the broad flat nose set between bright red cheeks, at her dark moustache, and down to her large breasts, which were suddenly pressed against him. 'We miss him,' went on the woman.

It took Healey a moment to realise that she was referring to Teague. 'He's working,' he said.

'So, you can have a good time with us while he is working,' the woman laughed. Beads of sweat appeared on her forehead and in her moustache. People at the tables either side had stopped talking and were looking up, listening to them.

Healey gave a small, tight smile.

'We are from Bulgaria,' continued the woman. 'I am Ludmilla and this is my friend Rosa.'

The friend, whose moustache also betrayed the falseness of her blonde hair, put out her hand to Healey, who struggled to balance the tray with his left hand while he took hers with his right. Looking past the two women, he saw Farrell watching from the table at the stern of the boat.

'If I could just squeeze past …'

'Squeeze …' said Ludmilla, putting her hands to her waist and making a squeezing motion. 'Squeeze,' she repeated, and the two women shook with laughter.

As Healey eased forward, they moved aside, pushing their bottoms into the heads of those sitting at the tables and their breasts into Healey as he passed.

'Well done, Richard,' said Farrell, as Healey set the tray down on the narrow table. 'Budge up, ladies,' he added, sliding along the bench seat that backed onto the window, and patting the space he left behind him. Sam, the course assistant, and the Italian woman, Silvia, followed him along, leaving Healey a small space at the end, next to the door to the deck at the stern. Healey took off his jacket and sat down beside Silvia. He poured Guinness from the bottle and held up his glass. 'Cheers!' he said.

'Cheers!' said the other three.

'Glad you could come,' said Farrell.

'Thanks for letting me.' Healey waved his glass in the direction from which he had come. 'You're just about full.'

'That's not a problem. Can always make room for an extra one. If we want to, that is. Funnily enough, the British Council woman asked me yesterday if she could come too, and I said no, we had a full complement.' Farrell made a grimace. 'I probably shouldn't have, but she's such an awful wet blanket.' He paused. 'And I don't like her.' He sipped at his Guinness. 'Luckily, she doesn't seem to like me either. It's poor old Sam here who has to deal with her.'

'She's not too bad,' said Sam. 'It's just that she's always worried that something is going to go wrong, and she gets stressed.'

'Tell Richard about the toilets,' said Farrell.

'Do I have to?' asked Sam.

'All right,' said Farrell, 'I'll tell him. There was a bit of trouble last year. The toilets got in a mess because some of the ladies didn't sit on the seat, they crouched over it somehow, and weren't very accurate. The cleaners complained, naturally, and she put up notices telling them how to use the toilet. Fair enough, I suppose, though it did cause ill feeling. So what happens this year? The day before the course begins, she gives Sam a set of notices to put up, telling them how to use a toilet. Sam tells me about it, and I say don't do it. The woman comes to me and talks about uncivilised and unacceptable behaviour. I tell her that putting up notices before anything happens is unacceptable.'

'And?' asks Healey.

'No notices and no trouble. Stupid cow!'

Healey wondered what then was the problem Farrell and Sam had had the previous morning, but he said nothing.

The boat chugged on along the canal, between parched looking fields. A little grey-haired woman walking a Dobermann along the towpath stopped and watched the boat as it went by, doubtless wondering at the noise coming from it. Farrell had begun to talk to Sam about arrangements for the following day, and Healey found himself asking Silvia about her life in Italy. She lived in Padua, she said, and taught English at the university there. She loved all things English. Even after being married to the Englishman who had left her. 'I still like Englishmen,' she said, looking directly into Healey's eyes over the wineglass held to her lips.

Healey said nothing, and she went on to ask him about his life. He told her he was married, forgetting that she already knew, and had two children.

'What do they think? That you are a policeman, I mean.'

'They don't mind.'

'Really?'

'Well, I doubt that the children think about it. And my wife accepts it.'

'But she doesn't like it?'

'Not very much.'

'Neither would I.'

'Why not?'

'You are too sensitive to be a policeman.'

'You don't know me.'

'I know you a little. And …'

'And what?'

'I shouldn't say this.'

Healey's throat was dry and his voice thick. 'Go on.'

She remained silent, still looking at him.

'What were you going to say?' he asked.

She put down her glass and placed her hand on his. 'I'll tell you later,' she said.

The boat bumped against the side of the canal at Burghfield Bridge, where stood the promised pub, The Cunning Man. Named after some local magician, Farrell had told them. As he climbed ashore, Healey was met by the two Bulgarians. 'I hope you will let Mike come to the party tomorrow,' said Ludmilla.

'The party? Oh, yes, the party.'

'And you, of course, Inspector.'

'We'll have to see.'

'Yes, we'll see you. That's good. Now, you'll have a drink with us.'

'Erm, thank you,' Healey looked round anxiously, 'but I have to have a word with ...' He caught sight of Mary Walters walking towards the door of the pub but separate from the general stream of people moving in that direction. 'With Miss Walters.' He smiled apologetically at Ludmilla and strode towards the door. He caught up with Ms Walters, as he remembered she preferred to be called, according to Rita at least.

'Could you spare me a minute, do you think?' he asked.

To his surprise, she smiled. 'Of course, Chief Inspector. But let me buy you a drink first. What would you like?'

A minute later, Healey was sitting on a bench outside a pub in rural Berkshire, drinking a glass of draft Guinness with Mary Walters, watching the sun go down. It seemed a very unlikely event. Unreal. She was wearing jeans and a stone washed denim shirt. The snood had gone and her sandy hair hung loose. 'Where's your friend?' he asked.

'Helga? She's already left. She couldn't get a flight tomorrow or Saturday, and she's going on holiday on Sunday.'

'Oh.'

'With her kids.'

'Her kids? But I thought …'

Ms Walters laughed. 'Don't look so surprised. It's not that unusual.'

'It's just that …'

'Of course.'

It suddenly occurred to Healey that the indiscretion she was showing was probably not unconnected with having drunk more than she was used to, and that this was his opportunity to get a less carefully considered view of what had been happening. 'So, you don't work with the others during the year, do you?' he asked.

'No,' she replied. 'I'm at the University of London. Peter Farrell asked me to teach on the summer school.' She took a quick sip of the large whisky she had bought herself. I *used* to teach with them, though.'

'Here in Reading?'

Before answering, she gulped down what remained of the whisky. Healey sensed that she was wondering how much to tell him. 'No,' she continued, 'I worked with Neville and Tim in Manila.'

'When was that?'

'About a year before Neville came back to England, and then three years after that with Tim.'

'So you know Mrs Crouch too?'

'Oh, yes, I certainly do.'

'You don't sound very approving.'

'Approving?' She shrugged her shoulders. 'She doesn't need my approval. She's got everything that she wants. Especially now, with Neville gone. You know she was a bargirl?'

Healey nodded.

'Well, compare the life she has here with the one she had then. I've only got admiration for her.'

'But you don't like her.'

'I wouldn't want her for a friend. I certainly wouldn't trust her.'

'Did Neville trust her?'

'I don't think he had a choice. He idolised her. And she did whatever she wanted.'

'Like go to the Philippines with Dr Farrell?' Healey ventured.

'You know about that?'

'I heard about it, yes. What happened exactly?'

'Not a lot.' She guffawed. 'He only got her pregnant. That's not much, is it?'

'Did she have the baby?'

'Of course.'

'Gia?'

'Yes. Gia.' Ms Walters looked down at her empty glass. 'I don't suppose you could get me another one, could you?'

By the time Healey got back with her whisky and his Guinness, Ms Walters had been joined by the two Bulgarians. He had wanted to ask her if Crouch knew that Farrell was the father of Gia but he couldn't now. Putting down the whisky, he made his excuses and went back inside the pub. Arriving at the bar, behind which were a Union Jack and the flag of St George, as well as framed photographs from what he guessed must have been the Falklands War, he sat down on a stool and looked around. Most of the course members were outside but a small group of men, central Europeans, he thought, or were they Scandinavians, were sat around a table, dourly drinking lager.

In an alcove two young men in camouflage jackets silently surveyed the scene; in another alcove was Farrell, deep in conversation with Sam. In the far corner was another couple: Silvia was sitting with what looked a lot like Tim Wright, who was holding a book. Could it be Wright? He hadn't seen him on the boat. As he watched them, they eventually fell silent. Silvia looked up, saw Healey, and said something to Wright, who didn't respond but continued to look at the glass in front of him. Silvia gave a small wave to Healey and he held up his hand in acknowledgement. Silvia said something else to Wright, stood up, and walked over to Healey. 'I'm just getting a drink for Tim,' she said. 'Can I get one for you?'

Healey gestured towards his still almost full glass. 'No thanks,' he said.

Silvia ordered half a pint of shandy and stood beside the seated Healey, tapping her fingers on the bar. She smiled briefly but neither of them spoke. When the burly, shaven headed barman, whose arms were heavily tattooed with patriotic emblems, placed the drink in front of her, she paid, picked up the glass and turned as if to go. Then she turned back.

'Come and join us,' she said.

'I don't think that would be a good idea.'

'I would like it. Please come.'

Healey was reluctant. He was getting more involved than he probably should, and he had already been warned by the Super. Still, it was a chance to learn more about Wright. He just had to be careful. He eased himself from the stool. 'All right,' he said.

* * *

'Wake up! Richard, wake up!' In his dream Healey heard the voice and felt his shoulder being shaken. And shaken again. But it wasn't a dream. He opened his eyes and saw Farrell leaning over him. He was still on the coach. Painfully, his hand gripping the seat in front, he hauled himself to his feet and stumbled along the aisle, down the steps, and onto the pavement outside the Hall.

Back at the pub he had followed Silvia from the bar to the table with a sense of unreality and the growing conviction that he was making a mistake. How was he going to learn anything useful while the woman was there to listen to them? Again and again in this case he had found himself questioning people in circumstances that favoured them rather than him. And it hadn't helped that he hadn't prepared properly.

Wright had been pleasant enough. He had put down his book, which he explained was a guide to Italy, where he was going to spend much of the summer, staying part of the time in Padua. Hearing the name of the city where Silvia lived, Healey felt a pang of jealousy, but asked politely when Wright would be leaving and was told that it would probably be Monday. He had already decided not to ask Wright where he had been during the day, but instead asked Silvia how she had enjoyed the course. Very much was the answer. And the lectures – Healey had attended the one on Othello – how were they? Variable – that Othello lecture she thought was dreadful, almost sent her to sleep. And today's, Healey asked, what was that about? The future of English language teaching, a large topic by a small man with a big reputation, very disappointing, she said, all about himself really. Much Ado about Nothing, the Italian course members had renamed the lecture.

Healey asked Wright whether he thought the same. Smiling, as if amused at Healey's clumsy effort, Wright replied that unfortunately he was unable to give an opinion as he hadn't been there to hear the great man speak. He'd gone to London first thing, for an interview for a job at the Institute of Education, but the Chief Inspector wouldn't be interested in that, would he? He continued to smile as Healey asked him how the interview had gone, and he said that, thank you, it had gone rather well actually.

Healey wondered who had taken Wright's class after the lecture, and why Farrell had let him go to London when he was already one tutor short.

The three of them were still talking, now about their holiday plans, when the arrival of the coach which would take the group back to Reading was announced by three loud hoots of the horn. Wright said he had his car there and asked if he could drive either of them back to the Hall. Silvia refused, as did Healey, who carried their three empty glasses to the bar and then stood at the door of the pub watching everyone else boarding the coach in the fading light.

When he climbed on himself, he was at once confronted by the sight of Silvia sitting by herself immediately behind the driver, looking straight ahead. If she had turned her head towards him then, he would have sat with her, but she didn't, and he made his way down the coach, until he found a seat near the back where he could be alone and think. The bus lurched forward and he sat down with a bump.

He was tired. It had been a long day. It had begun with the visit to Falstaff Avenue; then there was the awful interview at Gatwick; the flat in Hampstead; back to Reading; and now three hours on the canal and in the pub, listening to too many people talking, and drinking more than he should.

As he reflected on this, he remembered that Silvia had said she was going to tell him something. What could that be? He could go and sit with her now at the front of the bus, but she hadn't looked at him when he passed, and anyhow to do it now would be to make a statement to everyone else. He wouldn't do it. But what did she want to say? Something personal? To do with the case? Perhaps he could catch her when they got back to the Hall.

And then there was the Walters woman telling him about Farrell and Teresa. Was it true? If so, could it be connected with Crouch's death? He wondered how Teague had got on, whether he had been able to get into the rooms and, if so, whether he had found anything. He hoped that he would still be at the Hall. It was warm in the coach and the lights were dim. He had quickly fallen asleep.

Farrell walked with Healey as far as the main door of the Hall. 'I think that's it for me,' he said, yawning. 'I'm beat. I'd better get home.'

'All right, Peter,' said Healey, 'I need to check on a couple of things. See you tomorrow.'

He walked through the reception area and along the corridor to the incident room, where he found a constable, not Gifford, who handed him a message. The message, written in Teague's looping, rather childish hand, was brief: *Sir, W left in car and F on bus with you. Gained entry to there rooms Will report findings first thing, M.T.* Healey sniffed at his sergeant's misspelling (or was it bad grammar, he wondered) and the superfluous information about Farrell, handed back the slip of paper, told the constable to close up, and went in search of the toilets.

After washing his face and drinking water from cupped hands, he felt better. Nothing more to do here, he thought. He would start tomorrow by discussing everything with Teague. In the meantime he should get some sleep. He'd leave the car where it was and walk; it would do him good, and anyhow he'd had too much to drink. No point in risking it. He had just reached the entrance to the playing fields, when he remembered his briefcase, which he'd left in the boot of his car.

Walking back to where Teague had parked it, he glanced towards the hall and saw that there was a light on in one of the rooms on the top corridor. Whose room was it? Not Crouch's, surely. No, it was the one farthest from the stairs. Whose was that? What had the cleaner said? Sam's. That was it, Sam, the course assistant. As he watched, the figure of a man came to the window, stood there for a few seconds, and then drew the curtains.

'My God,' Healey uttered. The person who had closed the curtains was Peter Farrell.

FRIDAY

'Wake up … Wake up! Dick! Wake up.'

Healey struggled to break free from the deep sleep that enshrouded him.

'It's five past seven. Here's your tea.'

When he had got home, his wife had been asleep so he had left a note asking her to wake him at seven. Now he put out his two hands to clasp the mug of tea she was holding in front of him. Once he had taken it from her, she climbed onto the bed and over him to reach her cup of coffee (she had always claimed to loathe tea), which she sipped while nestling against his back. 'You got back late,' she said.

'About one.'

'How's it going?'

'Not bad. We're getting there.' He paused before adding, 'At least I think we are.' The tea was good, just what he needed for his parched mouth, but his head ached. 'Have we got any paracetamol?' he asked.

His wife leaned away from him and pulled open the drawer of her bedside table. 'Here,' she said, passing him a sheet of tablets. 'I suppose you want water now.'

'Do you mind?'

Before he left, Healey looked in on the children, both still in bed. His son was fast asleep. 'Daaad!' said his daughter in a way that he knew meant she wanted to engage his sympathy before she asked for something.

'Yeah?'

'Are we going on holiday?'

He had said a week ago that they would, but that had been before he was given this case. 'As soon as we can, love. I've got to finish what I'm doing first.'

'When will that be?'

'Soon.'

Downstairs he collected the mini-cassettes from his desk and put them back in the supermarket bag which Mrs Crouch had given him. He walked from the house out onto Beech Lane and immediately thought of Peter Farrell. He wondered where he had spent the night. He looked at the Farrells' house as he passed it but saw no one. It was another hot day and he was already beginning to sweat. As he walked into the cool shade of the Wilderness, his head began to clear. He felt better. Perhaps he had made mistakes this week (he could imagine Teague telling people that he'd been 'all over the place') but he had learned more than he would have if he'd simply followed routine. What he had to do now was sit quietly, order what he knew, then make a plan of action. Yesterday he had felt he was nearly there; today he wasn't so sure – the Reyes interview had thrown him. But still, he couldn't be too far away.

He walked on, now in the sun again, and had the sudden thought that perhaps Crouch *had* committed suicide – it wasn't impossible. This reminded him that the inquest was to be held that day. A formality – in the circumstances it would surely be adjourned – but he had better be there. But suicide, no. What was that letter all about, the one they'd found in Crouch's room? Could Reyes have written it? Seemed unlikely – if Reyes was running a drugs business and he wanted to get rid of Crouch, for whatever reason, he would hardly have written such a letter. Who then? It *could* be some disgruntled individual (who may or may not have killed Crouch) or it was someone, the killer, who wanted to suggest suicide or at least introduce a red herring. Someone over-confident in their own ability to deceive, holding the police in low esteem, certainly a risk taker. Well, every murder involved risk.

He made his way between various red brick buildings edged with lawns. Rabbits, probably unused to seeing humans this early on the campus, started in surprise at his approach, and hopped off to the cover of shrubbery, from where they watched him pass. Fifty yards ahead of him, a fox loped across the path, stopping only to briefly examine the contents of a litter basket.

Turning right, he arrived at a building on his left which looked as if it had been constructed out of Lego. Nineteen sixties, he thought, and wondered what it was like inside. He would probably never know. He looked around him and thought that this was a real university campus. If he was going to do a degree, it was somewhere like this that he wanted to do it, not a converted Tech on a busy main road. He peered through one of the windows of the Lego building but could see little more than an internal glass door and behind that a concrete staircase.

Then he heard the padding of feet and the blowing of breath, towards which he turned. A middle-aged woman with a very red face and a white bandana jogged past him, ignoring his 'Good morning'. Normal, he thought. Normal these days and in this town. It wasn't long since a young woman had been raped close to the path that he had taken through the Wilderness.

He walked quickly now across the games fields that stood between the University buildings and Shinfield Road. If he cut across the cricket pitch, as he had the other evening, that was the shortest route to the Hall but he decided to go straight on. Once he reached the road, he turned right. Coming up ahead was Christchurch Green, now just a triangle of scruffy grass and bushes, which had given its name to a row of shops that ran almost to the Queen's Head and which included a baker, an off-licence, a greengrocer that had a post office at the back, two Pakistani stores that stayed open all hours, and a newsagent.

He thought he would pick up a newspaper and crossed over the road. As he took a copy of the Guardian from the stand, he was reminded of the one that had been on Crouch's desk. Crouch had probably bought it at this very newsagent. While he was paying, Healey looked at the man across the counter and asked himself if he would remember Crouch or notice that he no longer came in for his paper. Probably not.

It seemed that nobody missed Crouch very much, not his colleagues or even his wife. How was the world changed by this man's death? To judge from what people said, he would be replaced in the Department by someone who would do a better job. And at home, would he be replaced there too? Had he already been? Healey thought now, as he had often thought before, that once you took away the emotive term 'murder' there were worse crimes. At least there were crimes that could have worse consequences. But now wasn't the time to be thinking that way. He rolled up the newspaper and strode off in the direction of the Hall, which he reached in five minutes.

'Sergeant Teague is waiting for you, Chief Inspector.'

Healey nodded briefly at Bird, as he walked through reception, but did not speak. What a pain the man was. Still, he had agreed to let Teague into the rooms last night, so one ought to be grateful to him. Ought to be grateful to Teague as well. If he hadn't buttered Bird up – something Healey could never have brought himself to do – there was no way they would have managed it without a search warrant. Miss Colgan would certainly not have given them access.

As Healey entered the incident room, Teague stood up from the table. 'Hope you don't mind, sir, but I didn't think it was worth waiting for you last night. Nothing we could have done at that time.'

Healey nodded in acknowledgement. Teague continued, 'But there *was* something interesting. Well two things actually.' From his pocket he pulled out a handkerchief, which he unfolded to reveal a brown piece of something, about the size of his little finger nail. He offered the handkerchief and its contents to Healey.

'Is that what I think it is?' asked Healey.

Teague held it to his nose and sniffed, then put it to his mouth and licked it. 'It certainly is. Grade one cannabis resin.'

Healey looked hard at his sergeant. Teague may be able to recognise cannabis resin but how the hell could he know that it was 'grade one', as he put it? 'Excuse me asking, Teague, but what is so interesting about *that*? Not a very exciting find, I'd say.'

Teague grinned. '*This* may not be much, I agree. It's the other two pounds or so of the stuff that's interesting.'

'Oh!'

'Yes. All neatly wrapped in silver foil.'

'And where did you find it?'

'Wright's room.' Teague took another sniff of the substance. 'This was in his desk drawer. The other was inside his guitar. As soon as I picked it up, I felt it move inside.'

'Not a very good hiding place,' said Healey, remembering that Wright had taken the guitar and strummed it in front of him. So he had been laughing at him again. Or perhaps not, perhaps the cannabis hadn't been in it then.

'No,' admitted Teague.

'Which suggests either that he's a complete amateur, or that he doesn't mind it being found.'

Teague looked doubtful at this suggestion.

'Don't you think?' asked Healey.

'Well I suppose there is another possibility.'

'Which is?'

'That somebody put it there so that it would be found. Somebody who wanted to take attention away from himself. Or herself.'

Healey drew a deep breath and exhaled slowly. 'But they'd need to know that we were likely to search Wright's room. Why should they think that?'

'I don't know, sir. But for all we know, somebody might be about to drop a hint that we should do just that.'

'Perhaps. But in the meantime …'

'There is the other thing, sir.' From the back pocket of his trousers Teague produced an envelope. He pushed his stubby fingers into it and carefully brought out something so fine that Healey had to put on his reading glasses to see what it was. It was a bright pink-coloured hair.

'Where was this?'

'Farrell's room. On the pillow of his bed. Which was unmade. More than that. The blanket was on the floor. The top sheet was pulled back and the bottom sheet was stained in two places, both near the middle of the bed. Pretty clear what had been happening there.'

Healey was still looking at the hair. 'Don't you recognise it, sir?' Teague asked.

Healey recognised it only too well. The only person he'd seen in his life, except on television, with hair that colour was the course assistant, Samantha. And he'd caught sight of her in the window of her room with Farrell only the night before. So that was going on, was it? Briefly Healey imagined the two of them together naked on the bed. 'Yes I do,' he said. 'And so do you. The question is – how does it help us?'

'It tells us something about Farrell, the kind of man he is.

And we might use it to put some pressure on him.'

'Hmm. Perhaps.' Healey felt uneasy.

'You know what, sir. It wouldn't surprise me if they were both in it, Wright and Farrell. Dealing in drugs. Mixed up with Crouch. Shagging his wife. Crouch gets awkward or greedy, threatens them in some way, so they decide to get rid of him. Wouldn't surprise me at all.'

Healey didn't contradict him. He had just remembered that he was about to ask Teague to do something that he had already said he would do himself. 'You may be right. And well done for getting Bird to let you have the pass key.' Teague beamed. 'Erm,' Healey continued, 'I'm going to be tied up most of the day. First there's the inquest. And I think you're right, I need to talk to Farrell again. So I was wondering if you'd mind taking back the cassettes I was going to listen to.' He held the bag that contained them towards Teague, who, with obvious reluctance, took it from him.

'Which ones have you already been through, sir?'

'I listened to a couple but I'm not absolutely sure which now, I'm afraid. Sorry. Best listen to all of them.'

Teague looked puzzled but said nothing.

'To be honest,' said Healey, 'I think you're probably better than me at this sort of thing. Attention to detail and all that.' As he spoke, a bulky figure appeared at the door. It was the Warden.

'Chief Inspector, I hope I'm not interrupting. It's just that I have some information for you.'

'Not at all. I'll be with you in a second.' Healey was relieved to escape from Teague's company. 'I'll catch up with you later,' he said. 'If you work here, I'll be back around twelve.'

The Warden led Healey into her office and motioned for him to sit down opposite her. She was wearing a lemon-coloured, short sleeved, cotton dress, which revealed a pair of podgy pink and freckled arms and a white neck, around which hung the same string of large amber beads that she had worn when he had first spoken to her. Her fair hair was short and thin, and curled in such a way as to reveal patches of scalp. Her eyes were dirty blue and the appearance of her yellow teeth was not enhanced by the bright red lipstick which surrounded them. Perhaps it was the contrast with the young women with whom the case had brought him into contact these last few days, but Healey couldn't help thinking what an unattractive creature she was.

She smiled. 'I'm sorry to have taken so long, but I've been terribly busy. I promised to speak to our senior porter, Bird, about Dr Crouch's relations with his colleagues. He tells me in fact that except for one altercation he observed between Dr Crouch and Dr Farrell, his relations seem to have been perfectly good with all of them.'

'That's interesting. Did he say what this altercation was about?'

'No, he didn't. He was too far away to hear clearly. Did he tell *you* what it was about?'

'I'm sorry?'

'Bird told me that he had already informed you of this.'

'Erm, yes, I believe he spoke to my sergeant about it. But I wondered if he'd been able to tell you more.'

'No, he hasn't, but there is something I've heard from another source. I'm not sure how relevant it is …' At this point the Warden leaned forward as if to whisper something highly confidential. But she remained silent and her face turned red. Suddenly she stood up, moved to the window, and opened it. 'So hot in here,' she said. As she came back to her desk, Healey became aware that it was not the heat but an escape of wind on her part that had driven her to open the window. He proceeded to breathe through his mouth.

The Warden sat down and continued. 'It seems that …' She paused again. 'It seems that there has been … or rather, it is generally thought to be the case that Dr Farrell has been having an affair with Dr Crouch's wife.'

'You mean, they were having an affair up to the time of Dr Crouch's death?'

'I don't know. That is, my source doesn't know. I did ask her. But it seems that it continued until fairly recently.'

'And how does your source know this?'

'Well this may sound a bit weak, Chief Inspector, but she's a friend of a friend of Farrell's wife. It was she who told her.'

'Farrell's wife or her friend?'

'The friend.'

'Is it known when this supposed affair started?'

'It's been going on for some years, I was given to believe.'

'So it's unlikely to be the immediate cause of the murder.'

'As I said, I don't know if it's relevant to your case.'

'No, but thank you, Miss Colgan. I appreciate your help.' Healey stood up to leave.

'Oh there is one other thing, Chief Inspector. I believe Miss Woods has been able to give you some information.'

'She told you?'

'Yes. She also told me that you didn't seem to give much credence to what she said.'

'Well, she did tell me amongst other things that she has Alzheimer's.'

'She doesn't have Alzheimer's.'

'No?'

'No. That's just an affectation. She may be a little eccentric but in my experience there is absolutely nothing wrong with her memory.'

* * *

Once it was confirmed that the body had been positively identified as that of Neville Crouch, the coroner adjourned the inquest pending further investigations by the police. Healey left the court immediately and waited on the steps outside. He had been there only a moment when Teresa Crouch, wearing a dark blue suit and a white blouse, emerged. As she came down the steps, she put out her hand, which he took and held.

'Are you all right?' he asked.

'I'm fine. Thank you.'

Healey released her hand. 'Are you in your car?' he asked.

'No, I came on the bus.'

'Can I give you a lift home then?'

'That's kind. If you don't mind. Thank you.'

They walked together to Healey's car, which he had parked at the back of the court. Once inside it, Teresa sat with her hands together on her knees, which she held close together. They drove in silence. It was only when they were turning into Falstaff Avenue that Teresa spoke. 'I'm glad that I went,' she said, not looking at Healey.

'Really? Nothing much happened.' Healey brought the car to a stop outside her house.

'No, but it helped me make up my mind.'

'About what?'

'To tell the truth.'

'You haven't been telling me the truth?' asked Healey.

Still not looking at him, Teresa shook her head.

'Why not?'

'I was afraid.'

'What were you afraid of?'

She turned and looked up at Healey. 'Neville was dead and I was alone. And I didn't know what was going to happen. I wasn't just frightened for me but for Gia as well. Do you understand?'

Healey ran his hand along the steering wheel. He didn't really understand but to say so might cause Teresa to stop confiding in him, if that was what she was really doing. 'Yes I do,' he said. 'It was an awful time for you.'

She seemed relieved to hear this and Healey decided to take advantage of the moment. 'So, can I ask you, *was* Tim Wright with you the night your husband died?'

'No.'

'Why did you say that he was?'

'Because he asked me to.'

'But why did you do what he asked?'

'I told you. I was frightened. I felt alone. And Tim is a friend.'

'Did he say why he wanted you to say he was with you?'

'No. He said I had to trust him.'

'But he might have been involved in your husband's death.'

Teresa looked shocked. 'Oh no. Never. That isn't possible.'

'How can you be sure?'

'He was Neville's friend too. Neville had always helped him. He would never ...'

'Was he just a friend to Neville? Or did they have some kind of business relationship?' Though he asked the question calmly, Healey felt excited. He sensed that the case was about to crack open for him.

'I think so. Neville was always very protective of me. He never told me things which might worry me. But, yes, I think they were doing something together.'

'I realise you can't be sure, but do you think it's possible that their business might have something to do with drugs?'

Teresa nodded. 'I think perhaps,' she said quietly.

'Is that why you were frightened when you learned that your husband was dead?'

'Yes.'

'You thought it might be connected with the business he was doing?'

'Yes.'

'But not with Tim Wright.'

'No.'

'Who then?'

'The others.'

'Not Roberto Reyes?'

'Yes.'

'But he's your cousin.'

'No. He isn't my cousin. Maria isn't my cousin either. That is just what Neville said whenever she needed to get into Britain. He used to say she was going to help me with Gia. When she applied for a visa.'

'Where is she now?'

'In the house. With Gia.'

'And you aren't worried?'

'I wasn't. But now that I have told you all this …' She paused. 'I'm going away, with Gia. To Neville's mum's.' Teresa made to get out of the car. Healey put his hand on her arm.

'How is Gia taking it, your husband's absence, I mean? You haven't told her that …'

'I've told that he's had to go away for work for a little while but she's still upset. I'll have to tell her in the end though.'

Healey nodded sympathetically. 'Can you give me an address and a telephone number for Neville's mother?' He handed her a notepad and a pen. She took a small diary from her handbag and began to copy from it.

As she handed Healey's notepad back to him, he said, 'There is just one thing I need to know, if you don't mind.' He took a breath. 'Peter Farrell. You went with him to the Philippines, didn't you?'

She nodded.

He decided not to point out that she hadn't mentioned Farrell when she had previously spoken of her visits to the Philippines. 'Did anything happen between you and him while you were there?'

Her answer came faster than Healey expected. 'Yes. We began an affair. Is that what you want to know?'

'And did it continue when you came back to Britain?'

'Yes.'

'And when did it end?'

'Two years ago.'

'Did your husband know about it?'

'That's when it ended. When he found out. I promised that it would end, and it did.'

'What was your husband's reaction when he found out?'

'He felt betrayed. By me. And by Peter.' Tears came to Teresa's eyes. Her hand went to the gold crucifix she was wearing. 'You may not believe me, but I loved Neville. He changed my life. He did everything for me and Gia. It's just that … he was never very interested in sex. It was hard at times. And when I was going everywhere with Peter in Manila, staying in the same hotel, having fun, it just happened.' She wiped her eyes with the back of her hand. 'I thought that when we got back to Reading, it would be all over. Neville ʍ ould never know, he wouldn't be hurt.'

'But …'

'Yes, we weren't going to but we started seeing each other again. Eventually Neville did find out. It was Peter's wife who found out first and she told Neville. After that he stopped sleeping with me.'

'And you?'

'I slept with nobody either.'

'Not with Farrell?'

'No.'

'Nor Wright?'

She smiled briefly. 'No, of course not. He isn't interested in women. You've met him. Couldn't you see?' Again she moved as if to get out of the car. Again Healey put his hand on her arm.

'You told me that your husband was particularly worried recently. Was that true?'

'Yes.'

'Do you really not know why?'

'No, though I know he was very frustrated at work. He had been working so hard, reorganising the administration of the Department, but when he asked to be put forward for a senior lectureship, he was told he didn't have a chance. In fact they said that it would be a good thing if he thought of moving on to another university.'

'Who told him this?'

'The Head of Department. Professor Bradshaw.'

'But that wouldn't explain why he called you the names he did. If he did, of course.'

'He did call me names, yes. But that was out of frustration. After he found out about me and Peter, whenever he was upset, he would always take it out on me.'

'And Gia. She isn't Farrell's ... is she?'

Teresa abruptly opened the door of the car and stepped out. Looking back in, her hand on the door, she answered, 'No, she isn't.' With which, she slammed the car door, turned on her heels and walked towards her garden gate.

Healey watched until she was inside the house. If it was true that she hadn't slept with anyone for years, perhaps that had something to do with the way she had behaved towards him the first time he had been to her house. And when she had handed him that bag. If it was true, that is. As he drove off, it occurred to him that the next door nosey parker had for once failed to put in an appearance.

Ten minutes later Healey was standing in the Farrells' open porch. The door opened and he was greeted with a smile from Farrell's wife. 'Oh, hello,' she said. 'Nice to see you. What's brought you here?'

'Sorry to bother you, but I can't find my penknife and the last place I can remember having it was when I was in your garden the other day. It wouldn't matter, only it was a present from my son and ...'

Mrs Farrell led him through the side gate and into the back garden. The incinerator still stood where it had been two days previously. Healey walked towards it.

'I had it in my hand just about here,' he said. He walked round the incinerator, looking carefully at the ground. There was no trace of the red object that he had seen there, though there were still half burnt twigs and leaves lying about. 'No,' he said, 'must have been somewhere else.'

'I hope you find it.'

'I'm sure I will. Probably in the house somewhere.' As they walked back towards the house, Healey asked, 'You haven't had another fire since then, have you?'

Mrs Farrell looked surprised at the question. 'No, but if we had, we'd hardly have burnt your penknife.'

'No, of course not. What was I thinking of? Must be the heat.'

Farrell's wife looked puzzled. 'You're right, it's hot, though they say it's going to break soon, did you hear?'

'Really? We certainly need the rain.'

'Yes. And I certainly need a drink. Would you like one?'

Healey glanced at his watch. 'I'm meeting my sergeant shortly, but a quick one, that would be nice, thanks. Maybe a fruit juice?'

The drink turned out not to be quite as quick as Healey had intended. For one thing, she pressed him to have a Pimm's and, against his better judgement (he hadn't had alcohol at lunchtime for nearly a month now), he said yes, and it took her all of a quarter of an hour to make it. For another thing, as soon as they had sat down on deckchairs on the lawn to drink it, she asked him if, as Peter had told her, he was seriously thinking about doing a part-time degree.

'I'm thinking about it. That's about all at the moment.' He drank from his glass. 'But you are doing a degree with the OU, aren't you? Are you enjoying it?'

'Yes. It's hard work but it's worth it.'

'Nearly finished?'

'Another year to do, if all goes well.' She sighed. 'I think deciding to do a degree was the best decision I've made in my adult life.'

'Really?'

'Yes. I love Peter, and of course I love the children, but it came to me all of a sudden that I was doing everything for them and nothing for myself. And really, that meant I had less to offer them, if you see what I mean?'

'I think so.'

'I was becoming, well I already *was*, an extension of them. I had no real sense of self. Of being an individual.' She stopped. 'I'm sorry, I don't know why I'm telling you this when I hardly know you.' She laughed nervously. 'That's something that *hasn't* changed. I've always talked too much.'

'That's all right.' Healey wanted to use her first name but he couldn't for the life of him remember it. 'In my line of work we much prefer people who talk to those who don't.'

She clapped her hands together and laughed again. 'Of course you do. Well that's all right then.' As she went on to tell him about the various social science courses she'd done or was doing, and how being registered for a degree had helped her get an interesting job at the Royal Berks Hospital, Healey looked at her closely for the first time. The most striking thing about her was her constant movement. Petite, red haired, with green eyes and sharp features, there was something bird-like about her. When at rest, her mouth remained slightly open and showed perfect white teeth. She wore no lipstick.

Quite the opposite of Miss Colgan, Healey thought. But quite like Teresa. Which made him think of Farrell himself and what he must see in the two women, and what he wanted from them.

Looking at his watch and realising that Teague would be expecting him by now, he gulped down the rest of his drink, stood up and said he must leave. Mrs Farrell said that she had to go too and pick up her youngest from nursery. As Healey walked back to his own house, he wondered if there was any connection between her husband's supposed affair with Mrs Crouch, which she apparently knew about, and her decision to do a degree.

Healey found Teague at the Hall and walked with him to the Queen's Head. In the gloom of the public bar they both stood waiting for someone to come through and serve them.

'Usual?' Teague asked.

'Mm?' Healey seemed lost in thought.

'Orange juice and tonic?'

'No. No thanks. I'll have a pint of Guinness.'

Teague raised his eyebrows but said nothing. Eventually they were served and, having ordered sandwiches, sat down in the corner beneath the dart board. On the way there Teague had reported that, though he had now worked his way through nearly half the cassettes, he had heard nothing that seemed relevant to the case.

'Stuff about language, about foreign countries ... football ...' Teague looked to the ceiling as he tried to remember what other topics there had been.

'Who was doing the talking?' asked Healey.

'Farrell I recognised ... Carter ... Crouch, I'm pretty sure ... one very posh bloke.'

'That would be their Head.'

'And an oriental sounding type.'

'Yeah, that's right, there's a Chinese.'

'I know that, sir. I was with you when Carter told us about him.'

'Of course. Sorry. What was his name, do you remember?'

'Was it Chow?'

'I don't think so, but go on. What did Crouch sound like?'

'Deep voice, northern …'

'Confident? Happy?'

When Teague did not reply immediately, Healey added, 'Depressed?'

'Well, actually, he sounded fine. Full of his own importance, though, is how I'd describe him.'

You'd know all about that, thought Healey. 'Of course we don't know when these recordings were made,' he said. 'He could have been okay then, and got depressed later.'

'You're not still thinking suicide as a possibility, are you?'

'Well, the blow to his left temple was the clearest indication that it wasn't suicide. But then we know he got a bang in that area when he was playing cricket.'

'But the pathologist said it was unlikely to have been caused by a cricket ball.'

'Oh, I didn't see that. Did he rule it out for certain?'

Before Teague could answer, their sandwiches arrived and they began to eat in silence.

'And what about you, sir? How did it go?'

Healey told Teague about the inquest and how he had driven Teresa home. He went on to tell him what Teresa had said.

'And you believe her?'

'I don't know. When I was listening to her, I did. Now, when I tell you, I'm not so sure.'

'We know she's lied before.'

'Yes. But what she's saying now makes sense of a number of things. At least it makes them fit together better.'

'And it gets you thinking either it was suicide, or it was something to do with drugs. Which she has got nothing to do with, and neither has Farrell. She'd have you believe.'

Healey nodded.

'Would you like me to talk to her again, sir?'

'No, I don't think that would help just now. In any case, she's gone to stay with Crouch's mother in Guildford. Let's leave her for the minute. Fancy another pint?'

'No thanks. It's hard enough already staying awake listening to those tapes.' They both stood up, Healey brushing the breadcrumbs from his jacket.

As they left the pub, Healey said, 'By the way, there's a course party tonight. We're both invited.'

'Yes, sir, a couple of people on the course already asked me to go.'

Healey thought of the Bulgarian women. 'You'll go, I hope?'

'Yes.'

'On duty.'

Teague gave a little smile. 'Of course.'

When they reached the Hall, Teague went inside, while Healey got in his car and drove off in the direction of Berkshire University on King's Road.

* * *

the man's a fool
soon be out of here
away
and it's all over
as if it never happened

* * *

Healey's visit to the King's Road campus turned out to be a waste of time. There was nobody at all in the Department of Communication Studies, not even a secretary. All of the office doors, each of which Healey tried after knocking, were locked. Wearily, he went back to his car and drove to the Hall, where he hoped he might find Wright. He walked through the reception area and on towards the bar. The door of the bar was open and he heard voices, hardly more than whispers, of two men. He stopped short of the door and peered in. Just round the corner, but with their backs to him, were sitting Farrell and Wright. Staying where he was, he tried to make out what they were saying but he couldn't. He was about to turn away and go to the incident room to talk to Teague but thought no, let's see what these two have to say for themselves. As he strode in, they both turned round in what seemed a rather furtive fashion.

'Oh, hello there,' said Farrell. Wright turned his back on Healey and said nothing.

'You haven't seen Teague, have you?' asked Healey.

'He was in the games room. The games room that was. The incident room you call it, I think.'

'Oh, thanks. He's more often in the bar.' Healey took a few more steps so that Farrell and Wright were facing him, looking up from the sofa on which they were sitting. 'I wonder if I might have a word with you, Mr Wright, when you've finished your business with Doctor Farrell, that is.'

'Hardly business, Richard,' said Farrell. 'We're just planning a quiz to start the party off with tonight.'

'I see. Well I'll just have a quick word with Teague. I'll be in the incident room when you're ready, Mr Wright.' Wright nodded but still said nothing.

Teague wasn't in the incident room. 'Said he could concentrate more on those tapes at home,' said the constable that Healey found on duty. Healey noticed a half-finished crossword that must have been hastily put aside.

Yes, I can imagine that, he thought. He sat down in front of a set of files and began slowly to turn over the sheets of paper that made up the first of them. He had hardly begun when Wright arrived. Healey wished Teague was with him; he wasn't feeling confident and he didn't fancy doing this by himself. Still, he would have to.

'Please sit down, Mr Wright.' Wright did so, placing himself across the table from Healey. 'Would you like to tell me what your role is in this drug business with the Philippines?'

'What?' Wright shook his head as if he could not believe what he had just been asked. The constable looked up from his crossword.

'You heard me. What is your role in the smuggling of cannabis into this country?'

'I don't know what you are talking about. What business? Why are you asking me this?'

'Two reasons. Yesterday you were in a house in Haverstock Hill which we know is used by drug smugglers from the Philippines, including your friend Roberto Reyes.'

'He's not my friend, as you put it. And I …'

'And second, you have a substantial amount of cannabis resin stashed in your room in this hall.'

'What do you mean?'

'Just what I say.'

Wright was disconcerted. 'You've been in my room? You can't do that.'

'No I haven't been in your room. The cannabis was discovered when the room was being cleaned and this was reported to me.' Healey felt safe lying in this way. If it turned out that Wright was involved in the murder, this wouldn't be important. If he wasn't, well the drug smuggling was for someone else to deal with. In fact Customs and Excise already were. Not his problem.

'All right, I do have a little cannabis, but only for my own use.'

'A kilo?'

'A what?'

'That's roughly the amount that was found inside your guitar.'

Clearly Wright had thought Healey had been referring to the smaller amount that Teague had found. Now he was completely at a loss. He said nothing. Healey kept looking at him but Wright averted his gaze. This was the moment for Healey to press home his advantage.

Before he could speak, however, Wright turned towards him, smiled broadly, showing his teeth again, and stood up. He pushed his chair under the table. 'I'm afraid I don't have any more time for your questions,' he said and walked past the seated Healey towards the door.

There was nothing Healey could do. Not looking round, conscious of the constable behind him, he simply said, 'You'll regret this Mr Wright.' He heard the door open and close. When he did get up and go towards the door himself, the constable was looking studiously at the printed page he held in his hands, as if nothing had happened. As he emerged from the room, Healey saw that Wright was already dialling a number on the public telephone. Who was he calling, he wondered. A member of the drug ring, his lawyer, or Mrs Crouch. He could hardly wait and listen so he walked past and out of the building, got into his car and drove home.

Going through the house and into the garden Healey found his wife, Pam Farrell with a little girl on her knee, Meg and Jamie, and two other girls of about Meg's age, whom he imagined must be the Farrell daughters. Could he remember their names? Was one of them Melanie? Polly? No, he couldn't. The children were playing tennis with a sponge ball and a low net. The women were at the table, drinking what looked like beer.

'Hello, Dick,' said his wife. 'Didn't expect to see you this afternoon.'

He smiled. 'You never know when to expect me, do you?' he said in what he thought was a self-deprecating way.

His wife frowned. 'Are you getting at me again?'

He was aware of Farrell's wife's bird-like eyes on him. 'Me?' he answered. 'You must be thinking of someone else.' He sat down beside his wife without looking at her. 'Another lovely day,' he ventured.

'For some,' said Mrs Farrell. 'Not for the farmers, or us gardeners.' She spoke as if to include Jill as a gardener, and exclude him.

'I'm sure you're right, but if the forecast is to be believed we're going to get rain today or tomorrow.' The three of them looked at the sky which remained cloudless.

'I'd better be getting along. Come on, Molly. Laura. Time to go.'

'Oh, Mum, do we have to?' one of the girls asked.

'Well,' Mrs Farrell looked at Jill, 'I suppose they could stay, if you wouldn't mind? It's not as if they've got far to go.'

'No, that's all right.'

The two women stood up and went into the house through the French windows, the youngest child following them. To Healey, who watched them, it was remarkable that two women physically not dissimilar could be so different in character. His wife, moody, endlessly worried, with little motivation it seemed for anything except the reading of trashy novels; Farrell's wife, lively, interested, clearly full of energy and now working for a degree. He turned his attention to the children. The three girls seemed to be getting on well, and Jamie appeared flattered to be allowed to play with them. Healey remembered his mother saying once that the only reason she had married was to have children. After fifteen years of marriage, he knew how she felt. He went into the house, climbed the stairs and lay down on the bed. The Guinness did its work and within five minutes he was asleep.

* * *

When Healey got to the Hall that evening, it was strangely quiet and he wondered if he had made a mistake of some kind. The reception desk was empty and so he made his way to the bar, where Farrell had told him the party would be taking place. Just as he was about to open the bar door, he heard voices from inside, singing softly, holding a low pitched chord, before beginning a slow melody. He pushed open the door slowly and stepped inside. The two Bulgarian women he'd met on the barge were standing at the far end of the room, with another five dark-haired, smaller women, all of them with their hands clasped in front of them, and singing a dirge whose tone was reflected in their mournful expressions.

There must have been at least fifty other people there, mostly women, sitting around the edge of the room, listening in silence. Bulbs had been taken from half of the lights, presumably to create a more intimate atmosphere but the result was to make it gloomy. The bar itself was just inside the door, to the left. Leaning against it, dressed in a blue velvet dinner jacket and a bow tie of the same cloth and colour, was Farrell. He mouthed an offer of a drink to Healey, who accepted, asking the barman in a whisper for a scotch and water. Sipping his drink, he leaned with his back to the bar and looked around the room.

In the darkest corner, just to his right, were three pairs of mostly fair-haired men and women, sprawled over the sofa that Wright and Farrell had been sitting on earlier. Along the wall next to them was a group of women whom Healey took to be of Latin origin. One of these was Silvia, who made a tiny wave to him with the fingers of one hand, to which he responded with a slight nod of the head. Next he saw Teague, who, pint glass in hand, was looking intently at the singers. Beyond him was an Asian contingent, all women, huddled together, the furthest of them only a foot or so from the Bulgarian singers, and looking as if they might burst into giggles at any moment. On the other side of the singers, along the wall leading back to the bar, stood a number of black Africans, a group of what might be people from the Middle East and finally a tall blond man who stood next to Farrell.

When the singing ended there was a silence followed by loud clapping. The Bulgarian ladies smiled and bowed and then immediately walked over to Teague and flopped onto the empty seats around him. At this, the group that included Silvia stood up and took the place of the Bulgarians and, after an exchange of nervous glances, began to sing *Guantanamera*. Healey moved along the bar to Farrell.

'Very impressive,' he said. 'Those Bulgarians, such beautiful sound from …'

Farrell nodded. 'Thank God that by the time it's *our* turn, everyone will have had a lot more to drink, including us.'

'So you sing too?'

'Oh yes. Rehearsals are in progress even as we speak. You'll notice none of the tutors is here.'

'None? Wright and Walters. Who else?'

'Good point.' Farrell looked somewhat the worse for wear. 'But there is one other member of the team. We've persuaded the lovely Olivia to step into the breach. Hence the need for rehearsal.'

'Olivia?'

'Of the British Council. And Sam as well.'

'But you're not taking part?'

'Oh I'll be taking part, don't worry.' Farrell then began to join in with the singing. 'Yo soy un hombre sincero,' he uttered in a loud voice which Healey, though he was no great singer himself, recognised as decidedly out of tune. The participants, who were almost all singing along by now, seemed not to notice his wayward notes. And nor did Farrell apparently.

Guantanamera over and cries of encore ignored, attention turned to the group huddled on the sofa. Someone shouted 'Come on Finland' and when there was no response from the group, chanting of 'Fin-land, Fin-land' began, to the obvious embarrassment of the sprawlers. Eventually, one of their number, a stocky middle-aged man, was pushed forward and he walked slowly to the other end of the room, to loud clapping. Putting up his hand for silence, and drawing himself up to his full but not very considerable height, the man began to sing in a rich, deep bass voice. He had only sung a few words, however, when he stopped, shook his head, and set off back down the room, where he was greeted with laughter from what Healey took to be his fellow countrymen and women.

'Finns,' said Farrell. 'They've been here three weeks, hardly said a word to anyone in public, including themselves, and all the time they've been having it away with each other. And getting pissed. On this.' He pushed a bottle towards Healey. 'They gave me this earlier. Whinberry liqueur, I think it is. Lethal. Try it.' He turned to the barman. 'Give him a glass, Mark, will you.'

Healey poured himself a small shot in the glass that the barman gave him.

'Take more,' said Farrell. 'You won't taste that.'

Healey did as he was told. Taking a first sip, he made a grimace. 'Tastes like disinfectant. Sweet disinfectant.'

'Don't sip, take a swig.'

Again Healey did as he was told. He coughed and screwed up his eyes. 'Powerful stuff,' he said.

'Have some more.'

And Healey did. 'How did the quiz go?' he asked.

'The quiz?'

'You said that you and Wright were planning a quiz.'

'Oh, that. We decided against it. Too much trouble.'

Seeing no point in pursuing this, though it made him think that perhaps it wasn't a quiz at all that Farrell and Wright had been talking about, Healey asked, 'Who is the tall blond fellow who was standing next to you?'

'Ah, that's Sven. The silent Swede. You won't hear anything from him tonight.'

By this time, the tutors had entered the bar, accompanied by Sam and the British Council woman, and Healey watched them split up and join various national groups. At the end of the room three tiny oriental women were singing what sounded like a lullaby, though in what language Healey could not guess. As soon as they had finished, the participants sitting next to where Farrell was standing, the ones Healey had thought were from the Middle East, rose and went to the far end of the room, where they began to fiddle with hi-fi equipment on a low table. People took advantage of this pause to come to the bar for drinks, including Teague. 'Enjoying it, sir?'

Healey, who had by now drunk three glasses of the Finnish liqueur, smiled happily. 'Very good. Yes, very good. Let me get you one, Mike.'

'Thank you, sir. I'll have a pint of Directors.'

While this was being poured, music came from the hi-fi and one of the women who had been involved in setting it up began to dance a belly dance. She was tall, young, swarthy and fleshy, and she danced with slow languorous movements, her hips rolling round and round. The others stood to the side, clapping, until at a certain point one of the men began to dance too. Eventually all of them were dancing. The young woman who had begun the dance then swayed across the room to the bar, where she stopped in front of Farrell and began to make suggestive movements and beckoned him to join her in the dance. Farrell smiled broadly but did not move.

Seeming disappointed, the woman was about to turn away when Teague stood up, stepped forward to her and began to move from side to side and clap his hands. This drew shouts of encouragement and soon Teague was dancing in the middle of the group, where one of the Bulgarian ladies (Ludmilla wasn't it?) joined him. The music ended, Teague returned to his seat with Ludmilla, to much applause and slaps on the back. Ludmilla gave him a quick peck on the cheek and Teague beamed.

Immediately, the Africans stepped forward and forming a line facing the bar, with no music, began to stamp their feet. They danced forwards and backwards and then from side to side, chanting in low tones. Healey decided he needed a pee.

When he got back, the Africans were no longer dancing. Their place had been taken by the tutors, Sam, and the lady from the British Council. Wright was dressed in a cream linen suit; Mary Walters and Sam in jeans and T-shirts; and the British Council woman in a beige jacket with padded shoulders, worn over a long floral dress. They stood in a line with Farrell and Wright at the centre. Farrell put up his hand and asked for 'a bit of hush'. The room went quiet.

The course members, said Farrell, were about to enjoy a rare cultural experience, one which he hoped they would treat with the respect and seriousness which it deserved. He nodded to his colleagues and they began to sing about a young maiden who encounters a certain Sir Roger. After each verse there was a brief chorus, the first being 'Oh, Sir Roger, do not touch me'. As the song went on, they proceeded to drop one word from their singing of the chorus. Soon they sang 'Oh, Sir Roger, do not touch'. Before long they had the young maid pleading 'Oh, Sir Roger, *do*', and they eventually ended with an orgasmic rendering of the single word 'Oh!' to the cheers and laughter of most and what seemed the painful embarrassment of a few, including the British Council lady, who broke away from the group and made for the door, swiftly followed by a short silver-haired man in a double-breasted blazer, whom Healey had not previously noticed.

So that was all that the English could contribute, thought Healey. But no, that wasn't all. Farrell was going round the room, pulling people to their feet and into the centre of the room. 'Ladies and gentlemen,' he announced, 'the Hokey Kokey!' He paused for the effect of his words to sink in. 'Come on everybody. In a circle. Arms round shoulders.' Once something like a circle had been formed, he began to sing, 'You put your left leg in, your left leg out, you put your left leg in and you shake it all about,' doing just what he said with his own left leg. The participants soon grasped what was involved and joined in with enthusiasm.

Healey stayed with his back hard against the bar. He may have drunk more than he should but he wasn't going to be drawn into this. It wasn't long before people were throwing their 'whole self' in and out, falling over and staggering to their feet again. Healey wiped his brow. God, it was hot in here. So many bodies in such a small space, with the windows shut, doubtless as an attempt to avoid complaints from the local residents. He took off his jacket and gestured to the barman that he put it behind the bar, which the young man did. 'Can I get you a drink?' asked Healey.

'Well I'd quite like to try that Finnish stuff, if you wouldn't mind.'

'It isn't mine, so I don't mind at all. And *he* doesn't look as if he'd mind either,' he added, gesturing towards Farrell, who was at that moment being dragged to his feet by Silvia and Sam. Healey pushed the bottle forwards. 'Help yourself.'

Once the English had completed their performance, the young man behind the bar went over to the tape deck. He put in a cassette and after a few seconds of hissing from the speakers, loud music emerged. It began with a couple of Rolling Stones songs and a Beatles number, during which people either sat in their groups or stood around the bar. Farrell went behind the bar and switched off more of the lights.

'That should help get them onto the floor,' he explained to Healey. Sure enough, three or four couples made their way to the darker corners of the room and began to dance. The music was all from the two previous decades. There were more songs from the Beatles and the Rolling Stones, and some from Queen. When Chubby Checker began to sing *Twist Again*, Teague, who until then had sat drinking with the Bulgarians, stood up and pulled Ludmilla to her feet, and the two of them began to gyrate vigorously, more or less in time to the music.

After a minute of this, Teague, still twisting, left Ludmilla and made his way to other course members sitting around the edge of the room and drew them from their seats. One after another, he convinced them to join in, until almost everyone in the room except the Finns was dancing. When the music stopped, there were shouts of 'More!' and the barman was persuaded to rewind the tape so that they could carry on twisting, which all of them did.

When the music ended again, Teague made his way to his seat and for the second time that evening was given a loud round of applause. Despite himself, Healey felt admiration for Teague. He was in his element and was helping to make a success of the party, something Healey knew he could never do himself. Picking up his pint of beer, Teague gestured with it towards Healey and gave him a big wink. Healey smiled back and nodded.

When ABBA began *Dancing Queen*, all of the Swedish course members (at least that was what Healey took them to be) stood up and joined in as if it were their national anthem, jiggling about in an awkward and self-conscious fashion. Healey wanted to point out to Farrell that he had been wrong about Sven; he was singing as loudly as any of them, holding the hand of one of his female compatriots. But Farrell was nowhere to be seen.

It was so hot in the bar, that Healey decided he had to get some fresh air. Walking somewhat unsteadily, he made his way out and down the corridor and through reception, where there was no one on duty. Once outside, he breathed more easily. There was a slight breeze. He looked up and saw that the sky was beginning to cloud over. It looked as if the weather forecast might be right. As he stood there, he heard what sounded like two voices in quiet but definite disagreement. A man was repeatedly interrupted by a woman saying 'No!' Moving round the corner of the building, Healey traced the sounds to the open window of the secretary's office. The light was on. From the shadow of a tree he could see Farrell and the British Council woman, standing face to face. Farrell was opening his arms in apparent supplication, while the woman shook her head. Behind them was Wright, watching them but making no contribution himself. Believing that whatever was being said could hardly be connected with the case, and therefore none of his business, Healey turned round and walked back to the entrance.

Approaching the bar he heard Boney M and *Rivers of Babylon*. As he opened the door, Farrell and Wright came up behind him. 'I was just getting some air,' said Healey.

'Don't blame you,' said Farrell. 'We need to open some windows but that bloody Council woman says she's agreed with the Warden that we shouldn't, so as not to disturb the neighbours with our noise. Tim and I have just been arguing with her.'

'So?'

'She still says no but we're going to open them anyhow. Bugger her.' Farrell and Wright then set off round the room, opening every window as wide as it would go. While they were doing so, Boney M stopped and Village People began *YMCA*. No one was dancing. Farrell turned from the window he had just opened and scanned the room. He walked across to where Mary Walters was sitting by herself and held out his hand to her. She shook her head. Healey watched as Farrell then approached Wright and the two of them went to the middle of the room and began to dance together, side by side, Farrell affecting an exaggerated butch manner, while Wright moved effeminately at his side. As the music ended there was a smattering of applause and the two men bowed deeply before making their way, holding hands, to where Healey was leaning against the bar.

'Something for them to think about,' said Farrell. Wright looked as if he were about to say something too but didn't.

'She seemed embarrassed, that British Council woman,' said Healey.

'What?' asked Farrell. 'Oh you mean when we were singing. I told you she was a wet blanket.'

'Who was the man who followed her out? Silver hair, blue blazer. I haven't seen him around before.'

'Oh, him. The great guru. He gave a lecture in the first week. Future of English language teaching. We had to pay him top whack to do it. Complete waste of money.'

'And is he connected with the woman?' Healey asked only out of curiosity.

'I doubt it. He's another wet blanket. Probably home now, drinking his cocoa.'

Healey realised that this 'guru' must have been the little man with the big reputation that Silvia had complained about at the Cunning Man. Then, for no obvious reason, it suddenly came to him who the jogger had been that morning. She was the wife of someone in the Criminology Department at the old university. They had invited Jill and him to a dinner party once. What an ordeal that had been. Dreadful food, cheap wine, and him going on about the need for the police routinely to carry guns and expecting Healey to agree with him, which he had resolutely refused to do. And then there was that framed certificate for Sexual Excellence on their bathroom wall, bearing his name and signed by the wife. He had never seen either of them since, until this morning, when she had ignored his greeting. Healey poured himself another whinberry liqueur.

The music was now slower. The barman had put candles on three or four tables around the room and turned off all of the remaining lights. At this point the Finns took the floor for the first time, pairs of them holding each other tight, shuffling about in nothing resembling any known dance step. Other couples got up to join them. Healey's mouth was dry and he asked the barman for a glass of water. Farrell was dancing with Sam, the course assistant. Teague was clutching Ludmilla, a dreamy expression on his face. None of the dancers bothered to sit down between tracks but remained leaning against each other until the next began. Healey felt someone take his hand. It was the Italian woman, Silvia.

'Will you dance with me?' she asked.

Healey was about to refuse but as she tugged him gently away from the bar, he relented. She folded her arms around him and whispered, 'Hold me, Richard.' He felt a lump come to his throat as they moved slowly around the room. Peering over her shoulder, Healey tried to see who was watching them but no one seemed interested. *Put Your Sweet Lips a Little Closer to the Phone* was playing, and Silvia murmured, 'Put your sweet lips a little closer,' and reached up to kiss him. Despite himself, Healey was aroused. Silvia smiled up at him. 'Will you come to my room? Two-two-one. Please come.' She released her hold on him and walked slowly out of the bar without looking round.

* * *

As he drew closer, Healey saw that the door to room 221 was slightly ajar. He tapped and pushed gently against it. There was hardly any light inside.

'Richard?' asked Silvia.

'Yes,' he replied huskily, and stepped inside. Barefoot and in a nightdress, Silvia came towards him, took his two hands and kissed him on the lips.

When Healey woke up, he smelled tobacco. He opened his eyes and saw Silvia, still naked, sitting beside him on the bed, smoking a cigarette. She offered it to him.

'No thanks,' he said, 'I don't smoke.'

She leaned over and kissed him gently on the cheek. Pulling back, she looked into his eyes. 'Why not? You think it is bad to smoke?'

Though he did think just that, he shook his head. 'No. I just don't like to.' As he said this, he was wondering what time it was. Resisting the temptation to look at his watch, he asked, 'Was I asleep long?'

'No. A few minutes, that's all.' Still looking into his eyes, she put her arm round his head and pulled it towards her. 'Relax, Richard. Take it easy.' Giving him a kiss on the cheek, Silvia took her arm from him, swung her legs over the other side of the bed, and stood up. 'Do you want a coffee?'

'Please.' He watched her go to the washbasin, pour water into a small kettle. As she stooped to plug it in to a socket near the floor, he looked quickly at his watch. Just after eleven. He should go down soon if Teague wasn't going to be looking for him, maybe even trying to phone him at home.

Silvia handed him a small cup of dark black coffee. It tasted bitter.

'So, Chief Inspector, how is the case progressing?' When Healey didn't answer, Silvia put down her coffee on the bedside table, climbed onto the bed and slid her hand up and down his thigh. After a moment, she looked down. 'Oh,' she said, 'I see that you are becoming excited. Are you thinking about your case?' She paused. 'Or is it something else?'

Healey put his arms round her and began to kiss her.

Silvia was lying beside him with her eyes closed. He looked at his watch. Half past eleven. He had to go. He leaned over the edge of the bed and searched for his underpants in the twisted sheets on the floor.

'You're leaving?'

'I have to.'

'Richard, you don't have to. You don't have to do anything. Just do what you want to do. If you *know* what you want.'

Healey continued to dress. Silvia got up and walked round to him. She folded down his collar and ran her hands down his shirt until they came to rest on his waist. 'You didn't tell me how the case is going.'

When Healey didn't respond, she continued, 'I can tell you something that you don't know.'

Healey looked down at her. She stepped back from him. 'Do you want me to tell you what it is?'

Healey nodded.

'Peter Farrell was in Dr Crouch's room on the night that he was murdered.'

* * *

Healey knocked at Sam's door and put his ear to it. There was no answer. He knocked again, louder and thought he heard the sound of a female voice. He knocked again, louder still.

'Who is it?'

'Chief Inspector Healey. Police.'

'Wait a minute.'

A few moments later the door edged slowly open and Sam's face appeared, her pink and blue hair tousled. 'What is it? What d'you want?' she mumbled.

'I need to talk to you. Now. It's urgent.'

'I can't. I've got someone with me.'

'Dr Farrell?'

'What? What do you mean? No!' She kept the door almost closed. 'Wait a minute.' She closed the door completely. A minute later she half opened it, looked back over her shoulder, and a figure, head down, pushed past her, through the door, and out into the corridor. Healey recognised it as one of the African students who had been performing at the party earlier. The man made off down the corridor and through the doors at the end.

'Come in.'

Sam seemed to be wearing nothing but what looked like a man's shirt. As he followed her into the room, Healey noticed the unmade bed, a towel on the floor beside it. He sniffed but smelt nothing. The only light was from an Anglepoise lamp on the floor, pointing down. 'I understand that on the night

Dr Crouch died you saw Dr Farrell come out of Dr Crouch's room. Is that true?'

Sam looked at him, down to the ground, then up again. 'Silvia told you.'

'Yes.'

'When I made my statement, I didn't …'

'I'm not interested in that now, just what you actually saw. *Did* you see Dr Farrell come out of Dr Crouch's room?'

'Yes.'

'You're sure? The light in the corridor isn't very good.'

Sam hesitated. 'Yes.'

'You saw his face?'

'No, but I saw the back of his head. And the raincoat he was wearing, the one he kept in his room. I'm sure it was him.'

'What time was this?'

'Midnight.'

'And where did you see him *from?* Show me.'

Sam moved to the door, opened it slightly and looked out into the corridor.

'Did he see you?'

'No.'

'Did you see where he went?'

'Through the doors at the end.'

'Why did you open your door?'

Again Sam hesitated. 'I had someone with me and he was leaving and I didn't want any of the tutors to see him.'

'Before that, did you hear anything? A bang? A shout? Any unusual noise?'

'When I first opened the door, I thought I heard Dr Farrell go into his room. I waited a minute in case he came out right away. Then I looked again, and that was when I saw him come out of Dr Crouch's room. He must have left his own room and then gone into Dr Crouch's.'

'You know this is a murder investigation?' Sam nodded. 'And how serious what you are saying is?' Again she nodded. 'Are you absolutely sure it was Dr Farrell?'

'Yes. Who else could it have been?'

'And that he was coming out of Dr Crouch's room?'

'Yes.'

'We'll take a statement from you in the morning. Stay at the Hall until we do, all right?'

Sam nodded and went back into her room. Healey headed towards the stairs just as heavy drops of rain began to beat against the windows of the corridor.

As Healey stepped downstairs there was a brilliant flash of lightning and trees were silhouetted against the sky. He winced. Even at his age he was still scared of lightning. Almost immediately there was a tremendous crack and a great roll of thunder. He got to the ground floor, looked into the incident room, which was in darkness. He tried the door. It was locked. He went to the bar, which was also in darkness. He slid his hand round the door and turned on all the lights, which buzzed and flickered before coming fully on. There were figures sprawled around the room, some lying, some sitting, some entwined with each other, some now turning towards him, blinking at the light. He walked around, looking quickly at each body in turn. No Farrell. No Teague.

Next he tried the reception desk. There must be a night porter. But there wasn't. He looked under the desk. Nobody. In the wall behind the desk there was a door which he hadn't noticed before. Perhaps only a cupboard but he opened it, and there in front of him, stretched out sleeping on the floor of what seemed to be some kind of storage area, his hands resting on his paunch, was Teague. 'Teague.' Teague moaned but didn't move. 'Wake up! Teague, wake up!' Teague opened his eyes but clearly didn't know where he was or what was happening. Healey grabbed him by the shoulder and shook him. 'Come on, man, we've got work to do.'

Teague stared at him. 'What time is it?' he mumbled.

Healey looked at his watch. 'Twelve.'

Teague slowly pulled himself to his feet. 'What are we doing?'

'I'll tell you in the car. Come on.'

As they got to the glass main door, there was a great crackling, a blinding flash and an instantaneous roar of thunder. 'Where's your car?' asked Healey.

'In the road. But I can't drive.'

'Why not?'

'I must be over the limit.'

'What! I told you not to drink too much.' Even as he shouted the words Healey knew that he had forgotten to. 'All right, I'll drive.' He thrust out a hand. 'Give me the keys.'

'Where are we going?'

'To see that bloody Farrell.'

SATURDAY

The storm had been brief but the morning air was fresh. They stood with their backs to the wall and watched the course members pass them and walk to the coach that was waiting for them just a few yards away on Marlborough Avenue. Sam stood at the foot of the coach steps, greeting each one of them, kissing most of them on the cheek. The coach would take them to the train station, from where they would go their separate ways, most of them to Heathrow and a flight back to where they came from.

A tall African approached the bus, pushed his case into the luggage compartment, and stepped to the front. He stopped in front of Sam, they exchanged a few words but did not kiss. This was the man who had been in her room the previous night. As he climbed the steps, Sam stole a glance at Healey, who acted as if he had noticed nothing. A few more students trailed out.

A hand touched Healey's sleeve. He turned to see Silvia looking up at him. She smiled. 'A kiss,' she said and he lowered his head and kissed her on the cheek. She smiled again. 'Goodbye, Richard.' He watched her talk to Sam, climb on board, and take a seat behind the driver. She did not look back at him.

'Good morning, gentlemen,' said a voice at the side of the two policemen. Teague continued to look ahead but Healey turned.

'Good morning. I wondered where you were.'

'Sorting out my room.' Farrell slapped the side of the briefcase he was carrying. 'Just some odds and ends.' Teague watched him out of the corner of his eye.

'Anyone left?' asked Healey.

'You mean course members? I don't know.' Farrell laughed apologetically.

Teague turned as if to say something but didn't, and turned away again. In the meantime Sam was watching them, looking first at Farrell and then questioningly at Healey. Hardly surprising, thought Healey, after what she had told him last night. He would have wondered what was going on himself. As it was, he felt distinctly uncomfortable.

* * *

The drive to Farrell's had been a nightmare. He was driving Teague's car, a Ford Capri, for the first time, he had been drinking, he was afraid of the storm, and his mind was racing with the implications of what he had just learned. Farrell, Carter, they had lied to him, one covering for the other.

The rain was streaming across the windscreen and Healey could hardly see the road ahead. Leaf-covered branches brought down by the wind spun crazily towards them. 'Mind, sir, you're close to the kerb,' called out an anxious Teague.

'You should do something about your wipers,' Healey growled as he wrestled with the wheel. Luckily there was no one else on the road. Eventually they got to Beech Lane and stopped outside Farrell's house. Behind the curtains there was a light in the front room. Thank God for that, he thought, pulling his jacket over his head, climbing out and slamming the door. He didn't hear Teague shout that he'd left his lights on.

Huddled with Teague in the porch, Healey rang the bell a second time and banged hard on the door. A light went on in the hall, the door opened. 'Richard, what's happened? Come in, both of you. What a night.' He waved an arm towards the sitting room door. 'I was watching telly. I must have dozed off.' Farrell slumped into the armchair, Healey and Teague sat opposite him on the sofa, water dripping from their sodden clothes.

'Could you switch it off, please,' said Healey. Farrell switched off the television and sat down again.

Taking a deep breath, Healey then warned Farrell that anything he said might be taken down and used in evidence. Farrell looked shaken. Healey proceeded to tell him that he had been seen leaving Crouch's room around the time of the murder. Farrell shook his head. 'No,' he said. 'No.'

'You were seen.'

'I wasn't there. I was here. Sitting in this very chair.' He patted the arms of the chair. 'Who says that they saw me?'

Healey looked at Teague before saying, 'I don't think I want to tell you that yet. But I will tell you that they saw you from the door of one of the other rooms.'

'Then it was Sam. Or Mary.'

'Whoever it was, they saw you.'

'But they didn't. I wasn't there.'

Teague joined in. 'They saw you in your raincoat, the one you kept in your room.'

Farrell looked down at the carpet between his feet. The rain had eased and it was possible to hear the radio from upstairs. He made as if to speak, hesitated, looked at Healey and then said, 'It wasn't me. It must have been Chris that they saw.'

He went on to explain that after they had left the Three Tuns and come back to Beech Lane, Carter had phoned his wife to say where he was and that he was going to watch the cricket with Peter and not to wait up. If his wife called, he asked Farrell to make some excuse for him. He had then gone straight off to the Hall on foot, to see one of the young women on the course, he had told Farrell. He came back towards one o'clock carrying Farrell's raincoat, saying that he had thought there was going to be a storm.

'Did you believe him?' asked Teague.

'I thought it was a bit odd, but that was all.'

'Was he carrying anything else?'

'No.'

Teague asked, 'Where did he get your coat from?'

Healey was about to interject but Farrell spoke first. 'It was in my room. In the Hall.'

Teague's eyes lit up. 'A locked room?'

'Yes.'

'And how did he get in?'

'He must have had a key.'

'Why did he need the key to your room, when he was going to meet a young lady, as you say? He wasn't taking her to your room, was he?'

'No, I don't think so.'

'So why did he need it?'

Farrell seemed confused. 'I don't know. He didn't ask for it, but I must have given it to him.'

'Yes. But why?'

When Farrell didn't answer, Healey asked if he had the key now.

'Yes, of course. I'll get it.' He left the room and switched on the hall light. 'Oh, hell,' they heard him say. 'I must be going mad.' He came back into the room, brandishing not one but two keys on the same ring. 'He said he might need the outside door key to get in, so I gave it to him. It was on the same ring as the room key and I didn't bother taking it off.' He offered the keys to Healey, who took and examined them, before handing them back to Farrell.

'And how did he seem when he got back?' he asked.

'A bit hyper. But you've met him, he's always like that.'

'Before he came in, when he got back, did you hear him open and close the door of his car, or the boot?'

'No.'

'Did you tell your wife about Carter going to the Hall?'

'No. She doesn't like Chris much and …'

'And?'

'I thought she might say something to Leila, or to someone else and it would get back to her. As soon as Chris heard about Neville he phoned to ask me to stick to our story in case Leila found out.'

'You weren't suspicious?'

'Not at all. Just a coincidence. And of course at first it wasn't clear that it was a murder. Once we'd made our statements to you we couldn't change them. And in any case it didn't occur to me that it was relevant. Chris hadn't seen anything, he said.'

Healey stood up. 'Well, we'll leave it there for the moment. You realise you committed a serious offence when you said that Carter had been with you until he went home?' Farrell nodded. Healey continued, 'Don't make it worse. Under no circumstances discuss what you've just told us. With anyone. And do not communicate in any way with Dr Carter. Is that understood?' Again Farrell nodded.

'Can I go to the Hall in the morning to see the students off?'

Healey hesitated. 'If I can trust you to speak to no one about this?'

'You can. Absolutely.'

Teague looked sharply at Healey, who ignored him.

Healey and Teague sat outside Farrell's house in Teague's car. 'What do you think, sir?'

'I don't know.'

'I don't trust any of them. They'd lie as soon as look at

you. Academics?' Teague turned his mouth down in disgust. 'I wouldn't give you tuppence.'

'Do you think he was lying just now?'

'Who knows? But let's ask the other bugger what he's got to say.'

Healey looked at his watch. 'Let's make it for seven. Gives us time for a bit of shut-eye. We've got his address, haven't we?'

'Yes.'

'Do you mind picking me up from home? Say half past six?' Healey got out of the car and closed the door gently. As Teague drove off slowly in the direction of Lower Earley, Healey noticed for the first time the 'Baby on Board' sticker in the back window. Typical, he thought, and walked the few yards to his own house. The rain had almost stopped.

* * *

When they got to Carter's house the next morning, Leila Carter answered the door. She told them that her husband was away at a conference in Birmingham but that he would be back later that day, sometime in the afternoon. Was it urgent, she asked. No, Healey said. Just routine.

That was how they came to be standing watching the course members leave. And why they weren't surprised that Farrell had put in an appearance too. Farrell must have seen Sam's expression because, as he looked in her direction, he said, 'So it was Sam.' Neither Healey nor Teague responded.

As they continued to stand there, they heard the sound of something banging against the glass door behind them. It was the suitcase of a young woman who was struggling to get through, another case trailing behind her. Teague stepped across and held the door for her. Young, pretty but red-faced and flustered, she thanked him, and dragged the two cases along the concrete ground, making her way, bent-kneed, as quickly as she could to the coach. Sam helped her put the cases into the luggage compartment, at which the driver stepped forward, closed the compartment, and climbed back on board. There were a couple of tiny waves from the nearside windows as the coach drew away but most people were looking straight ahead, no doubt already thinking of the next stage of their journey.

The glass door behind Healey opened again. 'Well met. How goes the world, gentlemen?' It was Carter, in an open necked blue and white striped shirt, and a linen suit. He smiled broadly.

'We thought you were in Birmingham,' said Healey.

'Birmingham? Why ever did you think that?'

'Your wife told us.'

'You've been speaking to my wife?'

'We were at your house earlier.'

Carter stopped smiling, scratched his head, then smiled again. 'Of course, yes, I understand. I *was* going to a meeting there but something else cropped up.' Now he scratched his beard.

'Well now you're here,' said Healey, 'we can talk. Would you mind coming with us to the incident room?' Healey held open the door for Carter to go through ahead of him. Turning to Teague, he said in a voice too low for Carter to hear, 'You come too, but tell Farrell and the girl to go to their rooms and stay there until we come for them. Politely.'

Once in the otherwise deserted incident room, Healey gestured for Carter to sit down at a trestle table near a window. He sat down himself opposite and waited for Teague to appear.

'What *is* this, Richard? You're being very formal.'

Healey ignored the question but, once Teague came into the room, he told Carter that he was arresting him in connection with the murder of Neville Crouch and gave him the standard warning.

'Arresting me?' Carter laughed out loud. 'What on earth are you talking about?'

'Tell me what you did from the time that you left the Three Tuns on Friday the 29th of July until you got home that night.'

'I've already given you my statement.'

'And we know it's not true.'

'*How* do you know?'

'At the time of the murder you were seen here in the Hall.'

'By whom, may I ask?' There was no reply.

Behind the thick lenses of his spectacles Carter's eyes darted from side to side. Eventually they stopped. 'All right,' he said, 'I take it you've spoken to Peter?' Again there was no response. Carter continued, 'As Peter will have told you, I'm sure, I came here to see a certain young woman.' He looked at Teague. 'In fact the young woman you just held the door open for. We spent some time together in her room and then I left the Hall and walked back to Beech Lane.'

'You'll need to give us details of the young lady later.'

'Gladly.'

Did you go to Dr Crouch's room while you were at the Hall?'

'No, I did not.'

'Did you go into the corridor where Dr Crouch's room was?'

Carter smiled. 'I think you know I did. It felt as if there might be a storm so I went to Peter's room to borrow his raincoat.'

'You knew it was there?'

'Everybody knew it was there. It was a course joke.'

'But you say you didn't enter Dr Crouch's room?'

'Absolutely not. Why should I?'

'You were seen leaving Dr Crouch's room at about the time of his murder.'

'Impossible.'

'We have a sworn statement that says you did.'

'No. If you have such a statement and you aren't just bluffing, then it's untrue. I did go into Peter's room but nowhere else on that corridor.' He paused. 'Look, I'm sorry that Peter and I misled you about our whereabouts but it really didn't seem important at the time. It was just meant to avoid embarrassment. We didn't even know that it was a case of murder, if you remember. And my wife is a very jealous woman.'

'Was Dr Crouch expecting you, sir?' asked Teague.

'No. As I said, I didn't go to Neville's room.'

'But you were seen coming out of it. That's a bit strange, wouldn't you say, sir?'

'I wasn't seen coming out of Neville's room. If I was seen coming out of any room, it was from Peter's. In fact that must be it. They are next to each other, as I'm sure you know, Richard. The lighting is poor. It would be an easy mistake to make. In fact from the other end of the corridor it would have been difficult to even recognise someone.' He paused. 'It was *me* they said they saw, was it?'

When neither Healey nor Teague replied immediately, he continued, 'Got it. So it wasn't me they said was there. It was Peter. And he put you on to me. Ha!' He slowly shook his head as if in sorrow. 'Oh dear, Richard. What do you think you're doing? Your informant makes a mistake about the person and you want to believe that they were right about the room they came out of. Well they weren't. You just haven't thought this through. He started to stand. 'I need to go now.'

'Sit down, Dr Carter. You're going to be here for quite a while yet.'

* * *

They did keep him there but in the end they felt that they had to let him go. Not before Carter had laughed in Healey's face. 'When you have a moment, Richard, perhaps you'd be good enough to tell me what motive I might have for wanting Neville dead. I'm not a policeman, but I should have thought that it's part of your job to establish a motive.'

As Healey walked home, he wasn't happy. That was obviously a serious problem, not having a motive. And Carter had quickly seen a weakness in the identification. That wouldn't look good in court. He must tell Teague to make sure that Sam omitted any mention of Farrell in her statement.

As he neared the end of Pepper Lane, on a whim he turned off towards Falstaff Avenue. He couldn't have said why he did it but doubtless it was something to do with the attraction of Teresa. He would probably slow down as he walked past, and maybe she would see him and … But he didn't walk past. He didn't even walk as far as the house, because there parked outside it was Wright's blue sports car. Healey swung round and walked back onto Pepper Lane and was home in five minutes.

His wife met him at the door. 'Oh, hello, this is a nice surprise. I thought you'd be gone all day.'

He put his hand on her arm. 'Just a second, love. I need to make a call. I'll be with you in a minute.'

His wife went into the kitchen and he stayed standing in the hall. In his notebook he found the phone number of the Customs office at Gatwick. Getting through, he asked for the officer he had dealt with on Thursday.

'Speaking.'

Healey introduced himself. 'I'm glad I caught you. I thought you might not be there on a Saturday.'

'I'm always here. What can I do for you?'

'You remember we spoke about someone called Wright?'

'Yes.'

'Well I think you might be interested in him. I believe that he's involved in bringing drugs into the country. Working with Reyes. I know for sure that he had a significant amount of cannabis resin in his university room in Reading. And I can tell you exactly where he is now, if you want to know.'

For the second time that morning Healey found himself being laughed at. 'Look, mate, we won't be doing anything about him. And we'd be most obliged if you didn't either.' That was when the man laughed. 'I thought you would have guessed. He's been doing a bit of work for us. He was our informant in the Reyes business.'

Healey quickly ended the call and put down the phone. While he was speaking, he had been looking out over the roof of his car, across the small lawn to the dying Leylandii. He felt low. He felt bad about the business with the Italian woman. Bad about the way the interview with Carter had gone. And now he'd made a fool of himself with Customs.

'Dad ... Dad.'

He looked round. It was his daughter. '*Are* we going on holiday?'

'We'll see.'

'When?'

'Later.'

'When later?'

'Tomorrow.'

'But Mum said we might be *going* tomorrow.'

'Tomorrow. I don't know yet.'

While his daughter stomped noisily upstairs to her bedroom, Healey went to the kitchen, made himself a mug of instant coffee, and stepped out into the garden. There was already a deckchair and, having set his mug down on the lawn, he let himself fall into the chair. He was soon asleep.

He woke to laughter and the feeling of a fly tickling his nose. The laughter was his son's; the fly was a piece of string that his son was dangling on his face.

'Stop it.'

There was more giggling. 'Mum says lunch is ready if you want some.' Healey's throat was dry and he had a headache. He heaved himself out of the deckchair, bent to pick up the now cold cup of coffee and followed his son into the house, his feet splayed, his head down. He poured the coffee into the sink, swilled out the mug and filled it with water from the tap. The others were already sitting at the kitchen table on benches. 'Gazpacho,' his wife announced.

'Not lentil soup,' Jamie added.

Healey smiled weakly. 'That's nice. Just the thing for a hot summer's day.' He squeezed past his son and sat beside the window that looked onto the garden, which was open as far as the latch would allow. He sprinkled chopped green pepper and onions onto his soup, dropped a handful of croutons into it, and took a spoonful. 'Mmm, this is good.' The children looked at their mother, who appeared pleased.

'So can we go on holiday, Dad?' asked Meg.

Before Healey could answer, the phone rang. 'I'll get it,' said Jamie. He came back. 'It's Teague for you, Dad.'

As Healey walked to the phone, he smiled to himself at his son referring to a grown-up by his surname alone. 'Yes?'

Teague was jubilant. 'We've got him. We've got the bastard.'

'Carter?'

'Yes. Mr Smart-arse bloody Carter. It's on tape. I didn't go home, I stayed here ...'

'Where are you?'

'At the Hall.'

'I'll be over.' Healey put down the phone.

'Sorry, I've got to go.'

'At least your soup won't go cold,' was his wife's parting shot.

At the Hall Teague explained again to Healey that after they'd released Carter, instead of going home himself as he said he would, he had stayed there and settled down with the mini-tapes from Crouch's bedroom. He'd spent a couple of hours listening to two more tapes. The usual stuff, boring people talking about boring things. Then it occurred to him to look more closely at the codes written on the cassettes. They didn't help him but doing this made him notice that one of the tapes, unlike the others, which had been wound to the end, had been stopped in the middle.

'I tried the wrong side first. Just the usual stuff. But when I turned it over – bingo! It was Crouch telling Carter that he knew that he had fiddled that Moroccan woman's marks. Said he knew that *he* had written her dissertation.'

Healey interrupted him. 'Can we listen to it now?'

The sound from the little tape recorder was tinny but clear. As Teague had said, Crouch accused Carter of altering Leila El Aloui's marks on the MA and of writing her dissertation. Carter denied nothing but simply asked Crouch what made him believe this, and he told him.

He had been looking through exam documents as he was filing them away and noticed some discrepancies. Then he had got a copy of the woman's dissertation, which it seemed Carter had not only supervised but also marked.

'Can you believe that?' exclaimed Teague. 'He supervised it, then marked it. And all the time he was shagging her! What kind of system is that?' Healey didn't answer but asked him to rewind so that he could hear what he had just missed. It was Crouch saying that there wasn't any need to make an issue of it, that he wouldn't report Carter, but that he wanted Carter to do something for him in return. Just let him have a few pounds now and again. Teague stopped the tape. 'So there's his motive. He was being blackmailed.' Teague took the cassette from the player, pulled a paper from a file in front of him, and offered both of them to Healey. 'There's just one date on the cassette. Have a look, sir.'

'I'll take your word for it.'

Teague seemed disappointed but carried on. 'Well the date is just three weeks before the first payment into Crouch's Isle of Man account.' The paper he waved in front of Healey was a bank statement. 'There's the motive,' he said again. 'He was being blackmailed.'

'But that's been going on for years. Why kill Crouch now?'

'Because he's being promoted. Crouch gets greedy and asks for more. Carter realises there's going to be no end to it unless he does something about it, so he does.'

'That's plausible,' said Healey, sounding unconvinced. Teague watched his face.

Eventually Healey continued, 'All right. So we have a motive. We've evidence he was near Crouch when he died but no traces of him in the room. There's the letter, written using a printer of the kind that he had easy access to. There's the fact that he was trained in karate, which would help explain why there was no sign of a struggle.' Teague frowned at the mention of karate.

'Sorry,' said Healey, 'I just happened to notice a photograph in his office and asked him about it. But what we want … what we want is a link between Carter and the missing bat and diary.'

'Search warrant?'

'Yes, but I'm sure he'll have got rid of them. He's too clever to leave them around.'

'He's clever, but not as clever as he thinks. If he was a bit more cleverer he would of kept his mouth shut this morning and called a lawyer.'

'Perhaps. Anyhow, let's take him in to the station. See what he's got to say this time.'

'Okay.'

As they walked to the door, Healey suddenly stopped. 'Hell, we didn't tell Farrell and the girl that they could leave their rooms. They'll still be there.'

'Don't worry. I told them when you went home.'

Healey chose not to look at the smirk that he knew would be on Teague's face. In fact there wasn't one.

* * *

Carter replaced his glasses after wiping them on a far from clean handkerchief. He blinked at the light that was shining in his eyes. 'Do we need the third degree?' he asked. Healey and Teague, sitting across the metal table, said nothing. Healey looked through a sheaf of papers. Teague turned the little tape recorder over and over in his hands. Eventually Healey spoke.

'We'd like you to listen to this.' He nodded to Teague who pressed the Play button. On the tape Crouch began to tell Carter what he had discovered. Carter showed no emotion, simply stared at Healey until Teague stopped the tape.

'Well?' he asked.

'You recognize the two people speaking?' said Healey.

'Of course.'

'You said you had no motive for killing Crouch. Well there it is. He was blackmailing you and you had had enough. You wanted to put an end to it. There's your motive.'

'Nonsense. First of all, that recording, which I have never heard before, incidentally, must be several years old. If I had been blackmailed, then I waited a long time to do anything about it, wouldn't you agree? That's one thing. The other is that I never was blackmailed. If you'd played the tape a little further you would have heard me telling Neville what utter rot he was talking. There was no truth in what he was asserting, none at all, and I told him so.'

Healey looked at Teague, who pursed his lips and shook his head.

'Have you listened to the end?' asked Carter.

'Yes,' replied Teague.

'And you're saying you didn't hear me denying what Crouch claimed?'

'Didn't hear anything like that.'

'Then the tape has been copied and cut. It must have been.'

'Why would Dr Crouch do that?' asked Healey.

'I've no idea. That's not for me to say. But I can tell you categorically that I told Crouch that he was talking nonsense, and that I never paid him a penny. I imagine you have forensic scientists who can help you.' Carter rose to his feet. 'If that's it, can I go now?'

'Stay there, Dr Carter. We have some more questions for you,' said Healey.

In fact there was very little else for them to ask. They asked him for details about the occasion on which Crouch had threatened to expose him and what had happened subsequently. They prepared a statement for him to sign as he sat silent, seemingly deep in thought.

Suddenly, quite out of the blue, he said to Healey, 'You realise that it may not have been me that went to the Hall that night. Have you thought about that?'

'What? You've just made a statement to that effect.'

'Yes, and I previously made a statement to the effect that I was with Peter Farrell in his house.'

'So?'

'So in both cases I could be protecting a friend.'

'Are you saying that Dr Farrell went to the Hall while you stayed at his house.'

'I'm not saying that. I'm saying that it's a possibility.'

'Why would he do that?'

'He could have been seeing a woman. He's not quite the lily-white character you probably imagine. Or he could have been meeting Neville. Have you considered that possibility? If not, I suggest that you do.' Carter was getting excited; his eyes gleamed.

'Do you remember when we first met, we talked about the pursuit of truth? I thought that was what you were involved with too. But apparently not. You gather a few scraps of information, make up a story that fits, and stop there. Aren't you supposed to look at alternative stories, alternative hypotheses?' He took the paper that Teague had in front of him, read it through quickly, took Teague's pen and signed. 'Could you show me the way out of here, please?'

'No, that won't be necessary, Doctor Carter. We'll be holding you here for the time being.'

'On what charge, may I ask?'

'Suspicion of murder. You'll be formally charged in a moment. And your fingerprints will be taken.' Healey nodded to Teague, who walked to the door and held it open for Carter.

'This way, please,' said Teague.

As the door swung shut, Healey was left sitting at the table, breathing yet again the acrid scent of Carter's body odour.

* * *

After setting in motion an application for a search warrant for Carter's house and office, and ensuring that any request for bail would be refused on the grounds of the seriousness of the crime and the fact that Carter had connections in Morocco, a country with which the UK had no formal extradition treaty, Healey and Teague had driven in their separate cars to Healey's house. Healey had left Teague sitting in the garden with a can of lager and then went off to Farrell's. Farrell answered the door.

'Oh, hello, Richard. Come in.' They sat in the front room. 'We've been talking to Dr Carter.'

'And?'

'He told us that we should be considering you as a suspect.'

'No.'

'Yes.'

'And are you?'

'Not at the moment, no. But unless we can tie a current suspect directly to the murder, then we'll have to look at other possibilities.'

'By current suspect, you mean Chris?'

'When Dr Carter came back from the Hall that night, you said you didn't hear him open or close a car door.'

'That's true. I didn't.'

'Did he bring anything into the house?'

'Not that I'm aware of.'

'Did you hear him go to the back of your house, into the garden?'

'No.'

'But he still might have done. Do you remember the evening that I came round and you were burning stuff in the garden? When we went to the Three Tuns.'

'Yes.'

'What were you burning?'

'Leaves, branches, general rubbish.'

'Not a cricket bat?'

'What? No. Of course not.'

'Why of course not? Dr Crouch's bat went missing the night he was killed. It could well have been used to render him unconscious before he was pushed out of the window.'

'But I had nothing to do with that. I wasn't anywhere near the Hall. I was here. I thought you accepted that.'

'For the moment, yes. But what if the person who killed Dr Crouch brought the bat here and took advantage of your fire to burn it? Dr Carter was here that evening you were doing the burning, wasn't he?'

'Yes.' Farrell looked uneasy.

'Well?'

'I saw nothing.'

'I think *I* did.'

'What, saw someone burning the bat?'

'No, but what I saw could well have been part of a bat handle grip. Red, like the one on Crouch's bat. Do you think we could go into the garden?'

'All right. But why?'

'Let's imagine that I was right. Someone was burning the bat. And Crouch's diary, possibly. I arrive in the middle of it. Not everything is burned. There could still be something here.' They were now in the garden. The ashes in the incinerator were sodden after the previous night's storm.

'Now if I interrupted the burning of the bat that night, where would the unburned parts be? In the hedge? Under a plant?' Healey asked himself aloud, as he continued walking down the lawn, past the incinerator. 'Or might it be in the shed? Is there a lock on it?' he asked Farrell, who had followed him down the lawn.

'A padlock but I never lock it.'

Healey stopped at the shed, opened the door, and stood looking inside. He stepped forward, put on his glasses, and dropped to his haunches next to the workbench. 'Look. Sawdust. And unless I'm mistaken, some particles of red rubber. Can you see?'

Farrell looked over Healey's shoulder. 'Yes.' His voice was hoarse.

Healey stood up. 'Now if we were to find the rest of the bat …' Stepping carefully round the sawdust, he craned forward, turned his head to look between a toolbox on the bench and the wall behind it.

'Well I never. A cricket bat with its handle sawn off.' Healey studied it without touching it. 'Gray Nicolls,' he read. He was pretty sure that was the make of the bat in the photograph in Crouch's house. Farrell stayed where he was. Healey turned towards him.

'You didn't know about this?' Farrell shook his head.

'No, I'm sure you didn't,' Healey continued. 'You and your wife were probably in the house and left Carter by himself in the garden for several minutes, didn't you?'

When Farrell hesitated, Healey added, 'If you were part of a strong case against Carter, it would make it easier to overlook your previous false statement. Otherwise the possibility of your being charged as an accessory might arise.' He paused.

'I hope you understand me.' When Farrell didn't reply, Healey touched him on the arm. 'You will do when you make your fresh statement. Come on, let's go back to the house. Can I use your phone? I need to get people to take these away and examine them.'

'Of course.'

'In the meantime, please don't enter the shed. And don't let anyone else there. All right?'

'All right.'

Farrell accompanied Healey to the front gate. 'Oh,' he said, 'I heard from the Research Council today. I've got the money for the research in Spain.'

'Congratulations. Are you going to go?'

'I think so. Pam is happy about it now. She can still carry on with her OU course. And she'll enjoy being in Spain.'

'I'm sure you'll all enjoy it.'

'Thanks. And what about you? Are you going to apply to us?'

'No, I don't think so, not this year. I've rather gone off the idea.' Healey didn't add that he'd rather gone off Farrell too.

He lied to him about Carter and he lied too about his relationship with Teresa.

'Well if ever …'

'Thank you. Of course.'

'Just one other thing before you go. You asked what the letters PF might stand for. It dawned on me, it probably stands for Pension Fund. The BC gave me my cheque for the course this morning. That's what made me think of it. Whenever we manage to make a bit of extra money, we always say it's for our pension fund. Neville did, I'm sure.'

Healey smiled. 'Really? Well that's very helpful. Thank you.' He set off along the pavement in the direction of his own house. Farrell watched him all the way, before walking back to his front door, a thoughtful expression on his face.

After Healey got back to the house and told Teague what had happened, he invited him to stay for supper. Teague accepted with alacrity. His wife had taken 'the littlun' to stay with her mother for the weekend, so he would only have had a take-away. Then, after supper and drinking a few cans of lager, he agreed to stay the night rather than drive home. He sprawled on the sofa, a can balanced on his little pot belly, his stockinged feet hanging over the arm. Jamie came in, supposedly to say goodnight. 'Teague,' he said.

'*Sergeant* Teague to you,' said his father.

Jamie ignored this and went on. 'What's pink and wrinkled and hangs out your trousers?'

'I don't know,' answered Teague, grinning. 'What *is* pink and wrinkled and hangs out of your trousers?'

Jamie roared with laughter. 'Not hangs out of your trousers. Hangs out your trousers.' Healey couldn't help laughing, and nor could Teague. The can of beer bobbed up and down on his belly. 'I don't know. Tell me. What is it?'

'Your mum, of course,' cried Jamie.

Teague laughed even more. 'That's a good one.'

'Yes, said Healey. 'That *is* a good one. And now *you* can have a good one, young Jamie.' He picked up his son and carried him to the door.

'A good what, Dad?'

'A good night. And now *say* goodnight.'

'Goodnight, Sergeant Teague.'

'Goodnight, Jamie.'

When Healey came back from putting his son to bed, Teague nodded to him, a grin on his face. 'So that's it. We've done it. Carter won't know what's hit him tomorrow morning. A job well done, I'd say, sir.'

'Yes, a job well done. Thanks for all your efforts. Really appreciate it.'

Teague was silent. Suddenly a thought struck him. 'How did you find out about someone being seen leaving Crouch's room in the Hall?'

'Sometimes it's not a bad idea to get close to people involved in a case. Whatever the Super says.' Healey smiled. 'Worth remembering that.'

If Teague thought he was going to learn about the circumstances in which Healey had been told of the sighting, he was disappointed. He asked another question. 'That dickhead Wright. I don't see where he fitted in. Do you?'

'Mmm. Remember the customs chap asking about him? Got his name wrong. Well it dawned on me in the end. He must have been working for them.'

'What, Wright working for Customs?'

Healey nodded. 'That's how they knew about Reyes and the cases at Gatwick.'

'You've got to be joking. Never.'

'He *was*. I actually rang them to check and they confirmed it.'

'Well I never did. I suppose that's why he didn't give a monkey's.'

Healey nodded again.

'And drugs had nothing to do with the murder.'

'No, we were wrong about that,' agreed Healey.

'And I was wrong about cherchez la femme.'

Healey looked surprised at this admission.

Teague continued, 'Yes, it was cherchez *two* femmes. There was Carter's wife. If he hadn't fallen for her, none of this would have happened. And Crouch's. She was the reason *he* did what he did.'

'I suppose so.' Healey was reluctant to concede the point but it would be difficult to argue against it. He looked at the crumpled beer can at Teague's feet. 'Fancy another beer?'

'Please.'

When Healey came back from the kitchen with the beer, Teague was clearly still turning things over in his mind. 'And that letter we found in Crouch's room in the Hall,' he said. 'The one in funny English. I suppose Carter wrote it.'

'Yes, and if he wrote it on his computer at work or one at home, it'll still be there, I'm told. There are ways of finding it, whatever he did to get rid of it.'

Teague nodded and then remained silent until another thought occurred to him. 'You know Farrell, you don't think he could have …'

'Don't even think of it.'

As he lay in bed that night, however, Healey did think of it. How likely was it that Farrell hadn't known what was happening to the bat in his own garden? And if he hadn't, would Carter have left the bat there for days without going back to burn it completely, or take it away? The more Healey thought about it, the more uncertain he became. But one thing he was sure of was that nothing useful would be served by investigating further Farrell's possible role as an accessory. Eventually he took his own advice to Teague, and quickly fell into a deep sleep.

* * *

no proof, they've got no proof
clowns
no logic to it
just bluff
no reasonable doubt? ha!
of course there's reasonable doubt
I'll show them
such utter utter clowns

SUNDAY

A metallic-green Vauxhall Cavalier sped down the M2 in the direction of Dover. Inside were a man, a woman, a boy, a girl and a dog. In the boot were a tent and various items of camping equipment. Healey's head nodded in time to a country music cassette. His wife dozed, as did the dog on her knees. The children were reading the books that had been bought for the holiday and which they hadn't been allowed to look at until then.

After spending the first part of the morning taking fresh and carefully managed statements from Farrell and Sam, the course assistant, Healey and Teague were confident of the case they had against Carter. They deliberately did not speak to him but learned that after a night in the cells he had asked for the first time to speak to his solicitor. Doubtless he would try some new trick or other but, however much he wriggled, he wouldn't get off the hook. They had him.

Soon after they had taken the statements, Healey received a call from his Superintendent. 'Well done, Dick,' he said, calling him this for the first time that Healey could remember. 'Very well done.' After clearing his throat, the Superintendent went on to say how draining the last week must have been for him, 'especially as you seem to have got involved emotionally, I understand, with the people you were investigating. Why don't you take a week or two's leave. You deserve it. I can look after the case while you're away, with Teague's help of course. How about that?'

Healey knew that he really had no choice and, in any case was ready for a break and said so. 'That's fine then,' the Superintendent continued. 'It will do you good. One other thing – keep it under your hat – don't be surprised if you hear very shortly that Mike Teague is being promoted. We're very impressed with his performance on this case. We see a bright future for the lad.' Healey did not respond, something which doubtless would not improve the Super's opinion of him. But to hell with that.

So that was how he came to be on the way to Dover, where they would spend the night at his wife's mother's and leave the dog. They'd catch a ferry to Calais in the morning. They hadn't booked anything, would go just where their fancy took them. There was nothing in Healey's mind but a sense of having completed something well and a feeling of freedom. Freedom from work, from worry, from the itch to know other women. The future was full of new possibilities. He began to sing along tunelessly with the cassette. His wife woke up and smiled at him.

AFTERWORD

The deleted file containing the threatening letter to Crouch was found on Carter's computer at the University. Carter was found guilty of murder and sentenced to life imprisonment.

No action was taken against Farrell.

Teague was promoted to Detective Inspector.

Healey returned from holiday and went back to work. He never did do a degree.